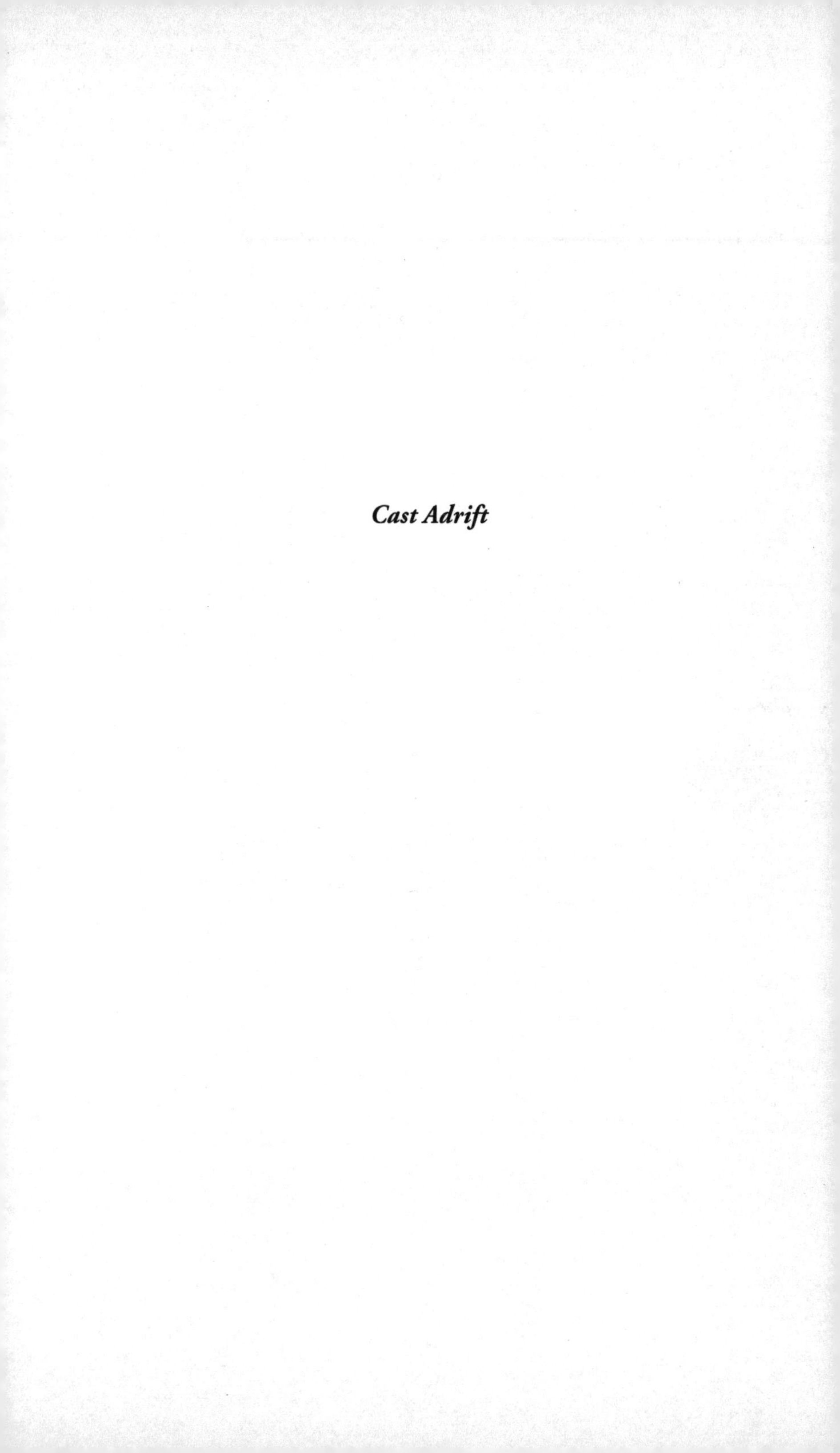

Cast Adrift

a&b

Cast Adrift

PETER GUTTRIDGE

This edition first published in Great Britain in 2004 by
Allison & Busby Limited
Bon Marche Centre
241-251 Ferndale Road
London SW9 8BJ
http://www.allisonandbusby.com

A catalogue record for this book is available from the British Library.

10 9 8 7 6 5 4 3 2 1

ISBN 0 7490 8355 7

Printed and bound by
Creative Print and Design, Wales

Sussex-based PETER GUTTRIDGE was born in Burnley, Lancashire and educated at Oxford and Nottingham Universities. He is the *Observer*'s crime fiction reviewer and the Royal Literary Fund Writing Fellow at the University of Southampton. He also writes about – and doggedly practices – astanga vinyasa yoga.

Chapter One

"Don't be irate
I'm just a pirate
It's what I was destined to be
I've pillaged and killed
I'm rather self-willed
But there's also a nice side of me."

At least this time I didn't have a lobster clamped to my testicles. Instead, I was thirty feet underwater looking at a fast-approaching sea monster. An enormous fish, six feet long, heavy, its cruel teeth bared. It was scything through a mass of brightly coloured snapper and surgeon fish *en route* to me.

Ask me again, Bridget, I thought to myself. Ask me again how I'd like being in the movies.

"How would you like being in the movies, Nick Madrid?"

Bridget Frost, aka the Bitch of the Broadsheets, my best friend, constant goad and accomplice in many an unlikely adventure, leaned over the table, grinned and smacked her lips. I looked at her, then past her to the long white curve of beach below. The sun was bright, the sky was blue, it was too hot to do anything but sit here in the shade, drink pina coladas and smile at the perks of being a freelance journalist with a best friend who is also a commissioning editor.

I waved my hand vaguely around. "Bridget, you got me down here to write a movie location piece. Now you're suggesting I could be the next Jude Law."

"You wish," she said, leaning back and stretching, thereby

attracting rapid eye-swivels from every other man in the bar. "No, what I was suggesting – what I've already suggested in fact – is that you take over as stunt man."

She leaned forward to display her breasts in a different way as I choked on my pina colada. I know it's not a fashionable drink these days but when in Mexico – the Caribbean shores of the Yucatan to be precise – you drink the local grog. I was saving the tequila for later.

"Yeah right."

"You know how to use a sword – well, after a fashion – and since this is a pirate movie there's going to be lots of that. You're supple because of that stupid yoga you do."

"Astanga vinyasa is *not* stupid."

"Yeah, yeah. Plus because of your – quote – *yoga breathing*, you can stay underwater for a long time – which is definitely a plus for a pirate movie."

"Are you saying the movie doesn't have stuntmen?"

"Stuntman – this is low budget movie-making, remember."

I raised an eyebrow.

"We did have a stuntman, big hunk called Larry, but he upped and went two evenings ago. Nobody's seen hide nor hair of him since."

"Why'd he leave?"

"No one knows – just disappeared. I was talking to Dwight and suggested – on account of the fact he's desperate – that he use you. At least until a real stuntman can be hired."

"You know how to build someone up and put them right down again don't you? And Dwight is up for it?"

"If I suggest it, why wouldn't he be?" she said, with what could only be described as a leer.

* * *

Time for a bit of what the movies call back-story.

Bridget Frost, deputy editor of a magazine in New York, invites me to write a location piece about the making of a movie in Mexico. Fair enough. I'm in New York anyway and in no hurry to go home since a woman called Mara I'm keen on is pissed off with me and my flat in London's Shepherds Bush has been trashed by the Russian Mafia – you really don't want to know. Hanging out on a movie set for a week or so in Mexico is not my idea of hardship. Then it turns out that Bridget is actually going to be *in* the movie.

"One minute you're a magazine editor, the next you're a movie star. How come?"

We're sitting in the restaurant of MoMa in New York, Bridget idly clocking everybody who walks in, giving them the old up-and-down look, then, having judged them, dismissing them.

She's wearing a tight-fitting top and skin-tight trousers but they're not right on her because Bridget is best described as voluptuous and she's bursting out all over. She is, of course, totally oblivious to how she looks.

"I didn't say I was the star," she rasped – always a bad sign, Bridget rasping – "I just said I was in it."

"How do you know this director?" I said, suddenly suspicious.

"How do you think I know him?"

I pondered for a moment.

"Married then."

She sighed, twisted a ring on her finger.

"Nick, it's something I do. You know about me and commitment..."

My turn to sigh.

"Only too well."

"So anyway, he discovered I could sing and got excited about giving me the part of the pirate's mistress – a hostage but one who's up for it."

"How did he discover you could sing?" I said absently, still digesting the thought of Bridget with yet another married man. "Bridget?"

She harrumphed. I'm glad to know people still do.

"I'll tell you some other time."

"But Bridget I have to ask – a low budget pirate movie? Geddouttahere."

"Why?" she said sharply. "You saw what a hit *Pirates of the Caribbean* was."

Oops. I'd assumed it was some kind of joke.

"That was a Disney movie with a big budget based on a successful theme park ride."

"*Master and Commander*?"

"Cost a lot of money but I don't think it did that well at the box-office."

"No sex in it, that's why."

"Several pretty young boys for a niche audience though."

"Mind your manners," she said, forking a big piece of lamb from her tagine and putting it in her mouth whole. "Go on," she said, whilst chewing. Nothing but class, our Bridget.

"Low budget and films made on water just don't go together. Big budget and films made on water usually don't."

"*Titanic*?"

"Massive exception."

"*Jaws*?"

"The film company was all for throwing in the towel it was such a long shoot and went way over budget. But so far as pirate movies go, until *Pirates of the Caribbean* had come along there hadn't been a successful pirate movie since Burt Lancaster sailed the seven seas in the 1950s."

She stifled a yawn, which is tricky when you're still chewing. I ploughed on.

"Remember *Cutthroat Island*, the multi-million pound project for director Renny Harlin and his wife Geena Davis? Hit a reef and sank with the loss of all hands."

"Nicely put," she said, still chewing.

"I'm a journalist. I'm supposed to be good with words."

"True – but I've read your stuff remember."

I took a sip of my wine and tried again.

"Fine that you're riding on the coat-tails of *Pirates of the Caribbean* and *Master and Commander*. But they were high budget, this is low."

"Are you done?"

Evidently I was. Bridget and I don't exactly have an equal relationship, caring though it is. Well, sort of caring.

"Yes," I said. "Go on."

"It's called *Blackheart*. It's about Edward Teach – know who he is?"

"Neat." Mel Gibson's *Braveheart*, although old now, was still in filmgoers' folk memory. They'd make the connection with the titles. I nodded. "Edward Teach, better known as Blackbeard, terrorised the Carolina and Virginia coasts in the early 1700s in a boat called the Queen Anne's Revenge. Although why Queen Anne should want revenge and on whom I've never been absolutely sure."

"On whom, eh?" More lamb forked into gob. "I was certain you'd have heard of him." I could hear the sarcasm in her voice through the noise of her mastication. Bridget thinks I'm a bit of a know-it-all. Who muttered something at the back there?

"Didn't know he'd gone down into the Spanish Main," I said.

"Yeah, well, he didn't," Bridget said quickly. "But that's

where people expect to see a pirate – in the Caribbean. This isn't a history lesson, you know, it's a Hollywood flick."

"Hollywood? On this budget?"

"Okay, off-Hollywood. Besides, Dwight says, how else is Blackbeard going to meet up with the French chap?"

"L'Ollonais?" I said, holding back the smirk. "You got Captain Morgan in this too?"

"You're such a fucking know-it-all, Nick."

Told you.

"Miserable childhood," I said gaily, though truthfully. "Best thing to do was keep my head stuck in a book."

"What – the *Encyclopaedia Britannica*?"

"In this instance, *The Boy's Book of Pirates* actually. The main characters were Blackbeard; a French sadist called L'Ollonais, who roasted captured Spaniards to death on a spit; Captain Morgan, who ended up as governor of Jamaica and gave his name to a rather tasty rum; and Captain Kidd. Is Kidd in your film too?"

She shook her head.

"We heard Ridley Scott had a film in development about him."

"I remember all about Blackbeard," I said. "Vicious and bloodthirsty as most pirates were, Blackbeard was the worst. Psychopath. Used to liven things up on board his ship by setting fire to pots of sulphur or by firing his pistols under his dining table whilst entertaining his friends in his cabin. Did his best to keep his men drunk so they couldn't plot against him."

"So the guy played a little rough to get a few laughs," a deep voice said.

I looked round. Bridget got up and hugged the man who had appeared beside us.

"Hi, Esther," the man said to Bridget. Bridget glanced at me and looked a little embarrassed. Esther?

"Nick, this is Dwight Brooks." She nodded at each of us in turn.

I stood up and we shook hands. He was tall, almost as tall as me and I'm six foot four". He was a craggy man, in his late forties I would judge, but in good nick. He was wearing a cashmere pullover over a pair of neatly pressed cords. He pulled over a chair, sat down and leaned back.

"Gather you've heard of Blackbeard."

I nodded.

"He wanted to terrify his victims into thinking he was a devil," I said. "Maybe *the* Devil. He had this long black beard that he plaited and tied with ribbons and he stuck long, lighted matches under his hat so his face was framed in fire. Dodgy juxtaposition, hair and fire, but it seemed to work."

"He carried three pairs of pistols," Dwight said, taking back the story. "And a heavy cutlass. When eventually they took him after a major struggle, they saw they'd inflicted 25 wounds on his body, most of them gunshots. He was still alive – though not for long. They executed him, took his head back to Virginia and stuck it on a pole."

"I was wondering how you were going to do this story given that the central character is a double-dyed villain. You're going to make him a Hannibal Lecter and turn him into a loveable monster?"

"Not just loveable – a lover!" Dwight said triumphantly. Adding: "He had 14 wives, you know."

"Wives is probably a bit of a loose term," I said. "So how you gonna do it?"

"I'm going to pit him against the Frenchie, who, believe me, was even worse."

He had a supercilious look on his face. He was holding something back, I could tell.

"There's more isn't there?"

He nodded.

"It's a story about a guy redeemed by the love of a good woman. And what has always been the best vehicle for that kind of story?"

I shook my head.

"Got me stumped."

"A musical."

Now I did laugh, a mixture of astonishment and, I don't know, admiration for his chutzpah. So that's why Bridget's singing had been a factor. But when was a musical a hit in the past forty years?

From brain to mouth.

"But when was a musical a hit in the past forty years?"

"*Moulin Rouge*?"

"That sold on Nicole Kidman's legs. And a *pirate* musical?"

Actually, why was I surprised? This was exactly the crass way film people thought. A pirate movie was a hit. *Moulin Rouge* had been a hit. Let's put the two genres together.

"This is a tax loss thing, right?" I said, not wanting to appear naïve. He was offended. He sat forward in his chair.

"Certainly not. This will be a major hit – and you know why? Because I'm going to redefine the musical." He paused and gave it the puffed out chest and tilted chin; the gaze off into the far distance. Well, into the corridor to the loos at least. "This," he declared in a deep basso, "is going to be the first brutalist musical."

"Brutalist musical?"

"Yeah – a musical with balls."

A musical with balls. How could it fail?

* * *

Down Mexico way, Bridget was still leaning over the table. Every man in the bar was gazing at her cleavage. Bridget is, as one of the techies had remarked to me the day before, "stacked". He was an older guy, natch. A younger guy had said to me: "Your friend Bridget, she's got great lungs."

"Good singer is she?" I'd said – well, this is a musical.

He smirked.

"Oh yeah."

When I caught on – I'm slow but not that slow – my instinct was to defend her honour. However, at the time she was wandering about topless on the deck of the galleon and I knew she'd wonder why I was bothering.

"Me a stuntman?"

"If you did the stunts it would make it an even better piece plus you'd get paid and hey, who knows, you might get spotted."

"But aren't stunts dangerous?" I said. Not that I'm a coward, you understand. Or maybe you don't.

"Why do you think they're called stunts? Because they trick you into thinking you're seeing something you're not really seeing." She squeezed my arm. "Nothing to it, kid. It's like David Blaine – do you think he was up in that box on the South Bank all those days? Come on – he was eating caviare and drinking champagne in the Savoy watching all the action. It was all done with mirrors. *Everything* is done with mirrors."

"And smoke," I added.

I must admit that for a few moments I sat there, looking down at the bay, imagining a life that didn't involve writing crap things to impossible deadlines. Even if I could forge a career simply as a stuntman, that would be enough. And as Bridget had said – how dangerous could it be?

I had my close encounter with the lobster the next morning. I was playing a pirate who is supposed to be dead but is actually lying doggo under the water. When the hero's back is turned I emerge from the water wielding my cutlass.

I had one line: "Die, you blackguard!" I'd been practising my deepest voice especially.

I was dangling off a ledge of rock for an interminable length of time as they fiddled with the cameras. When I got the action call I ducked down then pushed off the ledge to launch myself out of the water.

Unfortunately the lobster also heard the call for action. I felt an excruciating pain. I'll say this for myself: I was a trouper.

"Die, you blackguard!" I bellowed. Although, as everybody noted later, wetting themselves as they did so, it came out as: "Die you blackgeeeeeeeeeeeeee!"

It really hurt, dammit.

"The lobster must have felt threatened," I said to Bridget as we were standing around to do the shot again. Well, she was standing, I was in a semi-crouch. She raised an eyebrow, reached over, pulled my swimming costume away from my belly, peered down the front.

"Yeah, right." Let the elastic go with a twang.

Four hours later I was standing on this narrow plank sticking out from the waist of an eighteenth-century Spanish galleon. I was looking down at the turquoise waters of the Caribbean some twenty feet below me. I was bare-chested but behatted – a rather nifty black felt three-cornered job – and I was wearing a pair of droopy calico breeches that deserved to have seen better days but probably never had.

Brilliant sunlight. Vivid blue sky. A skull and crossbones hanging limply from the galleon's mainmast. Behind me on the main-deck, a line of rough-looking seadogs. Ratty long hair, lots of stubble. Big biceps. They were armed to the teeth – cutlasses, daggers, pistols and boathooks. They were swaying. Humming yet.

And suddenly they burst into song. For such rough-looking men, their voices were surprisingly sweet and melodic as they mouthed a refrain of which I could make out only two repeated lines:

"It's Blackbeard you can thank
He's made you walk the plank."

Their song was in counterpoint to another voice. Gruff, basso. The voice of a giant of a man in a heavy black frock-coat, long curly black hair framing his face, a tricorne plonked atop his head. His bandolier bristled with pistols and his black beard was plaited and tied with ribbons.

He sang:

"Don't be irate
I'm just a pirate
It's what I was destined to be–"

I didn't hear any more as a man standing immediately behind me prodded me with a cutlass and I dropped off the plank into the sea.

I sank like a stone. I saw a couple of bright lights directly ahead. I played to them, assuming the cameras were there too. I started to contort in a life and death struggle with what at that moment was an invisible creature. I made sure I kept my breathing steady – I was going to be underwater for some time yet.

Suddenly I felt a rush of water and I was caught in it, carried by this high-speed current into a funnel between submerged cliff walls. I was whisked down into deeper water and into the midst of thousands of brightly coloured snapper and surgeonfish: pink and blue and orange, hovering like a massive war party, swaying and feeding on the incoming tide.

I balanced myself and looked around. Just in time to see, heading towards me, the aforementioned primeval fish. It didn't look at all real but then I know mechanical fish are hard to make life-like. I upended myself and kicked frantically, coughing out air. I fended it off but it snapped at my arm before it veered away. Last I saw, its tail fin was disappearing back into the murk of the deep water. My lungs were trying to remember what air was like. I kicked for the surface.

The second I broke the surface of the water I gulped down big lungfuls of air. Only then did I look up. A line of faces peered down at me from the galleon. Dwight Brooks in a Hawaiian shirt loomed over them all.

"Cut!" he bellowed. And everyone applauded.

"You are Nick Madrid, journalist and yoga obsessive, and I claim my ten pounds."

I twisted round in my seat – something yoga-obsessives can do with insouciant ease – to see who was likely to have recognised me here in Mexico.

"Whatcha doing here, Blue?"

Ah. Her name was Stacey. She was a boisterous Australian make-up artist with whom I'd had a not altogether successful liaison at about four in the morning in a cramped caravan on the Brighton set of the eventually aborted film *The Great Beast.*

Sex with her had been going okay until she had totally put

me off my stroke, so to say, by asking at a critical point: "Have you slimed yet, Blue?" Slimed?

"No," I replied meekly, thinking: and nor am I likely to now.

She dropped onto my lap, put her arms round my neck, ground her buttocks into my crotch and kissed me open-mouthed, her tongue snaking down my throat. Good to see some things don't change.

"You're working on the film," I said when she'd allowed me to draw breath.

"Evidently," she said. "I heard you were here but somebody said you were doing stunts today."

"I got here the day before yesterday," I said. "I came to write a location piece but then your stuntman disappeared."

"Tell me about it," Stacey said, wriggling unconsciously but distractingly in my lap.

"Well, apparently the stuntman has done a bunk for no reason anyone can figure out. So because of my underwater swimming skills, my yoga, a background in competitive fencing and because the film company is desperate."

"I didn't mean tell me about it, I meant *tell me about it*," she said, rolling her eyes.

"Right. Sorry. Must say I was a bit surprised when I discovered the stuntman who has disappeared was *the* stuntman."

"Yeah, you'll have your work cut out doubling for some of the cast. Not sure you've got the tits for the pirate bride but I'm sure you'll manage."

She frowned.

"Nick, it is weird Larry disappearing like that. Not his style."

"Larry's the stuntman? You knew him well?" Silly question. Stacey, sweet girl, was the original good time had by all.

"We had a thing going, yeah. There was no reason for him to go off like that, no reason at all."

"You had a row?"

"No. He was supposed to come visit two nights ago but he didn't show." She pulled on a length of hair – it was hers, attached to her head, she hadn't just taken it out of her pocket or anything. "He was arrogant, lazy, shiftless, two timing, thieving, cruel."

"But you loved him, right?" I said, trying to keep the boredom out of my voice because, after all, how many times had I heard this from women about unsuitable men. I can come up with a similar list of negative traits for heart-breaking women, I hasten to add.

"No, I hated him. But he owed me money too. That's why I want to know what's happened."

"Could the money be his reason for skipping?"

"I've known him a long time off and on – for all his other faults he didn't seem that kind of person. Where women are concerned he's capable of anything. I caught him in bed with one woman. And I followed him and another floozy to the beach once. I was going to interrupt when they reached a climactic moment but the whole thing sickened me so much I went off and left them to it."

She clenched her jaw.

"Nick, you're a journalist. You know how to do this kind of thing. I know you're busy with the stunt-work but do you think you might – you know – investigate his disappearance?"

We were interrupted at that moment by Bridget wandering over in a low-cut blouse and long, muslin skirt. Since she has one of the world's great hip swivels, her skirt swayed as she walked.

"Hi Stace. Nick, you coming to dinner? Get your revenge on a lobster?"

"Ha ha."

"Everyone's going to the Artemio Cruz around nine." She wagged her finger at me. "Be there."

"You gonna come?" I said to Stacey when Bridget had gone.

"It'll take more than this," she said, continuing to wriggle in my lap. She gave a little gasp. "Though not much more." She leaned into me. "I don't get invited to the top table. I eat below stairs." She nuzzled my ear. "But listen, Nick, if you don't have to be at dinner until nine you have a few hours to spare. Do you fancy…?"

I did actually but I was remembering the disaster last time.

"If I'm encouraged in the right way."

"Oh darling, of course. I remember last time we had to do that because you were so – weren't very–?"

"Yes okay, I think we both remember." Frankly, Stacey hadn't been impressed by the size of me. And, frankly, she wasn't the first.

We went to her room. This time it seemed to go better from the start. Within moments she was gasping so excitedly it almost had nothing to do with me. She was very vigorous too, twisting her body and flinging her arms out. Hey, I was thinking, Mr Stud, until I realised she was having an asthma attack and was stretching desperately for the inhaler on the bedside table.

The restaurant was almost deserted when I got there. A striking blonde was sitting alone at a table for two, reading a book and jotting down notes on a pad of paper. Bridget and Dwight were at a much larger table with Chuck Johnson, the actor who was playing Blackbeard.

"Hey Nick," Dwight said. "Good job today. Esther said you were an eel and she was right."

There he was with the Esther thing again.

"I said 'heel' actually," Bridget muttered.

"Wasn't expecting that mechanical fish," I said. "I thought it was all going to be blue screen." My initial writhings in the water had been my half of a struggle with a giant octopus that would be added later thanks to the wonders of modern computer technology.

Dwight nodded absently. Then gave me a puzzled look.

"What mechanical fish?"

I laughed and he joined in.

Chuck smiled at me and made space on the bench on his side of the table. He was a big, broad-shouldered guy, pushing sixty. I wondered if he did my yoga, he sat so straight in his seat. He had a handsome, lined face and good teeth. He also wore a dreadful toupee that we'd been advised not to mention. He never admitted to it nor, more to the point, took it off – so when he was in costume his long, luxurious Blackbeard wig perched on top of his own like a bird's nest. When he wore his tricorne hat as well the result was truly bizarre, as if his head was about to topple off.

"How's it going?" he said to me with a nod, handing me a big plate of mixed tapas.

"Fine," I said, helping myself to some whitebait and grilled red peppers. "Is it true that you worked with John Wayne?"

He nodded. "A few times, later in his career. We were drinking buddies for a while. Did my first film with him and Angie Dickinson in 1958, I wasn't yet twenty. Don't recall the title."

"*Rio Bravo.*"

"Maybe so. Just remember the legs on that woman." He looked down at his food. Sat a little straighter and looked at me. "I tell ya, you should have been there."

"Are you looking forward to this movie?"

He lowered his voice.

"Tell you the truth, son, I shall endure. That's about the size of it."

"You don't like the part?"

"At my age any part is received with gratitude." He put a forkful of squid in his mouth. "But, see, I don't swim and, to tell you the truth, I don't much care for boats. In fact I get seasick real quick."

"So you agreed to it just out of gratitude?"

He shook his head, chewing the rubbery squid all the time. I saw his Adam's apple leap as the squid went down.

"Alimony, son, alimony." He clenched and unclenched his fist. "My three areas of expertise are the quick draw, fan-shooting, riding a horse and using a lasso."

"That's four," I said, without thinking.

He gave me a steady look.

"I kind of regard the draw and the shooting as one. Sure hope I get to use a lasso." He turned rather stiffly in his seat. "Hey Dwight – we got any lassoing scenes in this movie?"

"Just singing Chuck, just singing."

Chuck looked at the plate of tapas then at me. He lowered his voice.

"And I can't sing worth a damn either," he muttered. "Took my lead from old Lee. When they asked him how he felt about singing in *Paint Your Wagon* he said, 'If somebody's damned fool enough to pay me a million dollars to sing, I'll sing'." He leaned in and dropped his voice even further. Since it was already pure gravel it became pre-Cambrian. "Not that they're paying me anywhere near that much. But with three wives and a business manager to keep I got no choice." He was getting positively garrulous. "Business manager embezzled all my money. Me and Mitchum both. Hell of a thing when you're thinking of slowing down a little and you find you've got to start all over again."

A pitcher of beer was doing the rounds. I offered it to Chuck.

"No, thank you kindly. I swore off drink five years ago."

Dwight overheard this.

"You in AA, Chuck? Me too."

We all looked at the glass of beer in front of Dwight. Dwight caught our looks.

"Well, yeah but I'm there for the networking. I don't actually have a drink problem."

A waiter approached and hefted a large soup tureen onto our table.

"I took the liberty of ordering the speciality of the house for us all," Dwight said. He saw me glance at the menu and tapped the side of his nose. "You won't find it there. It's something you have to know about." He reached out and took the lid off the tureen. "Turtle soup."

At Dwight's last words the blonde at the nearby table looked up, her eyes – well, now I knew what the phrase 'eyes flashing' meant.

"If you've never had turtle soup before you're in for a treat," Dwight said, ladle in one hand, soup bowl in the other. He filled the bowl and passed it to me to pass down the table.

I was watching the blonde. She was standing now. She was wearing trainers but she was still about six foot tall. A heartbreak alert flashed through my body. Before I could respond to it she had walked over to our table, book and pad in hand, and stopped beside me.

"Hi – I'm Mollie, she said in a tight, harsh voice. "You know the turtle is one of the few creatures that cries. I've seen them hanging upside down, skinned but still alive, tears running down their faces."

"They skin them alive?" I said, trying not to look down at the soup bowl in my hand. Everyone was looking at the woman, Dwight with ladle and bowl frozen in mid-air.

"Slitting the throat of a turtle induces a chemical reaction that causes a nasty food poisoning if you eat it. So you need to cook the meat quickly. The only way to do that is to cut the turtle out of its shell when it's alive, so that when its throat is slit, it can be cooked straight away."

None of us spoke, held in the thrall of this woman's ferocity. I put the soup bowl down.

"Shit happens," Dwight said, an uncomfortable expression on his face.

"Shit happens," the woman repeated in a monotone, not looking at him. Then she bent close to me – close enough for me to smell her scent – and spat in the soup in front of me.

She straightened and gave me a hard look before striding off, half-turning her head to throw back over her shoulder:

"*Bon appetit.*"

Which would have been a great exit line had she been looking where she was going.

There were three steps from the restaurant down into the street. She missed all of them.

I was out of my chair as she gave a cry. When I got to her she was sprawled in a heap on the dirt pavement. I took her arm to help her to her feet. She glanced at me with tear-filled eyes and shook me fiercely off before stalking down the street in an ungainly but rapid stride. I watched her out of sight.

Bridget gave me a knowing look when I got back to the table.

"Woman spits in man's soup – now that's what I call meeting cute," she said.

Dwight was still standing with the ladle in his hand. We all looked at the tureen of soup.

"Shit happens?" Bridget said to Dwight.

"Was all I could think of at the time." He put the ladle down, slumped back into his chair. "What? Did you know that's how they killed turtles?" He looked round at us. Shrugged. "Still, so long as this turtle is already dead…"

He caught our looks. The soup went back into the kitchen. We were joined by the lyricist, Hal Jones. Not as an alternative dish; he'd just arrived. He was a striking man who looked like he was suffering from a wasting disease – hollow cheekbones, awesomely pale, raggle-taggle goatee beard, shaved head with a thick wedge of hair right down the centre of the back of his skull. He was thin and not exactly dressed for the climate – black T-shirt, black denims, black boots. He was carrying a black briefcase.

Settled at the table he handed a couple of sheets of paper over to Bridget.

"New lyrics for you."

Bridget picked the sheets up. Began to read out loud:

"I've lived in the tropics,
I've lived in the Indies.
I've seen exotic things.
Yet, strange as it sounds,
It's absolutely true,
I've never had a parrot
But I've had a cocka – I'm not singing this."

"Has a ring to it," Dwight said, putting his reasonable voice on.

"Then there'll be a chorus," Hal said, "repeating the lines 'I've never had a parrot but I've had a cockatoo'."

I must say I was confused about the musical element of this film. The song lyrics were, frankly, bizarre – although perhaps explained by the fact that Hal had admitted that his ambition was to work with the Coen brothers. In fact he was flying back to Los Angeles the next day for a meeting with them about their next film.

Mind you, the whole project was bizarre.

"I'm sorry, Dwight," I said. "I find it hard to even get the basic concept here – we're making a low budget musical biography of a mass-murdering, raping and pillaging pirate, right?"

"Sweeney Todd wasn't exactly a boy scout you know," Hal said waspishly. "Didn't stop Sondheim."

"But musicals on film have been dead in the water since *Star* in 1968. And any film made on or under water is a nightmare, Dwight, you know that. They always exceed their budget, from *Moby Dick* through *Jaws* and *The Abyss* to *Waterworld*."

"You're forgetting *Cutthroat Island* and *Pyrates*."

"I was being polite," I said. *Pyrates* was Roman Polanski's comic pirate film starring Walter Matthau. Polanski does comedy? 'Nuff said. "Look, the notion of a low budget movie on water is a contradiction in terms."

"Ridley Scott may be making *Captain Kidd*, a pirate movie about a Robin Hood of the sea who robbed from the rich to give to the poor."

That wasn't exactly how the books I'd read presented Captain Kidd. I made a mental note to check in that childhood copy of *The Boy's Book of Pirates*, which I happened to have brought with me. (Don't tell me I don't do serious research.)

Hal rummaged in his bag for a moment, came up with another

sheet of paper. He handed it to me. "You're doubling for Pierre le Peg tomorrow aren't you? Better get the hang of this."

"Read it out," Bridget said. "Let's see if it's up to the standard of my song."

"Pierre Le Peg?" I said. Hal shrugged. I looked at the paper. Read it aloud:

"You know what they say
Made the Royal Navy great
Is the lash, sodomy and rum.
Well two out of three ain't bad
You're not sticking that up my bum."

"You're not sticking that up my bum," Hal sang in falsetto.

"Neat," Dwight said as Bridget and I rolled our eyes. Chuck looked confused.

I tackled Dwight again.

"Hurricane season is almost here isn't it?"

"A while off yet."

"Not much of a while. Most of the budget for this movie has gone on the galleon and the seaport set, right?" He nodded. "If a hurricane were to hit it would destroy both and that would be it. Game over."

He looked at me. "I talk to you frankly, Nick, because Esther's given me the word on you and you're trustworthy." He nodded in Chuck and Hal's direction. "These guys I know I can trust. So here's the news. I got no doubts we can finish this film to time and to budget. What does piss me off is that Zane has a second unit doing underwater stuff about a mile out at sea that I have no control over. Don't even know what they're doing. They report directly to him – and that, my friend, I find a fucking profanity."

"Zane?" I said, unpleasant memories stirring.

"Zane Pynchon. The producer of this motion picture. What's that look for?"

"Nothing really," I said, in major memory mode. "I've met him before." On the set of that aforementioned unmade movie *The Great Beast*, which he also produced. I thought for some time that he was a murderer. I didn't think that now but I certainly didn't trust him.

"I'd tell him to fuck off, he did that to me," Hal said.

Dwight made a fist and looked at the table.

"Yeah, well. This is a chance for me. My last few films haven't exactly..."

He didn't finish his sentence. I could have finished it for him. What he didn't want to say was that his last few films had been box-office disasters.

"Pynchon's going along with the musical idea?" I said.

Dwight nodded. Another perplexing thing. Pynchon was about as canny as you get – a more-bangs-for-your-buck producer who mainlined commercial movies. I kept coming back to the same thought: why is *Blackheart* being made?

The cast-list gave no clue. It was a typical B movie mix of last chance, first chance and no chance actors. Chuck was last chance. Dwight had lucked out with his female lead, the pirate bride. Cassie Dexter, an actress on the way up. She would be arriving tomorrow.

The other major pirate part was that of a psychopathic Frenchman named L'Ollonais. He was to be played by Yves Delain, the alcoholic French actor who'd never recovered from being shafted by the media five years before when he was up for a Best Foreign Film/Best Actor Oscar double.

His ex-wife had blabbed on coast to coast TV about how abusive he'd been. He'd lost the Oscar and his US career had gone into a tail-spin. Ever since, embittered, he'd worked relentlessly all over the world, on anything, accepting every script he was offered.

I was pondering this when I saw Stacey run up the steps into the restaurant. She was distraught and out of breath.

"Dwight," she called as she neared the table. "They've found Larry."

Bridget glanced at me and, I must admit, despite the hardships I'd gone through today, my stomach lurched at the thought I was about to lose my job.

"Stacey, that's great," Dwight said, also flicking a glance my way. "Where is he?"

"Face down in Fuentes Bay, ten stab wounds in his body. Any one of four of them fatal."

Chapter Two

"I'm feeling topsy turvy
Is it love or is it scurvy?"

I was standing on the quarterdeck in a tight bodice with fitted falsies and a floor-length skirt. Bridget was facing me in a low-cut blouse and long gingham skirt. My back was to the camera because I was standing in for Cassie Dexter, the female lead. It was the Girl Fight scene and she was too expensive to do her own scrapping.

Not that I looked like her – she the hot new Hollywood babe, starting to attract a lot of media attention, shortly to be on the cover of Vanity Fair. I looked what I am: a red-blooded male. Pink-blooded. With child-bearing hips. But I do have broader shoulders than her – just. And I am The Stuntman.

I was talking to Bridget about fame.

"Does stardom beckon for me?" I said. "Is this the start of my movie star career?" Bridget laughed. "Hey, Burt Reynolds started his career as a stuntman."

She gave me her look. I ploughed on.

"Burt gets a raw deal because of those redneck car movies he made. He was the best thing about the film of Hiaasen's *Striptease*."

"That Demi Moore thing where according to her lap-dancing was both art and empowerment for women?"

"It was pole-dancing. Okay, bad example–"

"Demi Moore's a real inspiration to older women."

"She did well in a couple of roles but that was it."

"I'm not talking about her films, you moron. I'm talking

about the toy boy and all the stuff she's had done to make herself look so good."

"Since you mention the latter–"

"The latter?"

"The stuff she's done."

"I know what the word 'latter' refers to in a sentence, thank you. I just wasn't expecting to hear it in everyday speech." She shook her head. "But then you don't really go in for everyday speech do you? And stop fiddling with your falsies."

"They feel strange."

"Try having them sticking out of your chest all the time."

"You seem to like having them," I said, "judging by the way you flaunt them."

It came out peevish, which was not what I intended.

"Being censorious, Nick? I thought you yoga types were all for letting everything hang out." She looked at my crotch. "Maybe it's because you don't have much to hang out. Especially after the attack of the killer lobster."

"Let's go back to me making the transition from stuntman to leading man."

"Oh, we're still on the fantasy channel are we? Well, Kevin Spacey was a stuntman originally," she said, blowing smoke down her nostrils. That's a trick of hers I've always admired. Especially when, as in this case, she wasn't actually smoking a cigarette.

I had some difficulty getting round the Spacey-as-stuntman concept. I shook my head. "He has better toupees than Burt, that's for sure."

We'd been delayed for hours because the Mexican police had been questioning the production team about my dead predecessor. They would be taking full statements from everyone in the course of the week. Naturally, they were mostly interested in the last time anyone had seen him.

I thought Dwight might have suspended filming as a sign of respect but I guess there was too much money involved. We had two minutes' silence on board the galleon instead.

The galleon was an impressive location. Actually, we had one and a half galleons. The half was moored at the dock resting on big floats. It was turned either to face the sea or the dock depending on what shot Dwight wanted. The film production had taken over an entire bay a mile or so from Fuentes. The one road to it had gates erected to keep rubberneckers out – though to be honest, none of the locals seemed the least bit interested in us.

The other galleon – the one we were on – was an expensive replica of an eighteenth century Spanish galleon. It was sturdily built, but for our purposes carpenters had added various features for show on the deck and in the rigging. These features were less robustly made. Balsa wood featured heavily – or, I suppose, lightly.

This galleon was moored a few hundred yards outside the harbour so that, with cunning camera angles, it would look as though it were at sea, miles from the nearest land. The galleon and the assembly of period buildings on the dockside had swallowed up most of the budget. That was why there was no money to use the giant water tank along the coast at Fox Studios Baja. That had been built to film *Titanic* and was where *Master and Commander* was filmed. The Russell Crowe film cost $135 million. Ours was costing… less.

Actually, I don't know how much *Blackheart* was costing but from things Bridget and Dwight had said we'd be lucky if it was more than $10 million. Now that would be a lot of money if it were to be in your or my bank account but for a film it's nothing.

Spending the money on the set and the galleon (and a half) meant there was little money to pay cast and crew. The crew were mostly Mexican non-union, so they were getting even fewer peanuts than anyone else.

However, I had been surprised on my first visit to the set to see a large number of extras thronging the waterfront Dwight had built.

Bridget had explained.

"They're paying to be in the film."

"Paying?"

She shrugged.

"People want to be famous. We went up to Cancun where all the American tourists are. A lot of expats live there. We offered them parts as extras for $1,000." She raised an eyebrow. "Worked."

At the moment we were on the galleon just outside the harbour. The day was scorching hot so most of us had been hiding under an awning whilst we were waiting to shoot. We were actually waiting for cloud to match the previous shot.

There were two set-ups to do. The first had me in this catfight with Bridget's character, the lower class prisoner. She'd just been singing a curious song – "Use me/Abuse me" – to Blackbeard but he'd cast her down because he was obsessed with the upper class hostage he'd taken. The Pirate Bride, if you will. That was Cassie Dexter, who was yet to arrive.

"Pick it up from where Blackbeard has just rejected you, Esther," Dwight said. He was wearing a large palm leaf as a hat. Directors, eh? "You come up on deck and there, strolling along the poop, you see your nemesis. Without thinking, you throw yourself on her."

"What's my motivation?' Bridget said. I looked sharply at her. She'd clearly been reading too many copies of *Entertainment Weekly*.

"Your motivation is that you want to beat the bejesus out of the stuck-up bitch." Dwight looked at me. "You okay, Nick?"

I nodded.

"Sure, it has to be easier than wrestling with a mechanical fish."

Dwight stared at me.

"You know – like yesterday."

Dwight walked away calling back over his shoulder.

"We don't have a mechanical fish, Nick."

Bridget and I had rehearsed the various moves. The trick was to make it look authentic without actually making contact with each other.

"Then...Action!"

Bridget sashayed across the deck and stopped before me.

"No using this as an excuse to cop a cheap feel," she murmured, just before she punched me in the face. I stumbled back and she threw herself at me. We landed in a heap and she continued pummelling me with her fists.

Dwight only called *cut* when my wig fell off during my desperate attempts to get her off me. Made no bloody difference to Bridget, who continued whacking me.

As I tried to compose myself, my attention was drawn to a beautiful young woman in skin-tight jeans and T-shirt climbing aboard from the boat we used to ferry us from harbour to galleon. I saw her in parts, actually. One long leg draped over the side of the galleon. Her buttocks as she brought the other leg over. A Rita Hayworth as Gilda shake of her long hair as she stood with her back to me. And then she turned, just like Rita.

It was Cassie Dexter and she was a knockout. There was also

something most unusual about her. It took me a moment to realise what it was. Then I had it: everything seemed in proportion.

As a journalist I'd been noticing that women in Hollywood these days looked like stick insects except that they had breasts of an unlikely size. But Dexter wasn't skinny. She actually had hips – a rare sight in Hollywood – and breasts which, as the trade press excitedly pointed out, were natural. By which the press meant the breasts actually moved of their own volition, they weren't simply cemented on. Natural breasts in Hollywood are as rare as hen's teeth.

My distraction probably accounted for the fact that Bridget beat the bejesus out of me with the same level of violence for a further two takes.

After a couple of minutes of the third take when Bridget was, as usual, pinning me down and bashing me about, Dwight stopped the scene and came over.

"For God's sake, Bridget," I gasped, grabbing her fists and rolling her off me.

She lay on her back, arms stretched out either side of her, and burst out laughing.

"That was great!" she said.

"You were great," Dwight agreed. "You too, Nick, except I think you're forgetting one important consideration."

"And that is?" I gasped.

"You're supposed to win."

Whilst we were waiting to go again, I glanced over at Dexter. She had been watching the fight and I think she was in a state of mild excitement, her lips parted, her eyes shiny. Since she was staring straight at me, was I crazy to think she was excited by the sight of me? Of course I was crazy – I was wearing a skirt and falsies for one thing, and few people are known to fancy Widow Twankey – but that's what comes of being an optimist.

We did a couple more takes and finally got it. I'd been waiting to ask Bridget what was with the "Esther" business but didn't get a chance. As Bridget hip-swivelled off, with me hobbling behind her, Dwight introduced us both to Dexter.

"Hi," I said, in my lowest voice, giving her a sultry look.

"You feeling okay?" Bridget said.

Dexter tossed her hair and gave Bridget a big grin.

"You can surely kick ass, darling," she said. "Made me sorry I couldn't have been rolling around with you for real."

Bridget smiled demurely. Bridget acting demure was a first.

"Just getting into the role," she said. "I figured my character was at that place on her arc."

Dexter nodded.

"That's a meaningful nod," Bridget said. "What are you thinking?"

"A meaningful nod?" I said, bemused. A nod is a nod, isn't it?

I was ignored. Nothing new there, then.

"I so know what you mean," Dexter said, slipping her arm through Bridget's and leading her across the deck to the food counter beneath the awning.

I trailed behind, trying not to splutter as Dexter swung her hips with every step she took. She was indeed a beautiful woman. We joined the queue and Dwight joined us whilst Greg, his cinematographer, set up the next shot. Dwight and Dexter air-kissed.

"Great to have you onboard," he said, mopping his face with a handkerchief. We were all sweating.

"Is my lover here yet?" Dexter said.

She meant, I realised, her film lover. In fact, he was here.

Dwight had seen him on the dock a little earlier. According to Bridget, his name was Joseph Law and for that reason he often got parts destined for a couple of far bigger stars – Joseph Fiennes and Jude Law. No, honestly – casting agents in the States can be that dim.

In the movie business not just casting agents were dim. There's the legendary story of a diminutive star who had hired the wrong German director because he'd confused the names of the one who'd produced the powerful submarine thriller with the one who'd produced the respectful but deeply tedious arthouse book adaptation.

True horrors happened on a daily basis. But so far as our little production was concerned I was sure we had the wrong actor. Joseph Law's character was a swashbuckling hero in the Hornblower mould, the naval lieutenant who tracked down Blackbeard and killed him in a fierce battle in which the pirate sustained countless bullet and rapier wounds before finally succumbing.

According to Dwight, Joseph Law was a skinny runt. Sometimes that doesn't matter. The movies were invented by small men who wanted to be bigger. The history of tough guy movies is, in many ways, a history of hobbits playing tough, whether they were standing on boxes to make them bigger or not. Cagney, Edward G Robinson, Bogart, Alan Ladd, Dustin Hoffman, Al Pacino, Jo Pesci (excuse me whilst I snigger): harmless little fellows playing tough.

The more believable ones – Redford, Newman, De Niro say – were still well under six foot. As were the musclebound ones – Kirk Douglas, Schwarzenegger, Stallone. But they carried it off better.

And they still seem like gods when you look at the two dimensional guys you have now. Vin Diesel? Ahem.

Where was I? Oh yeah – so Joseph Law was a skinny runt and, according to the cinematographer, no way could you flesh him out to make him appear someone likely to take on Blackbeard and best him.

"He's back at the hotel," Dwight said. "You'll meet him at dinner. Time for you to get in costume."

I was still contemplating our romantic lead when it was time for me to do the next scene. I was standing in for Blackbeard this time. Chuck was no good with heights, so I had to go up in the crow's nest for a longshot of Blackbeard singing three separate songs at different points in the movie. He was supposed to be singing whilst looking down on Cassie Dexter's character as she stood on deck. Costume had decked Cassie out in a low cut dress to show off her best assets.

The songs were: "I'm feeling topsy turvy/Is it love or is it scurvy?"; "Weevils in my biscuits but love in my heart"; and "Up in the crow's nest but down in the dumps".

On the way up the mast I looked down on Cassie – for professional reasons, not because I wanted a cheap thrill. In any case my glance was diverted by what I saw elsewhere about her person. She appeared to have a hole in the top of her head, about the size of a ten pence piece, with her hair around it shaved away.

I have to admit I'm not great with heights so climbing up to the crow's nest took some strength of will. Discovering I had some strength of will came as a pleasant surprise. I clambered into the crow's nest and looked at the mast, which went up a further ten feet or so.

I took one look down at the deck and immediately grabbed for the mast. Which, even though we weren't moving, was swaying with the motion of the ship at anchor. After a few moments of this I was naturally feeling queasy. Growing nervous about the possibility I might sick my lunch over the assembled cast and crew some distance below I looked out to the horizon.

That seemed to settle me. In fact I could see for miles, breathtaking views back over the mainland and out to sea. The water was turquoise and so clear I could see the bottom. I could see what I assumed to be the second unit boat about a mile away, concealed from our people on deck by a headland.

"Okay Nick," the assistant director called through a megaphone. "Turn half on to the camera and throw your arms around as you're singing. Are you ready?"

I gave him an exaggerated thumbs up.

"Then, action!"

"I'm feeling topsy turvy," I bellowed, throwing my arms out to my sides. "Is it love or is it scurvy?"

I felt I put just the right amount of heartbreak in the second line, allowing my voice to break slightly. Not that I need have bothered since it wouldn't be my voice you'd hear on the soundtrack.

I did it a couple more times then there was a break while they set up the camera on the other side of me for a second song and a different sky. Except the sky was the same faultless blue as far as the eye could see.

By now I needed to go to the loo. I could guess what real sailors caught short up a mast used to do but peeing on cast and crew would be just as bad – or maybe even worse – than vomiting on them.

To distract myself I took the telescope I had as part of my Blackbeard gear and trained it on the second unit's boat.

"That's interesting," I thought to myself. (But then who else was I going to think it to.) "Very interesting."

I could make out four divers in wetsuits in the water around a rubber dinghy about twenty yards from the boat. The dinghy was lying low in the water and listing badly to one side from the weight of some lumpy, bulky objects individually wrapped in tarpaulin.

I wondered what scene they could be filming. I swept the telescope over the deck of the boat. Actually, I couldn't see any kind of film equipment on deck. I assumed it was all underwater.

"Okay Nick?" the assistant director called. "Ready to go with the next set-up. This is your *Titanic* moment."

Titanic moment? I cocked my head.

"Lean out over the rim of the crow's nest and put your arms back like wings."

I sneaked a quick look down at the matchstick people thirty feet below. Gave the balsawood crow's nest a little shake. Lean out over this – yeah right. Stay calm though Nick – you're a professional.

"Are you fucking bonkers?" I screeched. "If I put any weight on this I'm a dead man."

The assistant director cupped his ear and shouted into his megaphone again.

"Didn't catch that but I'll assume it was an affirmative. On my word, everybody. Standby. Roll and…Action!"

Oh fuck. Maybe there was a way I could do it without putting any weight anywhere but on my two feet. After all, I do yoga at an advanced level and that's all about balance. I planted my feet firmly, shoulder's width apart, bent forward from the waist, put my arms out behind me. I even tilted my face up to the sun.

"Weevils in my biscuits," I yodelled, "but love in my he-e-e-elp!"

So much for yoga balance. A motorboat zipping by had sent

out some swell which, at that moment, hit our boat. We bobbed, the mast wiggled, the crow's nest tilted and I felt myself fall out of the nest and head for the deck.

"Cut! Jesus, Nick, the line is 'love in my heart'. And since when did you start to sing falsetto?"

Since you fastened a safety harness between my legs, I murmured through gritted teeth. I was hanging like a giant spider with leather straps cutting into my shoulders and thighs and, frankly, sliding further between my buttocks than I was entirely comfortable with.

I know that the safety harness meant I'd never been in any real danger but I never said that I was brave, did I?

Slowly I swung back to the crow's nest and clambered into it. I leaned against the mast.

"It'll be five minutes before we go again," the assistant director yelled.

I looked over at the second unit's ship, took the telescope from my pocket and trained it on the divers. They were loading the objects onto a hoist which was dangling over the side of their ship. They were having trouble doing it. There was still no evidence of filming.

Over the next hour, between set-ups, I continued to watch the second unit. I began to wonder about them. What exactly were they filming? And then a different question occurred: were they filming at all?

Every early evening I liked to walk a few hundred yards along the beach to a bar by the water. Our location was a sleepy little village called Fuentes where tourism was just starting, so it was pretty quiet. Of course, being so near to Cancun it got busy at weekends.

This night I perched on a stool at the bar and ordered a

bottle of beer. I asked for a glass. I'm old-fashioned that way. The sun was sinking over the sea, sending sparkling slivers of pink and gold across the water. Someone was down near the water-line in a perfect headstand, face turned, in an upside down sort of way, towards the sun.

The bartender was a friendly young fellow, name of Carlos, who was trying to grow a moustache and failing – I'm sure much to his chagrin in this moustachioed country. He turned the stereo on. He was a *caribe* fan, that heady mix of all the music of the Caribbean – soca, calypso, merengue, zouk and reggae. I'd got into it when I was in South America a few years earlier with Bridget.

I tilted my head at Carlos as the music blared out.

"Clan Caribe and Grupo Caribe," he said. "Very old now. *La Chica de Los Ojos Cafés.*"

"I like it."

I should have known better than to encourage him. He started enthusing about Jorge Ben, Ivan Lins, Gilberto Gil then moved on to a range of home-grown singers and musicians. He would probably have gone on all night had not another customer come in.

When I turned back to the beach the person who'd been doing the headstand was walking towards me, the sun low in the sky framing her with a golden halo. It was a Hollywood moment – or maybe a hair advert one. I'd decided from the way the figure swayed her hips that it was a woman. As she drew nearer I could see she was wearing a bikini top and a lungi. She was tall and shapely. It was Mollie, the woman who had spat in my soup the previous night.

She was watching where she was walking so she only looked up and caught sight of me when she reached the entrance to the bar.

I couldn't quite interpret the look that passed across her face. I raised my glass and tilted it at her. She nodded and started across the bar. Then she stopped, turned and walked over to me.

Be still my beating heart.

"Hello," I said as she reached me. Not much of a zinger I know but I figured a neutral remark was safest.

She fixed her gaze somewhere over my left shoulder.

"I wanted to apologise about the other night–"

"No need," I said quickly.

"Can I finish?" she said with asperity.

I came to heel.

"I'm not apologising for spitting in your soup – frankly, you're lucky that's *all* I did."

"Hmm," I said.

"What does hmm mean?" she said.

"Just hmm." She'd get nothing out of me.

"No, I'm not apologising about the soup. I'm apologising because you came to help me when I tripped and I was rude. So – thank you."

Her cheeks were flushed when she started to turn away. I offered to buy her a drink. She shook her head.

"Please," I said, in a tone that I hoped avoided pleading.

"Don't wheedle," she said. "It's unbecoming."

Wheedle? At least I wasn't pleading.

She slid onto the stool next to me, her lungi falling open to show a long expanse of tanned thigh. Ulp.

"Why are you here?" I said.

"I'm a marine biologist working with Peace International."

"I know them – I once reported on their Rock Against Drugs tour of South America."

She didn't seem impressed.

"Are you focusing on anything in particular?"

"Can't you guess from last night?"

"Turtles?"

"Turtles and tortoises."

"Tortoises. I love tortoises. Me and my dad had a tortoise when I was really little. It ran away. That's what my dad said and I believed him. It was only when I was older that I realised that the pace it moved it must have taken about a week to get out of the back garden."

"A tortoise as a pet is bad enough but for centuries men have taken worse advantage of them. Sailors would go to the Galapagos just to take the tortoises for food."

"I wouldn't have thought a tortoise would be very filling," I mused. "Maybe as a starter…"

"The tortoises on Galapagos weigh around 70lbs," she said sharply. "Some of them grow to 400lbs. Sailors could only get them on board ship by carrying them on their backs. Ships would take a couple of hundred with them, stacked up in the hold like car tyres."

"Poor things – but why tortoises?"

"A tortoise can go without food and water for a year. That made them ideal food for long voyages because, unfortunately, their meat still tasted good. Plus you can get up to 10lbs of fat from them that tastes like butter."

She sighed.

"So what's the difference between a tortoise and a turtle?" I said.

"Do you really want to know? They're both chelonia but tortoises are usually land or freshwater creatures, turtles are marine."

"And the green turtle is an endangered species?"

She nodded.

"There were green turtles in the oceans before dinosaurs ruled the earth. They can live up to two hundred years. In the seventeenth century there were so many, Dutch sailors talked of being able to walk from one Indonesian island to another across their backs.

"But the turtle population has dropped by 80 per cent in the past fifty years. There's a ban on trading in them but illegal trading is a big problem. In Bali they've got a special dispensation in the form of a 5,000 animal annual quota. That's being massively abused. Then there's the trade in the eggs."

"So why aren't you in Bali?"

"I was, but others are working there now. I'm here to try to find the community that is carrying out the illegal slaughter and trade in this region."

"Sounds dangerous." She shrugged.

"They may be on one of the big islands in the Caribbean."

"What's mock-turtle?" I said, remembering my Lewis Carroll. It might seem an odd switch of topic but, crass man that I am, I was simply trying not to gawp at the long exposed length of thigh.

"Equally gross – they substitute a calf's head or some other meat in the soup."

We both took a drink.

"So there is a trade around here?"

"Oh yes – you saw proof of it the other night. But then there's a trade in everything round here. You know this area is known as the Yucatan Triangle?"

"I didn't. Because?"

"Small craft disappear in this area all the time."

I fluttered my hands.

"No, it's not anything spooky or mysterious," she said.

"Currents?"

She shook her head.

"These waters are like criminal freeways. Crooks of all kinds sailing here, all making an illegal living – drug dealers, treasure hunters, pirates."

"Pirates?" I said, trying not to scoff. "In this day and age?"

She held my gaze for a long moment. Guess I hadn't got the scoff quotient quite right.

"They're rife all over the world. In the China Seas they steal oil tankers, for goodness sake. Here they board expensive American craft, kill or cast adrift the owners and make off with the boats. But any or all of these criminals deal ruthlessly with people who get in their way."

An idea occurred to me.

"Tell me about treasure hunters."

"Loads of old Spanish treasure ships were wrecked in these parts. Their cargo is worth millions at current prices."

"Aren't they protected?"

She looked at me as if I was an idiot.

"In theory. The Titanic is probably the world's best known wreck. Doesn't mean that some of its best treasure hasn't been stripped from it – some 6,000 pieces at the last reckoning."

"These wrecks round here?"

"None have actually been identified around this part of the Yucatan but the whole area – the Gulf of Mexico and the Caribbean – was known as the Spanish Main. The Spanish treasure ships were regular targets for pirates based on Tortuga."

"I know, I know," I said. "That's why we're filming here."

"Thought you were filming here because it's cheap."

I flashed a glance at her. This sharp cookie.

"That too."

She still had that golden halo round her head, even though the sun had gone. Damn.

"Am I boring you?" she said. "You seem a bit abstracted."

"What you were saying made me think of something else and then – sorry, sorry."

"So what's your story, Nick?"

"The usual – a life badly lived. Hoping for better – for me to be better I mean."

"What do you reckon your chances are?"

I took a long pull of my beer. Set it down carefully and focused on the horizon.

"Slim," I said quietly.

I felt her watching me. I turned and grinned.

"But ever the optimist? Hey, I got attacked by this big fish the other day. Thought it was a mechanical one but apparently not."

"Bless," she said.

I looked at her sharply.

"No, it was really big."

"Well, do you know how big tuna are?"

I was thinking of the tinned tuna I had as a kid. Of the tuna steak I'd once had in a Washington restaurant on the recommendation of the maitre d' without checking the price: $80. Bastard.

"Oh, I'm sure they can be big," I said.

"They fished a bluefin up off the coast of Ireland in 2004 that weighed 88 stone. They were fishing for mackerel, caught it by mistake."

"That's a lot of tins."

"It was ten foot long, nose to tail. They sold it for £2,000 to make 5,000 tuna snacks."

"That's going to be quite a mark up."

"The average weight of tuna in British waters is around fifteen stone."

"But that's Britain, not Mexico."

She sighed.

"They usually roam the Pacific, the Caribbean and the Med, where temperatures are warmer. The bluefin tuna is one of the fastest fish in the world. They're pure muscle – and because they swim so fast cover thousands of miles in their lifetime."

"But would tuna attack a human?"

She shrugged.

"It's a predator."

I shook my head.

"I'm sorry, I can't take seriously the notion that I was savaged by something I'm going to be eating on another occasion." As I said this the image of the lobster came into my head. "Well, not this time. This fish was massive."

"Fish look bigger than they are – the water magnifies them."

She was beginning to irritate me, the way she assumed I was an idiot. I heard that.

"I know," I said patiently. "But this was never whitebait. It was about six feet long and four feet deep."

She took a sip of the margarita I'd ordered her.

"That's a big fish," she said solemnly.

She swirled her drink gently.

"You don't believe me."

She shrugged.

"Sure. If you say so." She tilted her head to look at me. "What's your involvement in making this film?"

I didn't know if I should say I was the stuntman – would she be impressed or would it come over as preening? Then I thought: what the hell. Preen – it has to be better than wheedling.

"I'm the stuntman."

She looked into my eyes. Did I see interest?

"How macho," she said quietly, looking away from me.

Clearly not.

"That's how I came up against the fish."

"Came up against the fish," she said slowly. "Was it – er – *mano a mano*? Or should I say *mano a fino.*"

"That's sherry." I have a sense of humour. I can cope with someone taking the piss. No, honestly. "I'm serious. This was big and it came straight for me. Had two rows of big teeth. Looked like something out of prehistory."

She nodded. She reached for her drink then seemed to hesitate.

"What?" I said.

"Nothing." She took a long sip of her drink then looked back at me. "So how does movie-making work? Did they film your encounter with this big fish?"

I shrugged.

"I'm not sure. A current took me away from where I was supposed to be. The camera may have been in the wrong place."

"Don't you have those things called rushes?"

I decided to be Mr Movie Expert.

"Sure. They're called dailies too. Raw footage of stuff we've shot that day."

"Wow – sounds really fascinating. Could I maybe see them sometime?"

There was something going on here, I could tell. Her enthusiasm sounded utterly false. But I ignored it because, frankly, I was smitten. No surprise there then.

"Sure," I said. "Don't see why not."

"That footage of the fish sounds interesting."

"Well, that's not current. I don't know how easy–"

She put her hand on my arm and gave me a warm smile. Ay caramba.

"I'm sure you can sort that out."

"I'm sure I can," I said. I was no longer wheedling. I was croaking.

She offered her hand.

"My name is Mollie Sanders."

"Nick Madrid."

"I just caught the end of your yoga practice the other day. On the beach in the morning? Was it Indian PT?"

I smiled and nodded.

"Astanga, yes. You do something gentler I'm guessing."

She ignored that.

"Listen, Nick – this fish that attacked you. I wouldn't go saying any more about it to the film people. As it wasn't a mechanical fish they might laugh at you, think you're making it up."

"But if it's in the rushes –?"

"Oh well, in that case, sure," she said airily.

She drained her drink.

"I've got to be getting back to my apartment. Do you want to walk me?"

Be nonchalant, Madrid. I shrugged.

"Sure."

"Why are you squeaking?"

She grinned as she walked off ahead of me. Then she slipped down the steps and landed in a heap in the street. This time when I got to her the tears in her eyes were of laughter. I helped her to her feet and when she'd stopped giggling she gasped:

"Oh, nice going, Mollie. Really cool."

She took my arm as we walked along the street. We walked in silence for a little until she said:

"So tell me, Nick Madrid, have you been a stunt man long?"

"A few days," I said, deciding not to lie. "The other stuntman was murdered."

"Murdered?" She looked shocked. "How do you know?"

"They found him face down in Fuentes Bay. He'd been stabbed to death. Pretty ferocious attack, apparently."

She looked pale.

"All the bad people around here…" Her voice trailed off. She stopped and held out her hand. She gave me a smile that didn't reach her eyes.

"Well, here I am. Thanks for walking me back. Let me know about the rushes."

"Sure. How?"

"Oh, leave a message with Carlos at the bar – he's my unofficial post-box."

I nodded. Hovered. Impulsively bent to kiss her on the cheek just as she turned her head. Caught her instead on the mouth. She jerked her head back.

"Okay, bye then," she said, turning and hurrying up the path to a small bungalow. Tripping on the step up to the door but righting herself and disappearing inside.

Back at the hotel bar I saw Greg, the cinematographer. He looked more like a movie star than most of our cast. There was something of Gregory Peck about him.

I asked him about my underwater stuff.

"Haven't looked at the footage yet. I know I got something through the viewfinder. But it was kind of murky because you were so far away so I don't rightly know what it is."

He put his glass down.

"But Nick – we *have* no mechanical fish." He winked at me. "Whatever attacked you was real."

"I know, I know. Dwight told me. I'd still like to look at the rushes though."

"I'll have to clear it with Dwight. If he says it's okay then, sure, I guess."

"Could I bring someone along?"

He shot me a glance and grinned.

"It's an expert on fish I've met."

He looked down at his drink, still grinning.

"Pretty is she?"

"Well, yes but–"

"The movie business is a lure, it surely is. So you hooked a fish expert?"

"Not exactly."

"Not exactly hooked or not exactly a fish expert? In fact no kind of fish expert at all?"

"No, she's a fish expert. Well, turtles really."

Greg thought for a second.

"Not the gal who spat in your soup?"

I nodded.

"Very pretty. Very pretty. Well, if it's alright with Dwight, it's alright with me."

He hoisted his drink.

"So how are you enjoying being a stuntman? Those lobsters really give a nip don't they? Don't suppose your friend is an expert on lobster nips is she?"

"Not that I'm aware. And being a stuntman is fine."

"You're doing a good job. Can't say I miss Larry. He did a good job too but he was a pain after hours."

"Who do you think killed him?"

"Don't ask me. Guess it's not safe here after dark. Lots of desperadoes. I was drinking with him, right here in this bar, the night before he disappeared. In fact he was standing just about where you are. Then he went over to the other hotel and that was the last I saw of him."

"Other hotel?"

"Where the second unit are staying. Think he was intending to hustle some work out of them too, to get more pay. You may have observed the pay rates are not exactly generous."

At that moment Bridget came in. Her entrance was, as always, presaged by a rush of wind, a fanfare and a shaking of the ground. She was looking pretty good.

"Hi Greg. Must be a slow night if you have to talk to Nick."

Greg gave her an admiring once over.

"Wait for me, darling." That was Cassie Dexter. She swung into the bar, still in jeans and T-shirt. She frowned when she saw me but beamed at Greg.

"Now if you're with Greg you must be talking about how terrible women are," Bridget said.

"Actually, we haven't had that conversation," I said.

"Well, here's my take. Ready?"

"Sure."

"You know the problem with men? God gives them a penis and a brain and only enough blood to run one at a time."

Greg nodded slowly.

"You're a one-off Bridget, you truly are."

Cassie looped her arm into Greg's.

"The very man. Wondered if I could have a quiet word about my close-ups tomorrow." She looked at Bridget. "If you'll excuse me for ten minutes, darling." As she drew Greg away from the bar he grabbed for his drink with his free hand and gave me a quick nod.

"Come to look at those rushes tomorrow night – around eight. Bring your fish expert."

"Fish expert?" Bridget said, helping herself to my drink. I ordered two more.

"It's nothing," I said. "What's with the 'darling' from Cassie?"

"She's a luvvie."

"Didn't think Americans did that."

"Depends if they've watched *Ab Fab* on cable."

"You and Cassie have bonded then?"

"Seem to have. Think she looks up to me as an older, wiser woman."

"Older, maybe…"

"Watch your lip, Madrid. I've seen you drooling over her. Forget it – she's out of your league."

"What is my league?" I said absently.

She took a long swig of her drink.

"Don't go there. Have you met Yves, yet. He's a dish."

"He's huge."

"Haven't got that far yet."

"L'Ollonais was this skinny young man. Aside from the fact Yves is twenty years too old and six stones too heavy to play him, it's perfect casting."

I sipped my drink and looked around the bar. Nobody else from the film was here as far as I could see.

"What have you heard about the second unit?" I said.

She looked at me cautiously.

"Only what Dwight was complaining about the other day. Why?"

"I'm going to pay them a visit – in my role as location reporter."

"I'm not sure that's such a good idea."

"Aren't you wondering what they're up to?"

She dipped her head to look at me intently.

"Not for a moment. Why should I? I've got bigger fish to fry."

"Well, I'm curious."

"Why do you always have to complicate things, Nick?" Bridget said.

"I'm not complicating things – I just want to know what they're up to."

"From your self-satisfied expression it sounds as if you already know. What have you figured out?"

"That was meant to be my sadly meaningful look–"

"Work on it. So what are they up to?"

I looked around. Still nobody from the film and nobody near enough to overhear.

"I think they're ransacking a sunken treasure ship."

I told her what I'd seen from my vantage point in the crow's nest.

"They were probably bringing up treasure."

"You mean jewels and gems?"

There was an acquisitive look in her eyes.

"Probably all kinds of stuff. It was under tarpaulin so I couldn't see. Whatever it is they're bringing up, what they're doing is illegal."

"Yeah right. Who cares, Nick?"

"I care – and I think Larry might have been killed because of it. Greg says Larry went over to the second unit's hotel the night he disappeared."

We to-ed and fro-ed on this for a little while then we sat there looking listlessly at each other.

"That's not all I saw from the crow's nest."

"Kennedy being assassinated?"

"Ha. Cassie."

"Oh what, you lecherous beast, you mean you were getting off on peering down her cleavage?"

"She has a hole in her head," I muttered quickly.

"I know she's not very bright but–"

"Who's not very bright, darling?"

We both swivelled on our chairs. Cassie Dexter was standing behind us.

Neither Bridget nor I could think of anything to say. We were saved by Dwight's arrival. He waved at us and strode over.

"Hey, the gang's all here," he said, doing some fluid hand gesture to indicate to the barman that he wanted his usual. He looked around. "And there's Jude."

I looked over to where he was looking. A skinny man was sitting in the corner of a big sofa, so sunk into it I hadn't actually noticed he was there before.

"Let me call him over." Then Dwight bellowed: "Jude!"

This spindly male, paler than anyone other than a vampire ought to be, shot off the sofa as if propelled and headed over. He was knock-kneed. I saw what the cinematographer meant.

Law was kind of a twin to Hal Jones, the lyricist, except that he had quite a handsome face. A totally unfamiliar one, which at that moment was frozen in a rictus of fear.

"Jude meet Cassie," Dwight said when Law reached us. "You two are nuts for each other."

Cassie looked Law up and down, clearly unimpressed. Law flicked a shy look at her. He was ginger-haired, a major no-no for movie stars.

He sat down, knees together, his hands clamped between them. Cassie looked at him. Smiled.

"You've changed a lot since *Talented Mr Ripley*. But then your marriage broke up – I'm sorry."

"My name's Joseph, actually. Not J-Jude."

Dwight obviously had a thing about misnaming people.

"No, no – you were the assassin in *Road To Perdition* – you were great."

He shook his head again.

"You sent Nicole Kidman shoes?"

"Not me. I'm Joseph."

"Joseph – of course." Dexter looked suspicious. "Didn't I see you in *Shakespeare in Love*?"

Law shook his head, his eyes on the ground.

"I've just left RADA actually," he said, daring to cast a glance at Cassie.

"Sorry to hear that. How long were you together?" Dexter crossed her long legs in such a way that all the males within a hundred yards were transfixed. Except Law, who wasn't looking. Instead he looked perplexed.

"I was there three years," he said.

"You were there?" Dexter said. "That's an odd way to talk about a person, even if she is a Hindu."

"What's a Hindu?" Dwight said.

"Anything he wants," Bridget said.

Who said music hall was dead?

Law looked from Bridget back to Dexter, total bewilderment on his face.

"Hindu?"

"I had a yoga teacher once whose name was Radha. It's the name of a Hindu god – means perfection or beauty or something. Her real name was Kelly so you could see why she changed it."

"RADA's a drama school in London," he stuttered.

Dexter spoke to him but looked accusingly at Dwight.

"You're fresh from drama school?" There was indignation in her voice.

"As if you knew what one of those was," Dwight muttered.

She heard.

"Yeah okay, I was a model. So what? I'm not that well-educated – so what? This isn't anything special."

Don't say it. Every molecule in my body screamed: don't say that fucking cliché. The one that even intelligent actors say as if they've just minted it when all it does is reveal they are also moronic.

"This isn't rocket science, you know."

Damn. She said it. I just hoped there wasn't going to be a double whammy.

"We're not trying to find a cure for cancer."

Oh, okay. I slumped against the bar.

"You okay, Nick?" Dwight asked.

"Sorry, sorry," I said. "It's an allergy." To clichés.

I could see how there might be one or two problems with Joseph. He was playing Cassie's lover, a priggish, upright and brave naval officer. Yes, I know, pretty much like the Jack Davenport character in *that* pirate movie.

"But here's the spin," Dwight was now saying to Joseph. "I want you to play him as a cockney wide-boy. A Keith Richards who's also a bit of a dandy."

Joseph nodded slowly. Bridget and Cassie smiled at Dwight. "Great idea."

"That's familiar."

"What are you saying, Nick – speak up, you're among friends."

"Well, forgive me – but that just makes him a cross between the character Johnny Depp played in that pirate movie and the foppish way Brando played Fletcher Christian in *Mutiny on the Bounty*."

Dwight looked winded.

"Is it that obvious?"

"Er, yes. Can't we come up with some original ideas of our own?"

Dwight looked at me for a moment.

"On this budget?" He turned to Joseph. "Ju-Joseph, how do you see your character? A Jack Aubrey as played by Russell Crowe? Or perhaps a ladies' man?"

"I wouldn't know about him as a ladies' man," Joseph said, "I believe in celibacy until marriage. But I could certainly make him foppish."

We all exchanged bewildered looks. Celibacy until marriage?

"Pinch me," Bridget whispered to me. "Tell me I'm dreaming."

I shushed her whilst Dwight nodded slowly a couple of times.

"Okay then, let's do him as a brave and fearless warrior," Dwight said. He looked Joseph up and down. "Okay with you?"

"Not foppish?" He sighed a long, drawn-out sigh. "I have a stunt double, though, right? For the fight scenes?"

Dwight glanced at me.

"Well, yes, but you'll be doing some yourself, won't you? I mean, I heard you were great with edged weapons."

Joseph looked at his hands.

"I don't know where you heard that. You expect me to do sword fights and stuff? I see myself as more of a Rock Hudson type."

More glances around the table. Dwight started to speak. I got in first:

"I don't think Joseph means the gay thing, he means Rock Hudson never did his own stunts."

"Nicholas, thank you," Joseph said.

Dwight sighed.

"I don't know how this is going to work in the climactic fight scene between you and Blackbeard. To be effective it really needs to be clear it's you. You kill him, you know. Slowly and messily."

"And you expect me to do that? How disgusting."

"He's raped your fiancée – you're out for revenge." Dwight frowned. "Jude, your attitude puzzles me a little since you're here primarily because of your talents as a physical actor."

We all looked at Law hugging himself.

"Joseph," he said timidly. "My name is Joseph."

"Whatever," Dwight said. He looked at the rest of us. "Ju-Joseph has a real talent for stage fights. He's the new Errol Flynn. Douglas Fairbanks on his best day should have moved the way this guy moves. Cinema history will be made in his duel with Blackbeard." Dwight leaned over and slapped Law on the back. "Right J-J … Mr Law?"

Law catapulted forward under the force of Dwight's slap. When he'd got his breath back and the colour of his face had calmed he croaked:

"But I have a stuntman, I believe?" he repeated.

I preened.

"For what he's worth," Cassie said.

I stopped preening.

"Nick can do whatever is required," Bridget said, bless her. "Can't he, Dwight?"

"Let's hope so," he said, shooting me a dark look.

"Good," said Law, sitting up straight for the first time, "because, to be honest, I'm terrified of pointed objects."

It was a couple of beats before anyone looked at him. Then everybody did.

"That could be a handicap in the sword fight scenes right enough," Dwight said.

"Not to mention the love scenes," Bridget said, thrusting out her breasts.

Law quailed. What a great word quailed is!

"Excuse me," he said, jerking to his feet and rushing towards the toilets.

We all looked at Dwight.

"Mexican food?" he said weakly, passing a hand over his brow.

Chapter Three

"When it comes to sex I'm just not fussy
Any other way is simply wussy
I jolly roger when I'm needy
All God's creations, yes indeedy
I don't just stick to women and men –
Kindly bring me that hamster again.
An Austrian gent named what I've got
There are lots like me believe it or not
But think it a blessing and not a curse
If you're polymorphous and perverse."

I did my yoga on the beach the next morning. The yoga I do has become very hip in recent years. This is a bit embarrassing as people think it's just a gimmicky thing. But astanga vinyasa, developed in Mysore in the 1930s, is a terrific sort of yoga, albeit a vigorous one. Those who do less physical yoga do as Mollie did and deride it as Indian PT.

It requires heat for best results. The heat allows the practitioner to get into positions that, frankly, there is no good reason for a person to get into. These days, as is the nature of things, there is an even more extreme form of yoga: Bikram yoga. It was devised in California. Ahem.

As far as I can gather, Bikram yoga is done in pretty much of a sauna. Whenever I do a yoga class in a moderately-heated *yogashala*, I shed rivers of sweat which sweep away the other practitioners. Bikram, therefore, does not appeal. I'd probably end up as a puddle on the floor.

It was already getting hot so I was in the shade of the trees. I was facing the sea and watching the surf flop gently onto the white sand. The humidity in this part of the Yucatan was enough to get me sweating within the first few postures. That's why, although I was a bit out of practice, I wasn't doing badly. Until Cassie Dexter speedwalked by. Speedwalking – yet another Hollywood fad.

Cassie crossed my line of vision just as I was in a rather delicately balanced position. I didn't fall too heavily and I knew it would only take a couple of days to heal. However, I made a mental note that if she was going to be speedwalking regularly I should encourage her to wear a sports bra for the good of her health. And mine.

She hadn't returned by the time I finished my practice so I limped back to my room and showered. As I was towelling myself down I watched the English-language regional news on TV. A story about the Yucatan triangle caught my attention.

The presenter, a pretty woman with unfeasibly big hair, emphasised words in a totally arbitrary way, in common with TV newsreaders the world over:

"News just *in* that the so-called Yucatan Triangle seems to *have* claimed another victim. This brings the *number* of craft that have disappeared without trace in *these* waters to eight in the *past* year. The best known *of* those who have disappeared *is* Los Angeles TV producer Neill Dodds. *He* was involved in developing *a* pilot for what at *the* time was the latest survival-*type* reality television show. He disappeared six months *ago.* It is assumed that the producer, a keen sailor, had either *been* sailing for the weekend *or* scouting locations for his show. *Neither* his family nor *his* business associates were *sure* which, however. The latest victim is..."

Later, a second story also interested me. It looked like the hurricane season would be starting a couple of weeks early this year.

Fuentes, the village we were staying in, was at the edge of a tropical rain forest. We were some miles south of Cancun, the tourist resort on the Caribbean coast of the Yucatan. It was a coast often hit by hurricanes, that I knew.

"Well, that's just fucking great."

Dwight was standing over the breakfast buffet, resplendent in a vomit green, purple and orange shirt and canary yellow shorts, his brown legs thick as tree trunks. His face was red with anger. He swung towards me.

"Nick, you're the film historian–" this was news to me but I nodded anyway, "–you know what happened to Francis in the Philippines and your man in Spain."

Chuck, Cassie and Bridget all looked down the breakfast table at me. We were sitting on the terrace of our hotel among the frangipani and bougainvillea. Greg and the crew were already breakfasted and out setting up for the day's shoot. Dwight had been with them but he'd just called back to prep Cassie and Chuck about their first scene together.

He was angry at the news of the hurricane season starting early.

"Francis is, obviously, Francis Ford Coppola or simply Francis Coppola depending on what period of his career we're talking about," I said. "These days probably known among younger filmgoers as much for being the father of Sofia *Lost In Translation* Coppola as for his own films."

"For fuck's sake, Nick, you pompous tit." My best friend Bridget was brandishing a pineapple in my general direction. "Get on with it."

"Okay, okay. *Apocalypse Now*, already horribly over budget.

Then a hurricane hits and totally destroys multi-million pound sets. Then, of course, Brando, who is to play a crack special forces commander, turns up looking like Orca the whale."

"Nick." This time it was Dwight.

"Shame he's dead," Chuck said.

"He's going to be," Bridget muttered, shooting a lethal glance at me.

"Always hoped he'd make one more decent film after the shambles of his career the past ten years," Chuck continued. "I made a film with him, you know. *Missouri Breaks*. Him and Jack Nicholson both. Brando was such a funny guy. Great mimic too. Had Jack right down – though I suppose that isn't very difficult. Decided to play the film dressed as a woman…" He frowned. "Never quite got that."

Dwight looked impatient.

"Yeah, okay, Chuck – thanks for sharing." He nodded at me. "Nick – continue."

"Right. My man in Spain is director Terry Gilliam who Dwight thinks, because of the Monty Python thing, is English but actually he's a Yank. Spent years putting together a film about Don Quixote, had Johnny Depp signed up. Had the sets built on the Spanish coast. Major storm destroyed the sets. No money to rebuild them. Film caves in. Depp goes on to be nominated for an Oscar for his role in the first successful pirate movie in decades – ouch!"

"Thanks, Nick," Dwight said. "And this hurricane season moving forward is going to be equally bad for us unless we get our fingers out. This is a six week shoot – ludicrous by current standards – but, boys and girls, we're going to have to try to finish in four. Are we up for it?"

Cassie, Chuck and Bridget all nodded. Dwight looked at me.

"Nick, don't sulk – are you up for it?"

All very well for him to say don't sulk. He hadn't just had a pineapple thrust at his crotch. Spiky end first.

After breakfast I went for a walk on the beach until it was time for the cars to take us down to the location. When I got back to the hotel, Bridget and Cassie were sitting on a sofa in the foyer and a large man was standing above them, a tumbler in his hand. He turned when I approached.

"Hello, we haven't met." He held out a thick hand. I caught a whiff of what was in his tumbler. It smelled distinctly like tequila. "I'm Yves."

Of course he didn't say it quite like that but I refuse to recognize his accent and won't attempt to describe it here because a) I hate all that phonetic patois stuff in books – 'Eet ees, 'ow you say, lovely you to meet' and all that rubbish; and b) I don't want readers swooning over this fat French lump when they should be getting on with the story.

Because, yes, he did have that heavy French accent that makes women go weak at the knees. Even Bridget.

"Lovely to meet you," she trilled. Trilled: a word I never thought I'd have cause to use in connection with Bridget and frankly hoped never to use at all.

Actually, her voice chilled me – it sounded as strange as Genghis Khan volunteering to read Thomas the Tank Engine in a crèche.

"Lovely to meet you too." That was Cassie. Ye Gods. She was simpering. Simpering and trilling and he'd only said one sentence. You got me at hello indeed.

I shook the hand that he'd held out to me several paragraphs ago but his attention had switched to the two women sitting on the sofa.

"Charmed," he said. "Bridget, delightful to see you once more. And you must be Cassie."

"I must be," Cassie said, giggling.

Yves looked from one set of breasts to the other. Threw back the tequila.

"Something tells me we are all going to get on very well," he said, sitting down in the narrow space between Bridget and Cassie.

"I'm Nick," I said. "The stuntman."

"Delighted to meet you," he said back, keeping his eyes on the women either side of him. He put his hand on Cassie's knee. When he moved from her knee up her thigh, she eased herself off the sofa and did a surprising thing.

She came over to me, put an arm through mine and kissed me on the cheek.

"Nick's a great stuntman," she said.

Woof.

Yves looked from Cassie to me and back again. He shrugged.

"I make movies so I know that appearances *are* deceptive. Even so…"

Cassie kissed me on the cheek again.

"I must get into costume for tonight."

She walked off. I must say she was managing a hip swivel almost as effective as Bridget's. Yves watched her retreating derriere with a tilted head.

One of our drivers wandered into the foyer and called for us.

It took Yves a moment to refocus.

"*Bien sur*," he jumped to his feet. "Of course." He turned and bowed to Bridget. "Until later."

"You bet," she said – but at least she'd stopped trilling.

When he'd gone she looked up at me from the sofa.

"And?"

"Why are you looking so cheesed off Yves has gone?" I said. "You're here with Dwight."

"Your point being?"

"Oh, Bridget."

We all piled on the boat to take us out to the galleon. The water was choppy and the small boat rolled a little in the swell. Chuck put his head in his hands.

"Feeling seasick again?" I said, commiserating.

"I don't do well on water." He put his hands down and clasped them. "God, I wish I was playing a cowboy. I'm desperate to be in a scene with a horse."

"Aren't we all?" Bridget said. She nodded at me. "Will you settle for a horse's ass?"

Everybody laughed. Rather too heartily I thought. Chuck smiled at Bridget.

"You're certainly a bright spark, Bridget. You certainly are." He looked back at me. "D'you ever see that film where John Wayne played a Mongol?"

"Now that's what I call miscasting," I said. "Aw c'mon, Genghis, we only need one more to make a horde."

I laughed – it was the punchline of an old *Private Eye* cartoon that I loved. Everyone else just stared at me. That's the problem with humour – it's so subjective. What I find funny others might not. Rarely do, in fact.

Chuck frowned, gave a little shake of his head, then continued: "That's about how I feel playing a pirate. I just wish I could show a Western roll."

"They just didn't have six guns," Dwight said. "Simple as that."

As it was so choppy we were sliding around in the cabin of the boat.

"You know," Dwight said, to nobody in particular. "When filming a sea movie a lot of directors get the idea they should go to sea."

"Understandable," I said.

"But wrong." Dwight slapped his hand against the side of the cabin. "You've got to resist that temptation because there are so many problems." He looked towards Joseph in the cockpit. He had just started throwing up. "Seasickness for one." He nodded sagely. "To tell you the truth, if I could have filmed this on land I would have been a happy man."

"A sea-story filmed on land is certainly an interesting notion," I said. "Couldn't you control it more by using a tank?"

"A tank would be good. But the producer nixed that on account of cost – d'you know how much Fox charge to hire out their big tank at Baja?"

"How much?" Chuck said.

Dwight frowned.

"Well, I don't know exactly but more than we can afford."

I spent the day running around like a mad thing. Dwight had really ratcheted up the speed of shooting so he could get the film in the can in four weeks. I was all over the place.

"I'm sure this isn't how films are normally made," I said to Stacey as she screwed on the peg leg I needed to play Pierre Le Peg, a pirate who was about to be keelhauled for daring to look at the Pirate Bride. "Ten set-ups in a day. Even Ed Wood didn't do so many."

"Welcome to the nouvelle fucking vague, pal." Greg was framed in the trailer doorway, leaning against the door jamb.

"Yeah, well," I said, standing and trying to walk with my

right lower leg strapped to the back of my thigh and my knee in the socket of the wooden leg.

"Five minutes," Greg said.

Bridget and Cassie were huddled down the far end of the trailer. I made my way down there.

"Hop it," Bridget said, without even glancing at the wooden leg.

Cassie ignored me and carried on with their conversation.

"Oh God, the Brazilian is *so* yesterday," she said. "My beautician told me my pubic styling was *so* old-fashioned."

"Pubic styling?"

Bridget glanced up at me.

"Private parts hairstyling, Nick – it's the latest thing."

"Sure," I said.

"Well, not the latest thing," Cassie said, glancing at my peg leg. "It's already old hat, actually. It's been around for absolutely ages." She waved her hand in the air. "At least a couple of years."

"Ancient," I said, trying to maintain my balance on the wooden leg. With the yoga I'm quite good at balancing on one foot but the conversation wasn't helping my equilibrium.

"But it remains important," Cassie continued. "These days if you want to keep up to date you need more than clothes and accessories."

"You need chic-slit," Bridget said solemnly.

"Chic-slit?" I said, bemused.

Bridget looked up at me wobbling beside her.

"Keep current, Nick," she said. "I read it in an article."

"So what's the latest thing?" I said. "Do tell."

Bridget flashed a warning look at me. My impudence, I guess. I tottered.

Cassie looked at me rather coyly. This was a surprise. I tottered some more.

"Bare," she said. "It has to be bare."

"Men too?" I said, trying for urbane. It would have worked too if my peg leg hadn't slid out at an odd angle and capsized me.

They both looked down at me. Pitilessly.

"But how's it done?" I said nonchalantly, as I scrabbled to get back to my feet. Well, one foot and a peg.

Cassie and Bridget burst out laughing. Not quite so nonchalant then.

"You look like a giant spider," Bridget said.

I managed to get my balance again.

"How is it done?" I repeated.

"With a lot of yowling," Cassie said. "Tearing hot wax off you with fabric strips – boys don't want to know, actually."

"Is it worth it?"

"That's a matter of opinion," Bridget said. She pointed at the peg leg. "As the man with the wooden leg said."

I spent a minute or so trying to figure that out. She watched my face patiently. Glanced at Cassie who wasn't even trying to work it out. I assume Cassie was so used to letting conversation go over her head, she didn't even think to try to make sense of what people said.

"Opinion," Bridget said. "*A pinion*? Wooden leg? Jesus, Nick, it's the oldest joke in the world."

"Very amusing," I said, applauding by tapping my peg leg on the floor.

"Don't get cocky," Bridget said as she saw me start to wobble again.

"Pubic hair changes from season to season," Cassie said. Clearly a single-minded girl. "If it's not bare, this year it's tufty – shaped and dyed."

"Bare or tufty," I said, totally out of my depth.

"I have a travel kit with stencils so I can style away from home," Cassie said.

I couldn't think of a response to that.

"If your little fairy is bare you can stick on crystals that spell words."

Ditto. In fact double ditto. Little fairy?

I looked at Bridget. Normally she would have had her finger down her throat at this point but, no, she was nodding lightly and paying attention to Cassie.

"What sort of words?" she said.

"Anything," Cassie said. She looked archly at me. "A lot of people do: *Fuck me.*" She kept her eyes on me.

"Written in crystals?" I said.

"What?" both Cassie and Bridget said.

I tried again, this time without croaking.

"Written in crystals?"

"It's a new world, Nick Madrid," Bridget said. "A new world."

Cassie smiled happily in agreement. Desirable as any woman I've ever seen. Beautiful as the morning sunrise. Thick as two short planks. With a hole in her head. In short, my kind of girl.

I did the Pierre le Peg scene. Rubbed my knee raw on the socket of the wooden leg. Between takes I was slumped in a chair, stretching the peg-leg out when Chuck came over.

"Hey, Nick, you're an educated man. What's this perverse thing?"

"Perverse?'

"I've got another song from Mad Hal. Polly – Polly…"

He was losing me.

"Polly put the kettle on?"

He gave me a long look.

"I haven't memorised it yet. Something about Polly being perverse."

Bing! I've read my Freud.

"Polymorphously perverse?"

"That's the one! What the heck does it mean?"

I looked around.

"Well, Chuck. Can you remember the lyric?"

He walked me through it.

How to handle this?

"Well, in this context it's being loosely used to suggest that you'll have sex with anything."

Chuck nodded slowly.

"That right?" He looked around. "Gol'darn." He raised his massive shoulders. "Well, I tell you, this is one heck of a peculiar movie. Reminds me of the film I made with Warren Beatty–"

"Chuck, can I ask you something?"

"I never saw Warren with any women," he said flatly.

"Not about Warren Beatty. Though I do know someone who years ago had a fling with him in London…"

"That's not a proper way to talk about your friend, Bridget."

I looked at him sharply.

"What's she been telling you?"

Chuck shrugged his big shoulders again.

"Okay. That aside, I wanted to ask you about this movie and the producer."

He tilted his head.

"Go ahead."

"Do you know what the producer is up to?"

He didn't hesitate.

"Shafting us, I assume. He's a producer – that's what they do."

"There's some stuff going on with the second unit."

Chuck held up his hand.

"Don't be telling me." He leaned forward. "Nick, I think I've said – I'm just here for the paycheck." He gripped my arm. "Don't complicate things."

I've been hearing that all my adult life. I took a breath.

"Man has to do what a man's gotta do, Chuck – you know that."

As I said it, I felt immensely crass. I was trying to put a twist on it but it didn't come out right. I was aware of Chuck looking at me. I couldn't read the expression in his eyes. He looked beyond me and down. Then he stood.

"Didn't take you for a wise-ass, Nick."

He walked away.

I was going to follow him but it was time for his next scene.

It was Yves's first scene and it was a big one – his character's showdown with Blackbeard. This came late in the film but directors always shoot scenes out of sequence.

Yves had been dressed as something of a dandy – lots of silk scarves, brocade waistcoat and a hat with a plume. He was leaning against the side rail talking to Bridget, his eyes flicking from her face to her breasts. She, of course, was loving the attention.

Stacey was trying to stop Chuck's tricorne hat from looking like it was perched on top of a bird's nest. She had the hat in one hand and the Blackbeard wig in the other. Chuck was sitting patiently, erect as always, little beads of sweat trickling from beneath his own wig. I assume it was sweat – maybe it was the glue.

Joseph was standing beside Stacey. He looked rather dashing in his naval outfit but that was because they'd padded his chest, padded his shoulders, even padded his calves and thighs so he didn't look ridiculous in his trousers and stockings. I think they'd overdone the shoulders and chest a bit – his thin face and neck sticking out of this massive upper body made me think of turtles again.

"Wouldn't it be easier without–" Joseph indicated Chuck's toupee.

"Without what?" Chuck said sharply.

"For god's sake don't mention the T word," Stacey warned.

"Without the wig," Joseph stuttered.

Chuck didn't say anything to Joseph. He simply stood up and stalked off to the other side of the deck.

Stacey sighed.

"Or the W word."

I felt bad that we kept upsetting Chuck but Dwight was in a hurry to get the next scene done. Yves stood facing Chuck.

"And Action!" Dwight called.

Yves, as L'Ollonais, hissed:

"I'm going to inflict famine, war and petulance on you."

I heard Dwight laugh.

"Keep it rolling," he called. "But, Yves, I think you mean 'pestilence'."

Yves shrugged – your actual Gallic shrug.

"Whatever."

He did the line again.

"And cut." Dwight jumped up from behind the camera. "And that's a wrap. Thanks everybody. I know it's been a long day but it's been a good one."

Bridget said under her breath:

"There's a man with a wooden leg with a view about that."

Back at the hotel we gathered at six to watch the dailies. This wasn't a regular thing but Yves was keen to see how his first scene had gone. Greg had also agreed that later Mollie and I could look at the fish footage.

Dwight and Greg had adjoining suites and they used the shared living room as a makeshift editing suite. We settled on sofas and chairs. Yves was sitting between Bridget and Cassie.

When L'Ollonais appeared for the first time, Yves spread his arms across the back of the sofa, behind Bridget and Cassie's heads.

"Hey," he said, laughing. "The money is finally on the screen. Now the movie begins."

As he laughed, I couldn't help noticing his arm had dropped around Bridget's shoulder. Nor could I help noticing that Bridget didn't mind at all. And neither, surprisingly, did Dwight.

At the end of the screening we all went our separate ways. I went to the bar to wait for Mollie. I took my drink to one of the sofas looking out to sea. The sun was near to setting so I sat there watching it sink beneath the horizon, all crimson and gold. It was beautiful. Then Bridget plopped down beside me.

"Hi, you."

"Hi, Bridget."

She leaned over and kissed me on the cheek.

"Nick, I'm sorry I've been so horrible to you. I haven't meant to be but I'm under a lot of pressure–"

"I know that," I said, touched by her frankness.

"Don't interrupt me when I'm apologizing!" she snapped.

I stiffened. No, not there. If only – I think the humidity had been getting to me.

"Sorry," she said, kissing me again and taking my hand. "You know, this film is my chance–"

"Chance for what? I thought you were just doing it for fun. This cameo role."

"Yes, of course," she said, releasing my hand then sitting up straight. "And I still think that. I'm being daft, I know."

She clasped her hands and looked down at them.

"You know, Nick, Dwight and I aren't really together any more."

"Was it because he kept calling you Esther? What was that about?"

"Oh. Nothing," she said. She sighed. "Not that I expected anything. I mean, I knew he was married. That was the deal – we were just together for the laughs." She sounded brittle.

"Are you okay?" I said.

"I'm fine – why wouldn't I be?"

I watched her hands clasp and unclasp.

"Bridget."

She slumped down.

I was aware of tears quietly spilling onto my shirt. My silk shirt, actually – damn.

I rummaged in my pocket, dug out a clump of tissues and passed them to her. She unfolded them and peered at them.

"They're clean – Jesus, Bridget."

"Sorry," she said as she blew her nose – more of a trumpet volley really.

I knew from experience that I had to handle Bridget feeling vulnerable carefully. She came across as so strong all the time and hated to appear weak. Or what she saw as weak.

"It's a full time job, directing a movie," I said. "He's got so much pressure on him. Especially on this budget, this schedule. And maybe his wife putting pressure on him."

"I finished with him, you dick, not vice versa."

She was sitting upright again. Silly me. Bridget was back.

"I want to shag Yves and I thought it unfair on Dwight to two-time him."

There's a complicated morality around a woman two-timing someone else's husband but I didn't want to explore it at that moment.

"Yes? But Yves is …"

"A little large, I admit. But that enthusiasm for life, that…joy de viver."

"*Joie de vivre*," I said – though what do I know about French pronunciation, a boy from Ramsbottom? Great that she was so moral. Great and … unlikely. "You've shagged Yves already, haven't you? Jesus, Bridget, he's only been here a few hours. When did you find the time?"

She leaned back and fixed me with her special stare.

"Oh what – you're giving me pointers on sexual etiquette when you've clearly got the hots for the Wildlife Woman who spat in your soup *and* Cassie "My Tits Wobble" Dexter. Who is, incidentally, totally out of your league. I won't even mention Stacey."

"What about Stacey?" I said indignantly, although why I was so indignant I don't know.

"I remember Brighton, mush."

"Mush?"

"I've seen my share of Sid James's films."

"You have slept with him, haven't you?"

"Sid James?" she said.

"You slept with Sid James?"

It was a woman's voice. We both looked up. Mollie was standing behind us. She flushed.

"Sorry, I didn't mean to interrupt." She walked round the front of the sofa and held her hand out to Bridget. "I'm Mollie Sanders. I love those *Carry On* films."

Bridget took her hand.

"Thought you were Catwoman the way you sneaked up on us without us hearing."

"I didn't sneak." She waggled a foot. "Plimsolls are quiet, I suppose. And you had your backs to me. I am sorry if I've intruded."

"Not at all," Bridget said, getting to her feet. She looked down at me. "Saved by the belle."

As Bridget waltzed away, Mollie leaned down and pecked me on the cheek.

"More," I blurted. She wagged a finger at me.

"We've got a fish to see."

As we were getting out of the lift Mollie said:

"Did she really sleep with Sid James?"

"Try Warren Beatty."

"Warren Beatty slept with Sid James?"

"Enough."

Greg called to us from the open doorway of the suite.

"Perfect timing."

He ushered us in. He looked Molly up and down with an appreciative smile, shook her hand, ushered her to the sofa then winked at me as she was sitting.

"So you're a fish expert, Miss," he said heartily.

"Turtles really but I know a thing or two about fish."

"I'm sure you do," he said. "I'm sure you do. Nick, why don't you sit next to Mollie there and I'll start the reel running."

There was no sound, just images on the spool of film. At first it was just a long shot of schools of fish, then suddenly I dropped into the water in a medium close-up. I began thrashing.

"I'd be grateful if you could identify this big fish, Mollie," Greg said cheerily.

"Had a man-of-war stung you?" she said, gesturing at my underwater St Vitus's dance.

"I'm fighting a giant squid," I said. "It will be added later."

"Dwight's decided it's going to be a shark," Greg said from over by the projector.

I came over all actor-ish.

"But I was imagining tentacles around me – I would fight a shark in a different way."

"Yeah right. Don't be petulant, Nick. Sharks are cheaper."

"I think you mean pestilence," I said.

Mollie looked puzzled.

"Film joke," I said.

Suddenly I whooshed away from the camera.

"That's when we lost you," Greg said. "Then you pop up again in the longshot among those fish. See?"

I could see me, scudding through the brightly coloured fish. Then I saw the big fish heading towards me, the small fish all darting away.

"Here he comes!"

"There he goes." Greg said.

He was right. The fish came towards me, veered off and disappeared in the murk, all in about seven seconds.

"Can you show that bit again?" Mollie said, leaning forward.

"Sure. But as you can see it's not very clear."

"Nevertheless."

"Nevertheless," Greg echoed. "Nevertheless."

He wound the film back and showed it again.

"Can you identify it?" I said to Mollie.

"It's not very clear." She'd been sitting forward on the sofa. Now she sat back in a waft of her perfume, her bare arm brushing mine. Steady, Madrid, steady.

"Looks to me like it could be almost anything," Greg said.

Mollie nodded.

"I'm afraid you're right."

We left Greg ten minutes later. As we came down the stairs to the foyer, me conscious of her perfume and her proximity, I said: "Would you like dinner?"

She stopped at the bottom of the stairs and looked at me. Wrinkled her nose.

"I don't think so, Nick. I like you but… you know. Maybe we could have a drink tomorrow evening?"

I watched her leave, half expected her to miss the step down into the garden. She didn't. She turned and waved, a grin on her face as if she knew what I was thinking. Turned back and sent a table and four chairs flying. Hurried out into the street.

I joined The Talent at the Artemio Cruz. Cassie Dexter was wearing a low cut, short dress which showed off her breasts and legs to, erm, startling advantage. Chuck was still the man in black, still very upright. Joseph was talking to Hal Jones, the lyricist. They looked like a couple of vampires out on a date. Yves was down at the end of the table, gesticulating wildly and speaking in a surge of words to Dwight and Bridget.

I couldn't help noticing that Yves's eyes were pretty firmly fixed on Bridget's unfettered breasts as he spoke to Dwight. I couldn't help noticing also that Cassie had noticed this and, I presume because she was not backward in that forward department, was looking pissed off.

I waved to Bridget and Dwight at the far end of the table and sat down opposite Cassie. Bridget and Dwight ignored me. So did Cassie. Life as I know it, then.

"How goes it with you, Nick?" Chuck proffered a basket of bread.

"Good, thanks. And you?"

"I'm getting paid, Nick," he said sombrely. "That's about the best I can say."

"How did your scene with Cassie work out today?"

I was looking at Chuck but really I was addressing both of them.

Cassie dragged her attention away from Bridget and Yves for a moment. Looked at me in a calculating way then said: "Oh it was great. Chuck's such a pro. And *so* sexy for a man of his age." She squeezed Chuck's arm. "Not to mention strong."

Chuck looked at her and smiled.

"Kind of you to say, sweetheart."

I could tell what he was thinking: he'd heard this shit from professionals. He wasn't going to be flattered by a model-turned-actress, however striking she was.

Cassie realised she wasn't going over so, after a quick glance down the table to Dwight, Bridget and Yves, she turned her attention to me.

Indeed, she spent the rest of the evening paying attention to me. Some might say she flirted outrageously with me. Now I'm a pretty cool customer. I've been round the track a few times. I'm not going to be taken in by the overt flirtatiousness of any woman, even if she's a Hollywood star of outstanding beauty and incredible sex appeal who is pretty much saying she's mine for the taking… What was the question?

Of course, there was mounting panic in me as well. The more she went on about tantric yoga and how great I must be in bed, the more I worried that a) Bridget would hear and pour scorn on the notion; and b) Cassie would be disappointed.

Because, frankly, I'm a disaster in bed. Always have been. My intentions are good but I'm just so astounded that anyone would want to go to bed with me that I blow it every time. I don't know what it is: I mean well. Nerves, I guess. So the thought of sleeping with a movie star…

"Escort me to my room, Nick," Cassie said, abruptly rising to her feet.

"Sure," I said as casually as I could.

"I didn't know you stuttered, Nick," Chuck said, concern on his face. Then he winked. Bastard.

Cassie draped herself over my shoulder. Ouf.

"'Night Dwight and Bridget and Mr Frenchman," Cassie said loudly as we staggered away from the table. Correction, I staggered. She was heavy, dammit.

"You going to screw me senseless, Nick?" she said as we waited for the lift.

"I very much doubt it," I thought, still reeling from the notion that this woman who had been so aloof with me earlier was now dragging me off to bed. The out of my league scenario came into my head again. What did she see in me?

"What did she see in you?" Bridget said next morning. "Hollywood star in the making. It bewilders me."

"Hang on."

"In fact, you and women bewilder me, frankly. How do you get off with any of them?"

I bridled. I do sometimes.

"Wouldn't you like to know?" I said stiffly.

"Well, clearly not or I would have tried to find out first-hand by now."

She almost did, actually, but now wasn't the time to remind her. We were sitting on my balcony overlooking this beautiful beach. I'd only been back in my room ten minutes but Bridget had clearly been watching for my return since she was hammering at my door after five of them.

When I opened it she barged past me, grabbed a small bottle of gin and a bottle of tonic from my mini-bar and headed for the balcony.

"Bridget! It's seven in the morning. Isn't that a bit early for your first drink of the day?"

"Who says it's my first? This day officially started at one minute past midnight. Between then and five am I must have had quite a number of drinks." She waved the glass in the air. "This comes under the heading of either continuing the party or hair of the dog."

I know from long experience that Bridget can drink anybody under the table. The bizarre thing is that it doesn't seem to have any effect at all on her. Mentally she can run rings round most people I know – including me, it goes without saying – and physically she's in damned good shape.

I slumped down in the beach chair opposite, an orange juice in my hand.

"So?" she said.

"So what, exactly?"

"What did she see in you?"

"You, as far as I can figure."

"What?"

"Just kidding. You seem very matey, that's all."

"It's an actor thing, darling. But sex with her? Can you imagine? We'd be fighting our way past each other's tits trying to kiss each other on the lips. We'd be a foot away from each other for the full frontal snog." She swigged her drink. "So come on, tell me about it."

"It's private, Bridget."

"You're not going to tell me anything?"

She was indignant.

"Okay. One thing."

She leaned forward, giving me the usual view of her cleavage down her low cut blouse.

"Which is?"

"Very nice," I said. "Yves is a lucky man. I assume that's who you've spent the night bonking and boozing with."

She looked down, waved her hand, ignored what I'd said.

"They serve a purpose."

I laughed.

"What's the one thing?" she said.

She took a swig of her drink, almost finished it off.

"I can confirm that she does have a hole in her head."

"Enough about that already!"

"No, honestly. She's been trepanned."

"What's that got to do with the hole in her head?"

"Ha ha. It's the old cure for mental illness. It involves drilling a hole in the head to relieve the pressure on the brain."

"Oh yeah – a Stryker saw."

"What?"

"A Stryker saw. I've read my Patricia Cornwell."

"Patricia *B* Cornwell, please. So have I. But a Stryker saw is actually for cutting the entire top of the skull off so you can remove the brain."

"Sounds right."

She saw my look.

"Are you saying," she said, "that Cassie Dexter, model turned Hollywood actress, has a brain?"

"Sharp. This hair of the dog thing is clearly working. Want another?"

"Make it vodka – I'm not filming today. I'm going back to bed once you tell me what happened."

"I'm not telling you anything," I said from over by the mini-bar.

"Well, tell me about this other bint – the one who spat in your soup. The Wildlife Woman. Greg said you were very pally with her."

"Bint?"

"Nick, get on with it. Give me something!"

"I told you – Cassie has been trepanned. Someone has drilled a hole in her head. Apparently it's the latest thing, the New Age way of releasing "creativity"."

Bridget slammed her drink down on the table.

"Bloody typical. I'm still trying to get the hang of the Kabbalah. I was always bloody useless at sums so pissing around with numbers is driving me bonkers. But what do you mean she's had a hole drilled into her head?"

"The kabbalah…the kabbalah. Aha – that's why the Esther – that's your Jewish name right?"

"Well, Madonna uses it…"

"Yeah, yeah. And yes she had a hole drilled in her head. Through the skull but obviously not into the brain. They did it to Apollinaire at the end of the First World War. Turned him into a vegetable."

"Use the wrong drill bit? Who's Apollinaire?"

"A poet."

I knew it was a mistake as soon as I'd said it. For Bridget poets, as she'd often remarked, were on a par with mass murderers and paedophiles.

She looked at me as she put her glass down, now devoid of vodka.

"You're *so* weird, Nick."

She stood and wrapped her arms round me, her breasts pressing against my chest in a worryingly pleasurable way.

"But I love you."

She kissed me on the lips and sashayed down the hall, her

hand raised in a little goodbye wave. When the door had closed behind her, I slumped back into my seat on the balcony and looked out at the sun already glittering on the turquoise waters.

That sex had been even more disastrous than usual with Cassie, which was not entirely my fault. It started well enough. For me, at least. Seeing this stunning woman shrug off her dress and turn towards me stark naked, one hand on her hip, the other acting as a fig leaf, was a good start by any man's standards.

"Why me?" I said, which is about the dumbest question any man can ask faced with a gift from God.

She didn't answer, thank that same God. Instead, she lay down on her bed, her legs crossed at the ankles, and looked up at me from under heavy lids. She beckoned.

Ordinarily, I don't need beckoning twice. But I was dazzled by how beautiful she was and still bemused about why I was here. She beckoned again, a look of impatience on her face.

The sex didn't last long. It never does with me, unfortunately. Afterwards we lay side by side.

"Can I ask you a question?" I said.

"Not: why me?" There was a harshness in her tone.

"No. When we came why did you cry out Bridget's name?"

She half-sat up and looked down at me.

"*We* came?" she said. "What makes you think I came? What makes you think I got any pleasure out of what just happened at all?"

Well, she was a straight shooter right enough. Usually, women wait for the second or third date to tell me I'm useless.

"I don't think that. Nobody else ever has – why should you?"

She softened.

"Nick, it's not you – it's me. It's just not my thing."

"Sex?"

She looked at me for a long moment.

"Men. But the world just isn't ready for the lesbian movie star. Anne Heche and Ellen Degeneres – where are you now? And as for the Big One, her career was wrecked because she wouldn't talk about her private life. Which was really dumb because her silence spoke volumes. One minute she was hot, hot, hot – *Vanity Fair* cover girl, *Premiere* cover girl. The next her films can't get arrested."

I knew who she was talking about. I thought.

"Yeah but the liposuction on her cheeks to make her cheekbones stand out more and the kick-ass attitude she adopted when she was under five feet tall might have had something to do with it," I said. "Audiences just thought she was ridiculous." I glanced at Cassie. "We are talking about the same person, I assume. Who were you talking about?"

"You think I'm going to say that out loud? She'd sue the ass off me – she's kept it out of the public domain so far. I assume she'll come clean when she's wrung her career utterly dry." She suddenly reached over and squeezed my hand. "It ain't easy being a gay woman anywhere – but in Hollywood? Whoosh."

"You should try crime-writing – I hear for some reason there are lots of dykes."

She gave me a look.

"Lesbians can call themselves dykes. Heterosexual men don't have that privilege. Besides – I'm an actor not a writer. And in answer to your question–"

"Question?"

"You asked: why me? Well, I would have thought that was obvious."

I was immediately nervous.

"I had to keep up appearances and of the men here you seemed the most harmless."

I sighed.

"I suppose it is obvious," I said.

She leaned over, her breasts pressing against my side. Ouf.

"Look, Nick, I need you to be my friend. I want to make a deal with you. And I'm being honest here – you already know enough to wreck my career before it gets to the next level – and I want it to get to the next level."

"What's the deal?"

"You can have me from time to time for the duration of the film but you mustn't tell anyone my secret."

Beautiful Hollywood star offers man her body with no strings attached. Ultimate heterosexual male fantasy, right?

"I won't tell anyone your secret."

"So we've got a deal?"

She took my silence for assent.

"Great – want to go again?"

I'm not a particularly moral man but this didn't feel right.

"I don't think I can just use you."

"But I want you to. You seem a nice, ineffectual guy" – she saw my look – "sorry, ineffectual wasn't the word I was looking for. You know, harmless. What, no better? Okay – just a nice guy. If I have you around I'm not going to be pestered by any of the other men. And everyone will think I'm hetero. It's a good deal for me and you get something out of it too."

"But if you're not going to get any pleasure out of it at all..."

"Hey, don't worry about me. I'll just grin and bear it."

"That makes me feel great."

"I'll think of it like a trip to the dentist. It will be fine."

She sat up in bed, her breasts jiggling.

"What's the problem, Nick?"

"I like the women I sleep with to enjoy themselves too."

"But I thought you said they never did?"

Hmm, suddenly she's a logician.

"Well, that's true."

"So what's the difference? With me you don't even have to try because you know it ain't going to work."

There was a subtle moral point I was sure I was missing here but I couldn't quite figure out what. I was thinking of seeing that old film *The Graduate* when I was a teenager. I couldn't understand why the Dustin Hoffman teenage character had such a problem being in a relationship with Mrs Robinson, this gorgeous, desirable older woman who just wanted him for sex. Wasn't that every teenage boy's fantasy? Was he mad? But now I found myself in an analogous position. I was being offered free sex, no strings attached – and I felt uncomfortable about it.

We went backwards and forwards on it. A hundred times she offered herself to me and a hundred times I said no. Well, 99 times – no point being a damned fool about it.

And afterwards she said just one thing:

"Do you think Bridget and I would make a good couple?"

Chapter Four

"I'm up in the crow's nest
But down in the dumps."

As I walked over to the breakfast table, Cassie, who'd been sitting talking to Greg, excused herself and hurried over to me. She put her arms round me and gave me a warm kiss on the mouth. Which fooled everybody but me since I could see her look over my shoulder at Bridget as she did so. Still, it had all the other men at the table looking at me in a new way. Joseph, in fact, was slack-jawed with surprise. He'd left the dinner table early the previous evening.

Dwight was talking to Joseph about his character, the Royal Navy lieutenant. Something occurred to me.

"Hang on," I said, frowning. "The man who killed Blackbeard in real life was an American naval officer."

"Nick," Bridget muttered impatiently.

"Yeah, right, and everyone knows about the American navy," Dwight said. "At the time we've set this film there wasn't even an independent America. Even American audiences will expect it to be the Royal Navy. It will be hard enough for them to accept a French pirate – 'What's a Frenchman doing in it?' they'll all be wittering. Talking of which, where is Yves?" Dwight looked round. "He's still on French time, I suppose."

Out of the corner of my eye I saw Bridget flush.

"How are you going to manage that sea battle, Dwight, between the Navy and Blackbeard? Where are you going to get the other boat from?"

"Miniatures – in a bath tub if our producer has his way."

* * *

At lunchtime I realised just how much Bridget was getting into this acting lark. I came back to the hotel to find her sitting very upright on the white sofa in the bar looking out to sea. She had one arm trailing along its back whilst she flourished her other hand in the air. She looked like she'd been transformed in the course of the morning into Gloria Swanson. I looked to see if there was a cigarette holder in her waving hand.

Dwight was sitting in a chair to her right. He had an odd look in his eyes. I couldn't figure out which cliché he most closely resembled: someone shell-shocked or someone hypnotized by a cobra that is about to strike.

"I mean the arc of this character has to be right, don't you agree, Dwight? She has to be in a different place at the end of the film from the one she was at the start."

"Right."

"And as things are, I just don't think that happens. Not on-screen anyway."

"Uhu."

"I mean we see her, this happy-go-lucky lower class woman fall head over heels in love with this pirate and she begins to change, begins to see there's another way of being."

Dwight nodded.

"Right."

"And then the Pirate Bride comes along." Bridget emphasized 'Pirate Bride' with a swirl of her hand in the air. "My character is threatened. She fights for her man." Bridget tilted her head to look up into the heavens – for which read a ceiling decorated with bull-fighting images – and pressed the back of her hand into her forehead. She'd definitely been watching *Sunset Boulevard.*

"She fights for her man –" she dropped her arm dramatically and sat forward on the sofa, fixing Dwight with a piercing look – "And then we scarcely see her in the film again!"

"Right," Dwight said after a pause. He looked uneasily at Bridget as she still fixed him with her gimlet eye. She was either Bette Davis being regal or Joan Crawford being mad as a bag of snakes, I couldn't decide which. Dwight swallowed audibly. "And your point is?"

"It's such a waste of a terrific character, such a waste of dramatic potential. You could do so much more with this woman. You waste her spirit, her courage."

Dwight sighed and picked at a loose thread on the arm of his chair.

"Bridget, you mean you want me to beef up your part."

"I'm not talking about me! I'm talking about her!" Bridget had both arms in the air now. "This magnificent woman who has so much more to offer."

"If you wanted me to beef up your part you should just have said."

"Beef up my part! I'm talking about what this character can bring to your film. She doesn't deserve to be tossed aside when she's served her purpose."

"It was always intended as a bit part. I thought you might have fun playing a cameo."

"Of course, it may be that through my insight into her passionate nature and desire for freedom I can bring something special to the role."

"I know she's a bit of a cipher but she's a means to an end."

"I think I can incarnate her in a way that might bear comparison with some of the great women of the silver screen." She looked down, clasped her hands in her lap. "Who am I to say?"

Dwight sighed again and saw what a mess he was making with the loose thread, which was by now about six inches long. He pressed it down onto the arm of the chair with his big hand.

"We don't have time either to rewrite the script or to shoot more scenes with her. Our schedule is too tight. The story is about Blackbeard and Cassie."

Bridget had been gazing off into the middle distance. If you'd seen her in a film you would have said she was gazing into the future or seeing her destiny. Now Dwight's words brought her back to the present.

"But this will enhance Cassie's role and her whole performance," she said quickly. "If the struggle with me continues. If I don't just – what is that beautiful line? – 'go gently into that sweet night'. It will be better for the film."

Egad – Bridget reciting poetry? Inaccurately, true, but even so. And now she was wringing her hands.

"I'm suggesting this for you, honey, for your film. I want this film to be the best it can be."

Dwight didn't say anything. Seemed, indeed, lost for words. Bridget glanced at him, thought she saw indecision.

"Look how it worked in *Chicago*. Zeta-Jones and that scrawny whatsername worked really well off each other. And there are hundreds of other examples."

"Such as?" Dwight's voice was a hollow rumble, as if he was dragging it out of some deep pit. I recognized the sound of a man beaten down by Bridget. Welcome to the club, Dwight.

Bridget was looking round for inspiration. Her immediate problem was that she didn't know anything about movies. She didn't like them much. All she knew about movie stars was what she got from the gossip columns. She spotted me, standing by a marble pillar, transfixed by her performance.

"Nick, darling, help me out here. My brain has gone temporarily awol. Movies with two strong women."

Dwight turned as I walked into the room. He nodded, started to rise.

"*Thelma and Louise, All About Eve*. Any Douglas Sirk movie, of course."

"Thanks, Nick, no need for more," Dwight said. He looked down at Bridget. "I'll think about what you said, sweetheart. Enjoy your afternoon off." He walked past me, resting his hand on my shoulder for a moment. "Nick, filming Chuck's close-ups in the crow's nest is taking longer than I hoped."

Chuck's close-ups of the crow's nest songs were taking place in a crow's nest some four feet off the ground, rigged up beside the hotel swimming pool. "I won't be needing you for the rest of today. Enjoy your time off."

I watched him go then turned back to Bridget. She had returned to sitting with one arm outstretched along the back of the sofa, her back arched and her breasts thrust out. Any memory of Gloria Swanson was wrecked, however, when she declared, loudly: "Fuck." She slumped in her seat, then gave me a hostile look. "Fat lot of good you were."

"I was struck dumb," I said. "That's the best acting I've seen since I got here. All that arc of the character stuff. When did you turn into Emma Thompson?"

"I was good wasn't I?" she said. She patted the sofa and, obedient as ever, I sat down beside her. "Thing is, I've twigged that this acting is a load of bollocks. It's what women do all the time with men: oh, do tell me more, no, no I'm really fascinated; oh darling size doesn't matter; no you were fantastic; no really, sometimes shorter is sweeter; no, of course I wouldn't rather be in bed with Brad Pitt." She shrugged. "Once I twigged that, I was fine." She looked around to see if we were being overheard. "Well, that and knowing where the camera is."

She swung her head back to look over my shoulder.

"You've got company," she said quietly.

I looked round. It was Mollie. I looked back at Bridget.

"Go on, piss off," she said. "I don't know where you get the stamina – and you'd best not let Cassie see you – I suspect she packs quite a wallop."

"See you later this afternoon?"

She shook her head.

"I doubt it. I'm going up to Cancun."

"Shopping?"

She nodded vaguely, looking slightly embarrassed. Maybe Cancun was code for spending the afternoon in bed with Yves.

I walked over to Mollie, kissed her on the cheek. She looked across at Bridget.

"Am I disturbing you?"

"Not at all. Do you want a drink? I have the rest of the day off."

"Not here. At Carlos's?"

"Sure."

"In ten minutes?" She turned to go.

"I'll walk with you," I said quickly but she shook her head then she was away. I looked back at Bridget and shrugged. Except that Bridget too had gone.

When Carlos saw me he immediately put on a record by that frisky Nazare Pereira. I nodded approval and picked up the beer he'd already poured. I shimmied my way across to Mollie, who was sitting at a small table on the edge of the beach.

"How are you?" I said as I sat down. Neutral-remarks-r-us.

"Can I trust you?" She flashed me a fierce glance. She was

holding the stem of her glass so tightly her knuckles were white.

I flushed. Had she found out about my night with Cassie?

I reached over and gently prised her fingers free of her glass. She looked at her hand for a moment then flexed it.

"I hope you can trust me." I said.

"Hope isn't enough."

"Okay – what have you heard?"

"What have I heard?" she said it almost contemptuously.

I was getting riled. I scarcely knew this woman, she'd indicated that there was no hope of us getting together and now she was being difficult because of something I did with someone else. Admittedly, at the time I did that something else I did believe myself to be in love with the woman sitting beside me now. But I didn't say I was perfect.

"Okay – trust me about what?"

She tapped her fingers on the table, then looked at me.

"That fish."

I sat back. Fish? It took me a moment to figure out what she was talking about.

"The one that attacked me? What about it?"

"I've identified it."

I frowned.

"And?"

"It's a coelacanth."

I nodded.

"Never heard of it."

"You've not heard of it?"

"Should I have?"

"It's the oldest fish in the world. Over six million years old – older than the dinosaurs. It really is primeval."

"God, and I thought turtles lived a long time."

"I don't mean the particular fish you saw is over six million years old, you berk – I mean the species. It was thought to be extinct until one was fished up off the coast of Africa in the 1930s. Then later others were found off Indonesia. And there's anecdotal evidence to place them off the coast of Mexico too. Nick, are you listening?"

"Berk?" I said.

She squeezed my hand. Adopted a childish voice.

"Has Mollie hurt little Nickie's feelings?"

"It was a simple mistake."

"That's better – huffing suits you better than sulking."

"Okay, so it's a very old fish – what's the problem? Is it a man-eater? Is the second unit's underwater crew in danger? "

"It's the fish that's in danger. It's good news there's another community here, but bad news because these fish are worth a lot of money and if word gets out they'll be fished back into extinction."

"So what do we do?"

"Keep quiet about it. And maybe try to find out where it lives."

"I would have thought that was obvious."

She gave me a frosty look.

"Yes, they live underwater but they're shy creatures – they live quietly in caves. I've been looking at some charts. There are caves marked over where your second unit is filming."

"I don't think they are filming," I said. "I think they're looting a sunken Spanish treasure ship."

She tilted her head.

"That could be awkward. But if you've got the rest of the day off, why don't we go out and see?"

I sat back.

"They wouldn't let us get near. The producer has declared the second unit off-limits."

"The sea belongs to all of us." She thought for a moment. "Can you scuba dive?"

I nodded.

"Then we'll go in underwater and they won't even know we're there."

Two hours later we were sitting in the back of a narrow boat with a tarpaulin providing shade above us and the outboard motor idling behind us. We'd anchored about a quarter of a mile from the second unit's boat. Even under the awning the heat was fierce.

Mollie was studying a chart whilst I was struggling to get my flippers on. I can scuba dive but I haven't for ages. I have done a fair bit of free-diving, where you descend without any equipment at all, but that wasn't appropriate for this.

"Officially we're in the Caribbean but we're so near the Yucatan Channel that links the Caribbean to the Gulf of Mexico it's hardly worth worrying about. Most of the Gulf is between 10,000 feet and 500 feet deep." She pointed at the chart. "But where we are it's much shallower – we're on a shelf. There are sloping beds formed by the silt poured in by rivers. So finding a boat under water isn't such a big deal. And here," she pressed one long finger into the chart, "are where the caves are."

"So if you were looking for a sunken treasure galleon, this is where you'd stand some hope of finding one."

She put the chart down and nodded.

"Local pirates used to infest the hundreds of inlets around here then come out to take the prizes by surprise." She sat on the side of the boat. "But, Nick, we're not here to see what your second unit is up to, we're here to find a fish. The caves should be between us and them."

"Looking for a fish in the sea – makes sense."

I sat beside her and we both put our masks on. She looked at me, gave me the thumbs up. I made the same gesture then we both toppled backwards into the water.

We had air for a good hour. It might be that at the extreme of our dive we would need to come up slowly to avoid the bends but we might not need to go so deep.

Visibility was good. We moved easily through schools of bright fish, keeping an eye out for sharks or any other predator we'd do better not to tangle with.

We reached the first of the caves in fourteen minutes. We both had torches. We beamed them into the mouth of it. Nothing there. I looked across at Mollie. I was nervous – I didn't really relish another close encounter with the coelacanth. If it felt we were threatening it in its home, there was no saying what it would do. As I was thinking these thoughts, Mollie was swimming into the cave.

Oh well. I swam in after her. The cave was about twelve feet high but it was hard to see how deep it was. Visibility was poor as there were sand particles in the water. We swam in about twenty yards before Mollie backed towards me. She shook her head and I led the way back out. I checked my watch. We'd used another four minutes.

Over the next twenty minutes we explored several caves without coming across anything approaching the coelacanth. We had eight minutes of air left before we would have to set off back to our boat.

As we came out of the last cave I saw four divers approaching us on those little scuba scooters. I touched Mollie's arm and pointed. We both trod water a few feet above the rocky plateau that hid the caves.

The four divers reached us, then circled us. They circled us tighter and tighter, forcing us close together. I couldn't make out the features of any of the divers but their eyes and their attitudes were menacing. I noted that each one of them had a harpoon gun strapped to the side of their scooters and knives at their belts. We had knives too but I didn't particularly want to get into an underwater knife fight. Any kind of knife fight, for that matter.

Mollie and I were back to back and I reached behind me to take one of her hands. She squeezed mine and we remained like that, treading water, whilst the four divers moved in and out around us. Then one of them pointed back in the direction of our boat and the others moved into a line beside him.

I steered myself so that I was alongside Mollie, which is how I saw her give them the finger. Oh dear. I tugged at her other hand to turn her. She tried to get free of my grip but I held on and started swimming back towards our boat, dragging her along behind me, her single digit still defiantly raised above her head.

I glanced at my watch. The divers had corralled us for thirteen minutes. That meant that we were going to have to do the last five minutes on the surface of the water. I was thinking maybe we could go faster then realised that would just mean we would use the air faster so it would come to the same thing.

When we bobbed to the surface we couldn't immediately see our boat. Mollie spat out her mouthpiece.

"Those bastards," she spluttered as waves raised her and dipped her down in the water again. "Who do they think they are?"

"Save your breath," I said, trying to get myself further out of the water so I could see the boat. I looked at the compass on my wrist. We had come in the right direction at least.

We swam on the surface of the water for five minutes, Mollie much faster than I. Then I bobbed up again and saw the boat a hundred yards away.

A few minute later we clambered aboard.

Mollie stomped around.

"Those bastards. Those bastards." She was shaking with rage.

"Hey, Mollie, we expected it. Remember?"

She moved quickly across the boat to the spare oxygen tanks. She kicked at one of them then hobbled away, yelling: "Bastards! Bastards! Bastards!"

"I think we've established that – what's the matter now?"

"They've emptied our spare tanks to stop us going back down."

She was furious. I could see the veins in her neck pulsing. The muscles in her arms were taut.

"Well, we'll fucking show them."

I put my hand on her arm. She jerked back.

"Back off," she snarled. And I did. Her beautiful face was horribly contorted. "We're going over there."

"Mollie."

"We're going over there and you're going to do your free dive down and you're going to find this fucking shipwreck."

"Mollie."

"This is outrageous! The oceans are for everybody. Warning us off – how bloody dare they?"

"Mollie."

She looked at me, her eyes hard.

"What?"

"We don't have to do this."

She looked at me for a long moment.

"Yes. We do."

It took her ten minutes to calm down.

"Do they live on the boat?" she said as she stripped off her wetsuit.

"I assume the crew do." I shrugged. "The second unit stay in a hotel over your side of town."

"Good. When they go back to the mainland, we'll go back over to the boat."

We spent the next couple of hours lying in the shade of the tarpaulin having a desultory conversation. Although I welcomed the opportunity to get to know her better, she wasn't in the mood for talking about herself. And since I had to put myself at risk shortly, I wasn't in a mood to talk at all.

"You ever seen corals have sex?" she asked at one point.

I wasn't entirely sure whether this was an eco-warrior's equivalent of a come-on.

"Coral sex?" I said cautiously.

"I saw it here last August. It only happens in the Caribbean. Happens for five evenings after the August full moon. Two hours an evening – mass sexual activity. The coral release millions of minute bundles containing eggs and sperm. It looks like a snowstorm as they drift upwards from the coral. Then they float on the surface of the water in a slick that smells quite sweet. It's fantastic."

"Sounds it," I said, unable to think of anything else to say.

Not long after we watched through binoculars as a motor boat left the second unit's boat and headed for the shore.

"You're up," Mollie said, starting the outboard motor.

We puttered to within a few hundred yards of the second unit's boat, scanning the decks for any sign of crew members. I was sure that even if we couldn't see them they could see us. Mollie remained insistent. But then it was easy for her to be insistent – I was the one going down again.

The dive wasn't a problem. Free diving is pretty easy, actually. Just a matter of slowing the heartbeat down by big, slow breaths then expelling carbon monoxide by quick breaths – then taking another big, big breath.

The problem with Mollie's free diving idea is that usually when you free dive you just go down and then back up again. You don't actually do anything when you're down there. Here I had to swim around to locate the wreck.

However, that took hardly any time. The wreck was only about forty feet down. I saw it in the distance – the water was remarkably clear around here – and approached gingerly. As far as I could see there were no salvage divers around.

I swam around the boat. It was precisely what a sunken treasure ship should look like. Lying on its side, half-covered in silt and sand, masts sticking out at odd angles, huge curved prow. There was a big hole in the side of the boat with fish flittering in and out.

Beside the wreck was the ship's massive anchor and rusted cannon piled at odd angles atop a huge mound of what looked like dull green copper ingots. I could see a thick cable anchored to the seafloor disappearing off up to the surface. I assumed the second unit's ship was at the other end.

I swam closer to the galleon and over to the big hole in its side. It's only in films, of course, that giant squid lurk inside a wreck to lunch on the unsuspecting explorer. Given that I'm a film buff, however, I wasn't taking any chances.

Instead of dropping inside I swam over to the cable and suspended myself in the water by holding on to it. I could probably last another couple of minutes as long as I kept my heart rate down. I peered around to see what else might have come out of the vessel to land on the seabed. I could see another large mound on the other side of the galleon. And then I saw something else.

Mollie looked anxious when I scrabbled back on board our boat.

"What is it, Nick? You look startled."

"It's a wreck alright," I said, trying to calm my rocketing heart rate.

"And?"

"Our coelacanth appears to be living in it."

"What?"

I looked across at the second unit's boat.

"Let's get out of here and I'll explain on our way."

She started the outboard and we puttered away.

"You saw it?"

I nodded.

"It didn't see me, thank goodness – God it's big. It came out of this big hole in the side of the wreck."

"It won't be living there," Mollie said.

"You said they liked caves. Maybe it thinks it's a cave."

Mollie frowned.

"No, I'm sure it would need more space. A wreck would be a bit cramped for such a big fish. It was probably just exploring."

"Do you think the salvage divers have already seen it?"

"Beats me. Unlikely, I would think – it would make itself scarce if it saw activity down there."

"So what do we do now?"

She laughed.

"I haven't a clue."

* * *

Mollie didn't want dinner with me so I mooched down to the Artemio Cruz. Bridget and Cassie were huddled at the bar with a stranger when I arrived back. I approached from behind. The stranger was talking.

"What's your internal barometer when you give yourself the licence to get a little big or be slightly somewhat self-referential in the theatricality of a moment –"

Oh dear.

"–because it delivers on perhaps a laugh or an audience-pleasing cheer-type moment that ordinarily as an actor one is never wanting to be conscious of kind of satisfying the audience in that sense."

"Right," Cassie said flatly, obviously with no clue what he was talking about.

"How true, how true," Bridget said. She caught sight of me.

"Nick – this is – what was your name again?"

"Mark Smythe, actor."

"Hello Mark Smythe, actor. You've just arrived?"

"No, no, I've been here from the start."

I frowned.

"Who are you playing?"

He was a handsome man. He flashed a set of good teeth that may or may not have belonged to him.

"Oh, I'm just an extra for the time being though Dwight thinks he might give me a line."

"You paid?"

"Cheap at the price," he said cheerfully. "Meeting these two very lovely ladies has already made it money well spent. Might I ask if you both are in relationships?"

Cassie gave him her full wattage movie star smile. I tried not to throw up.

"Kind of you to compliment us. So far as relationships go I love those wise words that Halle Berry uttered when her marriage broke down. 'The man for me is now the cherry on the pie, but I'm not the pie and my pie is good all by itself, even if I don't have the cherry.' Wise don't you think?"

"I'm speechless," I said.

We left Smythe and took our regular table.

"Anyone else coming down?" I said.

"Dwight and Greg are editing," Cassie said.

Bridget gave a small smile.

"And Joseph has gone out to dinner with Stacey."

"Well, that'll be a test of his celibacy rules. If he can resist Stacey, he is a true celibate indeed. Where's Yves?"

Bridget shook her head.

"You haven't heard? He fell off the prop galleon in the harbour, almost drowned. As the village's sewage system seems to centre on pumping everything into the bay, he's been taken to Cancun to have his stomach pumped."

"Poor guy. How'd he fall?"

"The tequila he'd been drinking since breakfast might have had something to do with it," she said shortly.

"How was Cancun for you?"

"Fine, fine," Bridget concentrated on her menu.

There was something odd about her tonight but I couldn't quite put my finger on it.

"Oh," Cassie said, "there's a terrific paedophile – no, paediatrician – no, paedologist – no, damn – you know, a foot guy there."

"Chiropodist?" I said.

"Podiatrician," Bridget said.

"Right. He did my heels and soles."

"Really," Bridget said. "Mine too."

"Really?" Cassie squealed. "What a coincidence."

"Small world," Bridget said, then dropped her eyes when she saw how Cassie was gazing at her.

"I just love high heeled shoes," Cassie said, "but they kill me so this was perfect. So comfortable now."

I was lost.

"What are you both talking about?"

"Collagen injections in the heels, dumbo," Bridget said. "Where have you been?"

"In a parallel universe, obviously."

"It plumps up the skin, makes the shoes more comfortable. Three injections per foot last three months."

"Took a while for the swelling to go down for me," Cassie said. "Did you have your toes done too?"

Bridget shook her head.

"That's too extreme for me."

"Plumped up toes?"

"No, dumbo," Cassie said. Great, now I had both of them insulting me. She slipped off her shoes and wiggled her toes. "See how my second toes are longer than my big toes?"

I did.

"Some women don't like that so they have a piece of bone removed at the joint to shorten the toe."

"Ugh."

"That's nothing," Cassie said cheerfully. "I know a few women who've had their little toes removed so they can fit into really narrow shoes."

"What if shoe fashions change."

Cassie looked blank. Around two minutes later she said: "It'll never happen."

It didn't sound like a ringing article of faith.

Whilst Cassie was ordering her meal I murmured to Bridget: "I need a word."

She ignored me.

In the course of the meal I muttered it to her a dozen more times.

She finally looked at me as if regretting not having a fly spray or a swat to hand.

"How about *pest*? That's a word – take that one."

"What are you two guys whispering about?" Cassie said, between mouthfuls of her fish dish.

"Oh, just talking about the Kabbalah?" I said.

"You're into the Kabbalah? I used to be but I felt it was time for me to move on."

"I'm interested but I'm lousy at maths," Bridget said.

"What's that got to do with anything?" Cassie said, frowning.

"Well, it's all about the significance of numbers," I said. "Hidden correlations?"

"Don't know what they are and that's not the way we did it. We did twenty-second speed meditations. And we didn't need to read the ancient texts – we could just run our fingers over them to get the hang of them. It was brilliant."

"I'm sure it was."

When Cassie excused herself to go to the bathroom, Bridget turned and punched me on the arm. Hard.

"So what's so important that you hiss in my ear all evening."

"You've got to tell Dwight."

She shifted in her seat.

"Tell him what?"

"The second unit isn't filming anything. They're salvaging treasure from a wrecked Spanish galleon."

She shifted again.

"Nick, why are you always trying to make things difficult?"

"What do you mean? Do you mean Dwight is in on it?"

She looked indignant. She does indignation well.

"Of course I don't mean that. I mean here we are playing at being in the movies, having a perfectly lovely time. You're shagging every woman that moves – as long as they don't move too much, presumably. And you have to uncover secret plots."

"It's not my fault the stuntman was murdered by a person or persons unknown. And what they're doing is illegal. The wreck is in Mexican waters. That wreck belongs to Mexico. They're in big trouble if the authorities find out. And don't you think there might be a connection between a highly illegal operation and a murder?"

"Yeah, yeah." Bridget sighed, running her hand down her thigh like some old-time vamp. "But you know, you're as likely to see Dwight as me. I'm not sharing his suite any more."

"Are you with Yves?"

She gave me a withering look, although it looked slightly odd for some reason I couldn't figure.

"Nick, although my sex life is none of your bloody business I have not in fact made the beast with two backs with Monsieur Delain, much as he would like to. For a time I thought I would also like to – but as our Gallic heartthrob loves drinking above all else that has not been a practical proposition, if you get my meaning. And now I've gone off the idea."

I saw Cassie striding back to the table. Bridget glanced over to the bar where Martin Smythe was still sitting, nursing a drink.

"However, I definitely have an urge so I'm thinking I might invite Goldilocks over there to share my porridge."

"What – an extra?" I said, then flushed at my sudden snobbery.

"Noblesse oblige," Bridget said as Cassie sat down again.

At the end of dinner, Bridget did indeed go over to join Smythe at the bar. Cassie took me back to her room, making sure everybody saw her draped over me in the street and in the hotel foyer. Once we were in her room she undraped herself and walked over to the bed.

She stood with her back to me as she slipped off her dress.

"God, what's that?"

She looked back over her shoulder and tried to follow my gaze.

"Oh those – they'll have gone in a couple of days."

All across her back she had large circular purple weals.

"I was cupped this morning."

"Cupped?"

"Yeah, my qi had stagnated."

"I'm sorry to hear that."

"See how purple those rings are? That shows I was really stagnant."

I nodded, distracted even more by the sight of her bare bum and shapely legs.

"Poor thing."

"Gwyneth had it when she had headaches after the birth of her child." She saw my look. "Paltrow."

"Okay. How's it work?"

"This woman put rounded glass cups on to my back and buttocks and used a lighted taper to suck all the air out."

"Aha."

She turned to face me.

"Well, that's it. It encourages blood flow and eases aches and pains. Gets rid of your toxins."

"Great," I said.

She stepped forward and pressed her naked body against me.

"Well," she said. "Let's get it over with."

She certainly knew how to excite a man.

"Look," I said, gently disentangling myself. "You don't need to do this."

"I gave you my reasons," she said. "You're reneging?"

"No. Look, we can keep up the pretence out there but you don't have to pretend in the bedroom."

"Well, what are you going to get out of that?"

Good point.

"Er, nothing. But that doesn't matter."

She examined my face for a moment or two then she hugged me to her again. I tried not to groan.

"Wow," she said. "Do men like you really exist then?"

"Only outside Hollywood," I said.

She stepped back.

"What do you want to do then? Do you want to watch a DVD instead?

"Sure," I said, trying to feel good about being honourable. "Do you think you could put your clothes back on?"

"Oh, I'm sorry." She slipped on the big fleecy bathrobe from the bathroom. It reduced her sex appeal by a nano-fraction, especially when she bent over to look at the DVDs lined up on the coffee table.

"Let's see, I've got the remake of *Casablanca* with Nicole Kidman and Vin Diesel set in Detroit not – erm – wherever the original was set; Tarantino's lesbian kick-boxing remake of *Love Story* with Uma Thurman and Lucy Liu; *Kill Bill 7: the film without end, however much you pray …*"

On and on she went with a list of remakes, sequels and pre-quels.

"None of these films are out yet," I said.

She straightened up.

"Zane Pynchon lent me them. They're pirated, I guess."

We settled on the one original film she had. Which turned out to be a reworking of *Brief Encounter* set on a space station.

Cassie was a sweet woman if you could get behind the New Age babble and the fact that she wasn't very bright. She still pined for Bridget.

I left her at about 1 a.m. and walked back across the hotel's central courtyard to my room. I hopped over my balcony onto the narrow verandah and gave a little gasp when I saw a bulky figure sitting in the chair there.

"You Nick Martini?"

"Madrid," I said.

"Madrid Martini?"

I pressed the lightswitch on the wall.

"Well, well, Zane Pynchon. You haven't changed a bit."

I'd last seen him three or four years ago when he was just another producer off the assembly line: overweight, dressed entirely in black, wearing shades in and out of doors, full of shit.

He peered at me.

"Do we know each other?"

I could tell he didn't recognize me at all. That would be the cocaine consumption, which also added to the cliché that was his character.

As I was deciding how to answer he moved on.

"Martini, do you know what a producer does?"

"I wonder about it frequently."

"He has vision. You ever read Hemingway's *Last Tycoon* about Monroe Stahr?"

"Scott Fitzgerald."

"No, definitely Monroe Stahr. De Niro played him in the movie. That guy had vision. It was based, as best I recall, on Zanuck."

"It was based on Irving Thalberg though Zanuck fired Fitzgerald from *Gone With The Wind* just because he could."

"You've got everything cock-eyed here, my English friend. Anyway, the public has this notion of the producer as this showboat impresario, drinking banana daquiris, smoking big cigars and having cocktail parties."

"That sounds like Zanuck or Louis B Mayer." I pointed at his cigar. "But you try?"

He looked at me, waved his cigar.

"You're causing me some inconvenience," he said.

"I hope so," I said.

"Why? What do you have against a man trying to earn an honest living?"

"Isn't a man earning an honest living an oxymoron in Hollywood?" He frowned. "Skip it. What you're doing is illegal."

"Why do you care?"

Why did I care, come to think of it? Because I didn't like crooks ripping off treasure that belonged in museums? Actually, yes, I am that much of a geek.

"Do you know what we've found down there?"

I shrugged.

"A treasure ship."

"Not just any treasure ship. A very famous treasure ship. A very famous treasure."

"That's good to know."

"It's Captain Kidd's treasure down there."

He sat back with a self-satisfied expression on his face.

"Bollocks," I said, before I could stop myself.

"And you are suddenly an expert?"

"I know about Captain Kidd." And not just from my *Boy's Book of Pirates.* There had been that talk about Ridley Scott's film about Captain Kidd in which he was going to be represented as some kind of seafaring Robin Hood. This piqued my interest since there was nothing in the little I knew of Kidd to suggest he was anything but the usual piratical cut-throat, out for whatever he could get.

"You'll know he killed his gunner in a fight and his crew deserted him off Madagascar then," Pynchon said.

"I do."

"You'll know he was hanged for piracy in England."

"I do."

"You'll know he was the most successful pirate ever. That he amassed a massive hoard of treasure. That the legend goes that rather than his treasure fall into the hands of the government he scuppered his ship in the Gulf of Mexico and his treasure sank to the bottom of the ocean."

"What, you mean it's in Davy Jones's locker?"

"Are you being deliberately obtuse?"

"Obtuse – impressive word to come from a Hollywood bottom-feeder."

"Fuck you, pal. I heard it in a film, as a matter of fact."

Of course: key word in *The Shawshank Redemption.*

"I'm only being deliberately obtuse a little. All that you've just said is garbage."

I gave Pynchon a brief account of what I knew. Kidd, who was born in Greenock, Scotland around 1645, had been a successful privateer for England in the West Indies – a private captain hired by the English government to attack enemy ships. He made so much money doing that that by 1691 he could retire. He settled in New York, where he married. He clearly got bored because in 1695 he sailed to England and offered his services to William III. The king hired him to capture pirate ships in the Indian Ocean.

Kidd crewed his ship – called *Adventure Galley* – with men from both England and New York. Instead of attacking pirate ships, however, Kidd attacked merchant ships in the Red Sea and later off the coast of India. Some of these were French and since England was at war with France that was fine. But Kidd attacked the ships of England's friends too – in fact he attacked everything he came across. And that was piracy.

"Cut to the chase, for God's sake," Pynchon said.

"Okay, then there was the mutiny. Facing down the gunner William Moore, Kidd snatched up an iron bucket and whacked him over the head with it. Killed him. When Kidd's ship landed in Madagascar, most of his men deserted.

"Kidd and the crew he had left sailed to the West Indies. When he got there he found he'd been declared a pirate."

"Which is when he scuppered his ship full of treasure."

I shook my head.

"Kidd sold most of his cargo and went back to New York. He hid some of his treasure with friends then sailed to Boston. He was arrested there and sent to England for trial. At his trial he said he'd been forced to commit the acts of piracy by his mutinous crew. Actually that's what he wanted to say but he wasn't allowed to present his evidence. He was found guilty; he was hanged."

"And his treasure?"

"The government seized most of it. This definitely is not Captain Kidd's treasure."

Pynchon was both pissed off and piqued.

"Well aren't you the fucking know-it-all? Okay, whose damned treasure is it?"

"Why does it matter to you? It's still treasure."

"Yeah but who is interested in some anonymous Joe Schmo's treasure? I want a name attached."

"But it isn't yours anyway."

Pynchon's sucked on his cigar but it had gone out. He lay it down on the table beside his chair.

"Look, can't we come to some arrangement here? You're a bright kid – tell you what. Why don't I give you an associate producer credit? It'll give you a good start in Hollywood."

I laughed.

"Do I look stupid?"

He looked surprised.

"Well, yes."

Hmm.

"Well, I'm not that stupid." Associate producer was a vanity title, bestowed on the star's brother-in-law or some guy the director slept with or the producer's secretary. It's a little gift. Everybody in the business knows it's meaningless and valueless.

Zane looked at me.

"Do you know how sick I am of bog snorkelling? Do you know how much I want to be able to say to people 'Okay, this is what we're doing – give me the money' – and then just get on with it? But I can't. I fucking can't. It used to be a jungle out there. These days it's a cesspit."

"You don't think you've played your part in making it a cesspit?"

"You're being impudent – in your position? You creep. If I were you I'd be grabbing the knee pads." He shook his head. "Man oh man. This wreck is my chance to get out of this frigging business."

Pynchon smiled. Thinly.

"You think I'm going to be hurt by your words. Sticks and stones, my friend." He turned up his hands. "I'm from Hollywood. They bite the heads off snakes there."

"They missed one," I said.

Pynchon shook his head and pulled himself to his feet. He was about six inches shorter than me but much wider.

"Lot to learn, Martini. Lot to learn. I hear you and Bridget are buddies from way back. And then there's that little eco-warrior with the great ass you brought out to our boat earlier today. That's a lot of responsibility for one man to handle. Are you up to it?"

I wasn't quite sure what he meant. He saw my puzzlement.

"These are dangerous waters. A dangerous town, for that matter. I hear your stuntman turned up dead."

"I thought you might have first-hand information about that."

He picked up his cigar, sucked on it and blew a plume of smoke into the air.

"I advise you most strongly not to interfere with our little enterprise."

"Why – will I get what the stuntman got?"

"I know nothing about the stuntman. I just wanted to remind you that you bear a heavy responsibility in the lovely – albeit very different – shapes of the one with the great tits and the one with the great ass."

"Which movie did you find 'albeit' in?" I said, but he could see I knew I was outmanoeuvred.

"I don't know, but try this from any number of old movies: keep quiet or the dames get it."

"'Girls Get It' would be better – the alliteration trips off the tongue," I called to his retreating back. He didn't break step but waved his hand in the air and flipped me the bird.

"Eat shit, shit-heel," he called back. "How's that for alliteration?"

Then he was lost in the trees.

"Marginally better," I muttered. Pondering the fact that when Pynchon had leaned forward to get out of the chair I couldn't help but notice he too had a hole in his head.

Chapter Five

"All I wanted during years
Of plundering and pillage
Was to settle with a wife and kids
In a little country village
And run a little tavern
Offering sandwiches and beer
To be a friend to every man
So they'd have no need to fear
Though if from time to time
When I was too full of rum
I felt the need to keelhaul one –
Well, that's just harmless fun."

The next morning I found out what was odd about Bridget.

I slept badly and wasn't in the mood to do my full yoga practice in the morning. I did the Five Tibetans instead. It's okay, it's legal. The Five Tibetans are five specific yoga positions that, repeated enough, provide a pretty vigorous work out. Frankly, they nearly kill you.

I wanted to ask Bridget about her full body work out with Smythe but she wasn't at breakfast.

Otherwise breakfast was a familiar scenario. As usual, Cassie made a point of coming over, putting her arms round me and kissing me on the mouth. And Chuck was sitting erect. But then Joseph was sitting at a separate table gazing into Stacey's eyes.

Way to go, Stace.

I walked over to where Dwight was talking to Greg.

"Can I have a word, Dwight?"

"Not just now, if you don't mind, Nick. Greg and I are planning the final battle."

I sat between Chuck and Cassie.

"Dwight wants to hire a helicopter," Chuck rumbled. "Shoot the final battle from above."

Dwight overheard.

"It's pure Busby Berkeley," he said. "Forty sailors thrown overboard form a big circle to fight off mechanical sharks whilst dolphins leap and sperm whales spout." He looked from one to the other of us. "Can you picture it?"

"Horribly clearly," I murmured.

"But I'll never get the money for it. That damned producer Pynchon."

"It was Pynchon I wanted to talk to you about," I said but Dwight was talking to Greg again.

Bridget only appeared as we were all on the boat and were about to cast off at the dock. She was wearing big dark glasses and an enormous floppy hat almost completely hiding her face. That didn't bode well.

"So how was your night?" I said.

She was po-faced.

"You like to live vicariously through me don't you?" she said through gritted teeth.

"Didn't pan out well, then?"

"Not that it's any of your business but I changed my mind. Smythe regards himself as a ladies man. Quote: 'my mission is to show women what they're missing.' Then he couldn't get my bra off."

A man after my own heart.

"Oh you got that far then?" I said, obscurely jealous.

"That far and no further."

She was talking in a curious clipped way – tight mouthed. I wondered if it was some Bette Davis thing she was trying.

On the trip to the galleon, Dwight was still talking to Greg. I sat next to Stacey. She was on her own because Joseph was outside throwing up, as usual.

"You and Joseph seem to be getting on," I said.

Stacey nodded sombrely.

"Nick, he's opened my eyes."

"I bet you've opened his too."

She shook her head.

"No, no. You know, I thought I was a free spirit. I didn't want commitment, just enjoyed sex. But Joseph has made me see there's another way of being. The celibate way."

Stacey and the celibate way. I was trying to digest this when she changed the subject.

"Chuck looks great for his age, doesn't he? Look how erect he sits, thanks to his corset."

"Corset?"

"Sure," she said, getting up to go to help Joseph.

Aha. I looked at Chuck. He too went out to help Joseph. I watched him pat Joseph gently on the back. He seemed to regard him in a fatherly way. Now he came back inside and sat beside me. I couldn't resist glancing at his flat belly but his shirt was too thick to make out any whalebone or whatever modern corsets are made of.

"How were your crow's nest scenes, Chuck? Did you endure?"

Chuck had been doing the close ups for the songs I had mimed a couple of days earlier. The techies had rigged up a crow's nest beside the hotel swimming pool, so that the blue of the water might be mistaken for the ocean. Chuck had been there all yesterday afternoon, singing Hal's ludicrous songs.

"That I did, son, that I did. I've been given some very odd lines to say. How about: 'There's a man can't find his sealegs because I threw them overboard yesterday'? I mean: what is that? "

The first scene on the galleon was between Bridget and Chuck. Unless Dwight changed his mind it would be Bridget's only big scene. She'd been worried about it at the start of the week because she had to be quite emotional – it was the scene when she confronted him about the Pirate Bride and pleaded her cause.

Bridget came out in her costume. She'd taken her hat and glasses off, of course. There was still something odd about her face.

Chuck called Action. I was over at the other end of the deck, getting into costume for some stunt-work later in the morning, so I couldn't hear the lines.

I wandered across just as Dwight called Cut.

"Bridget, darling, I need a bit more emotion. And your voice sounds a bit strangled."

"I don't want to overdo the emotion," she said tightly. "You know, Dwight, in film acting, less is more. "

"So I've heard," Dwight said quietly.

Chuck turned to me.

"I acted with Mitchum, late on in his career. We did a scene and he gave nothing. He was really flat. I thought it was the booze and old age catching up but when we saw the rushes it was all there, on the screen. Told me early in his career directors used to get furious with him until they saw the rushes. Maybe it's the same with Bridget."

I was looking at her intently. I realised what the problem was.

"You're not showing any emotion on your face," Dwight said.

Bridget flushed and I knew I was right. At any other time Bridget flushing is as likely as – well – me satisfying a woman in bed.

"I think this has something to do with Bridget's trip to Cancun yesterday," I said to Chuck.

Bridget leaned in to Dwight, whispered in his ear. He pulled back and peered at her face. Reached out and touched her cheek. Then he wandered back behind the camera and stood looking out to sea, clearly perplexed about what to do.

I walked over to Bridget.

"That podiatrician in Cancun…"

"Don't say a fucking word," she said. It sounded like she was talking through gritted teeth but in fact it was a frozen jaw. Her face was totally without expression.

"Did he do botox on the side?"

"I'm going to kill that fucking surgeon. I just wanted to lose a few lines on my forehead and round my eyes. Last night it was fine – just my forehead had gone numb. I woke up this morning and I couldn't even feel my nose. I'm going to be eating my food through a straw."

"It'll wear off."

"Yes, in three bloody months."

I squeezed her arm.

"Why did you do it now, partway through filming?"

She flashed her eyes at me. At least she could still do that.

"Are you kidding? Have you seen Cassie? You think I'm going to go onscreen with that bitch and not look as good as I can?"

"Oh, Bridget. Her selling point is that she's natural. There's this backlash in Hollywood – they're looking for women who haven't had stuff done."

"What, you don't think Cassie has had stuff done aside from her feet?"

"She's only twenty-five," I protested.

"Don't be naïve, Nick."

I frowned.

"Shouldn't that be naïf," I said. "Masculine case?"

She slapped me across the side of the head. At least it was with her open hand. The fact that it cracked like a pistol shot across the deck was by the by. Everybody looked over.

"It's okay, Bridget," I said. "I know you're just taking out on me the anger you're feeling for your incompetent surgeon."

"Thanks for that insight, Sigmund." She prodded my chest. "Now, do you want to leave me alone so I can get in character?"

In fact, Dwight abandoned that scene for the day. I did a bit of stuntwork clambering up and down the rigging for an hour or so then we broke for lunch.

It was then I finally managed to speak to Dwight about Pynchon. I told him what I knew and what I suspected. He went pale beneath his tan. He clenched his fists and worked his jaw.

"That bastard, Pynchon. I should have known better than to trust him." He walked away then walked back. "Well, I'm going to go over right now and sort this out. Order the boat someone. Filming is over for the day. I'll drop you off on shore then I'm going to have it out with my producer."

That was the last time I ever saw Dwight.

Most of us went to the hotel bar straight from the boat. Bridget kept her hat and sunglasses on. For the next couple of hours she, Joseph, Greg and I got quietly loaded whilst Chuck and Cassie swigged herb teas. The sight of Chuck trying to fit his big fingers in the handle of the teacup was entertaining for a while, but in the end we just sat watching the surf down on the beach.

Then the bar phone rang. It was for me. A spaced out voice.

"Zane Pynchon."

"An unexpected pleasure," I said. "Not. What do you want?"

"I have news."

"Where's Dwight?"

He cleared his throat.

"He's on his way back to LA."

"Why would he be going to LA?"

"He lives there, dipstick."

"He's shooting a film."

"Not any longer. I fired him. Clearing your desk and being escorted from the building happens just the same in the movies as in any other major industry."

"He's gone?"

"This film is on hiatus until I can bring a replacement in. And that's assuming I can hold the money together." He cleared his throat again. "See what your meddling has done. Now I'm going to go out to the second unit to get on with our work. I don't expect any more foolishness from you."

There was a click on the other end of the line. I put the phone down and looked across at the group. All but Bridget had moved out on to the terrace and Greg had joined them. Would Dwight really have gone without saying anything to anybody? Even though he and Bridget were no longer a couple wouldn't Dwight have spoken to her?

I went over to reception, asked if Dwight had checked out. Affirmative.

"In person?" I said, puzzled. How had he got past us?

The receptionist shrugged.

I went over to Bridget and bent down beside her.

"Have you got Dwight's mobile number?"

"Sure. Why?"

"I need to get hold of him."

"He's with the producer."

"Apparently not any more."

She fished out her phone and dialled him. The phone rang but there was no answer until his voice-mail cut in. She asked him to call her back as soon as he heard the message.

"What's going on?"

I told her what Pynchon had said.

"Poor Dwight," she said. "I know he was a big lunk but he was *my* big lunk. Fired from his pet project."

"Would he have gone without saying goodbye?"

"He's a proud man. We're not that close anymore. It's possible."

She picked up on the tone of my voice a beat later.

"Why? Do you think Pynchon might have done something to harm him?"

"I'm sure not. But Larry disappeared when he went to see Pynchon."

"According to what Pynchon told the police, Larry had never reached the hotel."

"Well, he would say that, wouldn't he?"

"None of the hotel staff had seen him either."

"Dwight seems to have got in and out of here without being seen too," she said. "Oh God, something has happened to him hasn't it."

Bridget burst into tears. Well, she would have had she been able to move her face. Instead tears suddenly welled up in her eyes and spilled down her face. This was so unexpected and puzzling that I was slow to respond. She reached into her bag and pulled out a large handkerchief to mop her eyes with. I could only assume she'd got it from Chuck. Who under sixty still carries a handkerchief?

I sat down and put my arm round her. I hated to see her upset. Bridget and I have our difficulties but, essentially, we love each other. I think. She leaned into me.

"What do you want to do?" I said gently.

She straightened and set her shoulders back.

"I want to see the producer."

"Have you not met him yet?"

She shook her head.

"Briefly. And Dwight has hardly seen him."

"But you know him from Brighton."

"Brighton?"

"Yeah – Zane Pynchon was the producer of that film about Aleister Crowley in Brighton. When we ended up on Crete? The kickboxing zebra?"

She waved her hand at me.

"Darling, enough. I think that was more your adventure than mine. Weren't you madly in lust with that sexy Asian girl?"

The temptation to go down memory lane was almost overwhelming, especially when that memory involved Priya, that self-same sexy Asian woman. But I resisted. Instead I just noted that Brighton is the California of Britain – you'll find any weird philosophy or lifestyle takes root there first. We'd got involved with Pynchon in an adventure we'd had a while ago when the Old Religion met New Age with fatal consequences. That was my first meeting with Stacey, the make-up artist. And that kick-boxing zebra. Don't ask.

"But actually, yes I do remember meeting him," Bridget said. "Damn – I *knew* I'd seen him before. Bastard. Dwight should never have gone to work for a murderer."

"He wasn't a murderer – we just thought he was."

"That was prescient of us."

I flashed her a look.

"Prescient?"

She shrugged off my arm.

"Fuck off, Nick. Every time I come up with a big word you look all surprised. Just because you went to Oxford – which I still can't believe, incidentally, given you're a moron – you think the rest of us are thick."

"That's not true."

"So why the snideness?"

She'd shuffled to the far end of the sofa and now was leaning towards me in her aggressive pose. Her fists would be up in a moment, I knew.

"I didn't know what the word meant," I said, as meekly as I could. She whacked me across the side of the head with her fist. Not meek enough, then.

"If he's harmed Dwight I'll bloody 'ave 'im."

There were a number of ways to calm her down. I opted for humour.

"Consonants, darling, consonants," I said, in my best Rex Harrison.

She swung back towards me.

"And you can fuck off too, you useless length of spaghetti."

Okay: bad choice.

"I want to help," I protested.

"Don't whine." She suddenly stood up. I put up my arms to protect my head, just in case. She stood over me and looked at my arms.

"What's this?"

"Precautionary,"

She kicked me between the legs.

"Good thinking."

Bridget finds it hard to express her emotions verbally. Physically, she doesn't have quite the same problem. And I'm a good outlet for her emotions. Unfortunately.

"Sorry," she said, when I was able to sit upright.

"Let's join the others," I said, my voice more or less in its normal pitch. Safety in numbers.

Chuck was as upright as ever; Joseph was hunched up at the end of the table, the worse for drink. Cassie was leaning back against the wall, her breasts thrust out.

We filled them in on Dwight's firing and rapid disappearance. Well, Bridget did. Then we filled them in about what we thought was going on and how the film was funded. Well, Bridget did.

I couldn't get a word in edgeways. No change there, then.

"Seems to me, since we haven't got a director, we might as well pay a visit to our producer on the second unit."

That was Chuck, his voice a dark rumble. Nobody else spoke. Cassie seemed to have mislaid her brain – she was tilting her head as if looking for it. Joseph was trying to roll himself into the tightest ball he could manage. Only Greg was nodding in agreement.

"We have no other choice," he said.

"The police?" Joseph croaked.

"That would cause us major problems," Greg said. "We want to get this picture made."

"I'm not sure there is a picture anymore," Chuck rumbled.

"But won't it be dangerous?" Joseph again. I liked Joseph. His utter cowardice made me seem almost heroic.

Bridget looked around the table.

"Well, alright then," she said through her frozen jaw. "More than anything I want to be sure no harm has come to Dwight.

We'll go to see Pynchon and if he's not convincing we'll go to the police."

I'd like to think the six of us walked down to the dock like the four hombres in Peckinpah's *The Wild Bunch* heading for the last gunfight. But, in truth, footwear was against us – flip-flops and thonged sandals don't create quite the same effect as cowboy boots and a snare drum on the soundtrack. Plus, Cassie and I were half-carrying, half-dragging Joseph.

We climbed in the boat down at the dock.

"We need to go out to the second unit," Greg said.

The man at the wheel, a thin, bald-headed man, exchanged a glance with his colleague. His colleague scratched his beard.

"Sure enough," he said. "Though I don't think you'll be welcome."

We went below decks into the cramped cabin and sat hunched side by side. The man with the beard cast off and within minutes we were powering across the bay.

There was quite a wind across the water so the ride was choppy. I could see Chuck looking a little green. He could ride horses all day and all night but put him on a boat…

Bridget has, of course, the constitution of – well, if not an ox, then something equally solid. There was a fridge on the boat stocked with snacks and drinks. She was eating ice cream out of a big tub with a beer by her side. She burped occasionally but that was just to clear her digestive tract, not because she was feeling poorly.

I told myself this was her way of coping with worry about Dwight but in fact it was just Bridget being Bridget. Cassie Dexter was leaning against me, ever the performer. However, I couldn't help noticing that, as usual, she had her gaze fixed on Bridget. Maybe it was lust, more likely it was awe at the amount Bridget was putting away.

Joseph didn't stay in the cabin because, of course, he was going to be sick. I joined him on deck, just in time to see him throw up over the side. Greg was also on deck standing, head back, his profile like the prow of the ship. He looked great. It was just unfortunate that he was standing downwind of Joseph. Ugh.

It would have been wonderful scudding across the water, the spray flashing in the sunlight, if we hadn't been heading for some sort of showdown.

Within half an hour I could see the second unit's hi-tech vessel riding high on the water. We got to within a few hundred yards of it before we first heard the pops.

Bridget had come up on deck.

"They have fireworks?" she said.

Chuck joined us.

"That's gunfire," he said. "Small bore, semi-automatic and automatic."

He said it with such certainty none of us questioned it.

"Could it be filming?" I said.

Greg shook his head.

"Not underwater and this unit isn't doing any other sort of filming."

"Or any filming at all," I said. "Plus, I don't think Blackbeard's pirates used sub-machine guns often."

"So what's going on?" Bridget said.

Greg had a pair of binoculars out. He was focusing on the middle distance. He lowered the glasses and shook his head.

"Well, I don't mean to sound insane but I think they're in a fire fight."

"A fire fight?"

He nodded.

"They're under attack."

"Take us closer," I said to the man at the wheel. He looked at me as if I was mad. "Just a little," I said.

"We should call the authorities," he said.

"Yeah, in a minute. Go near enough so that we can see what's going on."

He took us a further hundred yards. We all watched as we saw two speedboats circle the second unit's boat about fifty yards out. There was a regular crack and pop of small arms fire and then the occasional chatter of automatic weapons. I thought I could see one man in the nearest speedboat with a rocket launcher on his shoulder, though he was finding it hard to keep his footing as the boat bounced across the waves.

Joseph was standing beside me. "What's going on?"

"I think they're being attacked by pirates. Or a rival salvage crew."

"Pirates?" Joseph squeaked. "What do you mean pirates?"

"But they're defenceless," Cassie said.

Just then people on the film unit's vessel started to return fire. I saw one speedboat veer away as someone dropped off the side of it.

"Apparently not." I looked across at Chuck. "What do you think we should do?"

He looked at me.

"Get the hell out of Dodge."

The man at the wheel didn't need any second bidding.

"We'll call the coastguard on the way back in."

We headed back to shore at full speed, the outboard motor churning up the water behind us in long white plumes. Full speed didn't mean much, of course – this boat wasn't exactly top of the range.

The man at the wheel was fiddling with the radio with one hand whilst he held the wheel with the other.

"Can't raise the coastguard – the frequency is jammed," he said. He sounded jittery. Given that he knew these waters, that didn't help my confidence any.

I kept scoping the sea around us to see if we were being followed. We were running close to some islands dotted on the sea to our left. Excuse me, port. They made me nervous, even though ahead I could see the mainland, only some fifteen minutes away.

I was right to be nervous because two minutes later the pirates were alongside us.

One moment the sea was empty, the next these two speedboats shot out of an inlet on one of the islands and bracketed us.

Men standing in them pointed rifles at us. One bare-chested skinny black man jumped onto the back of our boat with a rope that he used to secure the two boats together. Two other men also jumped across. Both were armed. Chuck and I put ourselves in front of Bridget and Cassie. So too, I was surprised to see, did Joseph. I glanced at him. Good to see I wasn't the only one quaking in my boots.

The black guy moved the crewman away from the wheel. He looked over at us, gestured with his gun.

"We got a motto: Shoot first, you won't need to ask questions later. Doing as you're bidden is best." Another gunman herded us down the three steps into the cabin then sat in the doorway, machine pistol pointing in on us.

I saw our crew transferred to the other boat. Our engine cranked up and we set off again.

"Should we be worried?" Cassie whispered to me.

"What're you asking him for?" Bridget said. "He doesn't know shit from Shinolah."

"Who does?" I said, wondering what that strange expression meant.

"Nothing we can do until we find out where they're taking us," Joseph said, sounding reasonably calm.

The local television station had suggested piracy as one reason for the Yucatan Triangle. It had given some statistics which, if I best remembered them, suggested that there are hundreds of incidents of piracy a year and that the number is increasing at forty per cent a year.

I knew from my conversations with Mollie that there are different sorts of modern day pirates. At the lower level there's a new breed of speedboat buccaneer. These pirates will zip up in a speedboat, point a rocket launcher and demand money. At the high end organized crime syndicates slaughter entire crews to steal multi-million dollar vessels. Some guys over in the China Seas stole an entire oil tanker carrying jet fuel and diesel oil.

I thought maybe we were involved at the low end.

"You can understand piracy in a way," I said. "Expensive ships plying the waters in areas ringed with poverty, envy and desperation. Usually they're carrying goods that sell easily on the black market too: jet fuel, alkali, aluminium ingots. Sometimes they want the cargo, sometimes they want the boat. They might repaint the boat and sell it on or keep it for their own use."

"We don't have any cargo and these guys have already got boats far better than this one," Bridget pointed out.

"We're the cargo," Cassie said. "Are they going to shoot us or drown us?"

"I don't think we need to worry yet," Chuck said. He was standing looking out of the porthole. Occasionally he looked up at the cold-eyed man with the semi-automatic. "Let's all just take it easy."

So we tried to. As a matter of fact, Cassie seemed to swing so far away from being frightened she was enjoying the boat ride.

"Do you think we'll see any dolphins," she said, from her seat beside a porthole. "I love seeing dolphins."

Bridget looked at me. She wiggled her ears, which seemed an odd thing to do in the circumstances.

"Damn," she said through her frozen jaw and I realised the ear-wiggling had been a by-product of trying to raise an eyebrow.

Seeing Bridget with an immobile face was only seeing a partial Bridget. Her grimaces, scowls, frowns and gleeful grins *were* Bridget, dammit. Now she patted Cassie on the arm.

"Is it the hole in your head, dear?"

"Or is your qi stagnating again?" I said.

Bridget looked at me.

"She had stagnant qi," I explained.

Cassie looked from one to the other of us. Her eyes looked wider than usual. Staring. Had she dropped something? I hadn't thought of her as a druggie but there is all kinds of stuff available in Hollywood.

"You know," she said to Bridget. "The life force in Chinese whatsit."

Bridget nodded, tried for a facial expression; failed. She growled.

After an hour our engines were cut and we banged against a much bigger vessel. Out of the portholes on the starboard side all I could see was grey metal.

"What now?" Cassie said, back in panic mode. I knew the feeling.

"Sit tight," Chuck said.

A few moments later the man sitting on the steps gestured with his gun for us to come up on deck. Chuck and Greg led the way, the women next, with Joseph and I bringing up the rear. I looked up at the starboard side and did a double take. The grey metal vessel towering above us was a submarine.

I moved closer to the women. I wasn't being gallant, I was trying to be safe – either one of them could kick ass far better than I. However, some rough-looking men standing in the conning tower did have their eyes fixed on Cassie and Bridget.

A lean Rastafarian about six feet tall, with dreads almost down to his waist, was standing on our deck with armed men spread either side of him. He was bare-chested and barefoot and his hands were in the pockets of his baggy chinos. His pupils were like pinpricks.

He tilted his head to the side and looked from one to the other of us. Then he tilted his head back.

"We have a motto," he said.

I think all of us were surprised, though it didn't seem to phase Chuck.

"We've heard it already," he said.

I must admit I was impressed by Chuck. He was an old man in a corset and ridiculous toupee but so far he'd been the epitome of that Hemingway thing: coolness under pressure.

The rasta tilted his head again and stared at Chuck.

"Our motto is: *sagittas prius non indigeas interrogare posterius.*"

Chuck nodded.

"Very clever."

Joseph looked perplexed.

"That's not right. Surely first should be *imprimus* not *prius* and you should use a different construction for 'ask questions later' – the noun *percontator* followed by a different verb."

"Joseph," I hissed.

The Rastafarian looked at him. Joseph shrank back.

"I was just saying," he said in a whisper.

By now the synapses of my brain were more or less crackling again. The reason for my surprise – and that of the others, I think – was that this rasta pirate had a cut-glass English accent. The Queen would have been struggling to sound as posh.

"You presume to correct a Balliol man?" the Rastafarian said.

A Balliol man. Okay, that explained the poker up his bum but there was something else too. I needed him to tilt his head back again to be sure.

"Yeah, well what do you want with us?" It was Bridget, light under a bushel as usual.

"I do not talk to women."

Bridget flared.

"You won't talk to me because I'm a woman?"

The rasta suddenly dashed towards her, his arms raised. He looked at her with interest when he saw no change of expression on her face. She showed no sign of being startled by him. Little did he know. He tossed his head back.

"I thank you. I am Cecil, the Pirate King."

"Sounds like a Disney movie," Bridget said.

I shushed her.

He didn't have nostrils. Well, to be strictly accurate, he didn't have a septum so his nostrils had become one enormous orifice, an amazing black hole. Okay, so we were dealing with a man who had stuffed a lot of drugs up his nose. You see people like that all the time in Hollywood. The difference was that this drug abuser had, at a rough estimate, around twenty armed men under his command who looked, judging by their expressions, equally drug-crazed.

"I played football with Bob Marley once," I blurted out.

One by one my gang turned to look at me. Equally bewildered was the Pirate King.

"Who is he?" he said.

"A Rastafarian who hasn't heard of Bob Marley?" I said, astounded. "You don't listen to reggae?"

"We've heard of it. We prefer BBC Radio Three. I learned to enjoy classical music when I was at Balliol." He gestured back to the submarine. "We listen to that and the BBC World Service online. And we watch the Discovery channel."

Okay, a cultured, drug-crazed pirate chief.

"Oh," was all I could think to say. So much for my attempt at bonding. I tried a different ploy.

"I was at Oxford."

He looked at me with his pin-prick eyes.

"Indeed. Which college?"

"Keble."

He snorted – a risky thing to do when your nose is like a vacuum cleaner hose.

"Yes, well…" he said, his voice trailing off. "You know, they've found a worm that is related to humans."

"You only need to go to Hollywood to know that," Bridget muttered.

"It has a basic body plan with no proper sex organs, stomach, excretory system or brain."

"Ditto."

I shushed her. I was wondering about the link between my going to Oxford and worms.

"People used to think it was related to bivalve mollusks such as mussels and oysters but it is now one of our closest relatives. It is fascinating to think that whatever long dead animal this simple worm evolved from, so did humans."

"Fascinating," I said, musing on what a very strange day this had been.

"Actually, maybe it should be *principalis* for first," Joseph said.

Now we all looked at him. What was with the boy?

"What do you want with us?" This from Chuck.

The rasta pointed at his boat.

"Do you like our boat? It was once in the Russian navy. I bought it from the Russian mafia. In perfect condition."

"Is this the future of piracy?" I said. "Submarines?"

"Perfect condition," he repeated. "Except that it is unable to submerge."

"I think you need to reconsider your notion of perfection," I said. "Not submerging might be considered a major flaw in a submarine."

He shrugged.

"It's for show really. We have other vessels."

"What do you want with us?" It was Greg's turn now.

"You're my hostages."

We looked at each other.

"Who's going to pay to release us?" I said.

The Pirate King swung his head back from one to the other of us.

"You had better hope that somebody will. You will remain on this boat for the time being."

"But there's only one bathroom," Cassie blurted out. "You can't expect six of us to share one lavatory. That's disgusting." I felt she was not perhaps focusing on the right priorities but the Pirate King ignored her anyway.

He climbed up the ladder back onto the submarine and shortly afterwards we heard the strains of Sibelius drifting out of the conning tower.

"They haven't a fucking clue what they're doing," Bridget said as she clomped back down the stairs into the cabin. "Who's going to pay for us?"

"They're going to swap us for the treasure," Chuck said.

"Of course," I said. "Or at least they think they are."

"What do you mean, think they are?" Cassie said. She sounded frightened again.

"He means that no way is Zane Pynchon going to cough up anything to save us." Bridget, savvy as ever. "He doesn't give a shit about anyone but himself."

We all nodded sombrely. Cassie was a beat behind.

"But we were trepanned together!" she said. "That's supposed to form a bond."

None of us could think of anything to say to that.

I did try a few minutes later.

"Cassie, can I ask a stupid question?"

"Do you ask any other sort?" she tossed off without even pausing for thought. Oh, okay – not too frightened to be horrible to me then.

"Having a hole in your head and all – doesn't it make your brain vulnerable?"

"Vulnerable?"

"Yeah, you know if someone bops you on the head or – well – what if it rains?"

"What if it rains?" Bridget said with a sigh. "What if it rains? Sometimes, Nick, I despair."

"Actually," Joseph said timidly, "I was wondering the same thing."

"What do you think umbrellas were invented for, you pair of morons!" Bridget spat.

"Steady, now," Chuck said. "We're all getting het up but it isn't about dodging the raindrops it's about our predicament here – we're just directing our fears elsewhere."

"Since when did you turn into Oprah, Chuck?" Bridget snapped, attempting to scowl and giving up on the attempt. Those ears were really going to ache after a while.

"Skin has grown over again,' Cassie said. She dropped her head. "See?"

It was true. There was a medallion of pink skin, pulsing slightly in rhythm with her heartbeat.

"Touch it if you want," she said.

I reached out my finger and touched the skin. It depressed slightly but felt pretty firm.

"It's like a baby's skull – babies start out with a hole here before the skull knits properly."

"Remind me: why'd you have it done?" Chuck said but I could tell he wasn't really interested in the answer.

"Well, I'd tried pilates and power yoga, scientology, sweat lodges and the kabbalah but none of them seemed to give me that creative uplift I was looking for." She touched Chuck's arm. "I'm a very creative person, Chuck."

"I'm sure you are darling, I'm sure you are."

Cassie was sitting on the floor of the cabin. She reached up and squeezed my knee.

"What do you think they're going to do with us?"

She was sitting in a way that she hoped wouldn't draw attention to herself. Fat chance. She was a beautiful woman and I knew what she was thinking.

Greg was the other side of her.

"Danger is only what you make of it," he said.

Bridget bent to look up at the pirates – armed and barbarous – on the deck above.

"Yeah, right." She looked at Greg. "You've only ever been around movies haven't you?"

"What do you mean?"

"You talk in movie language."

Greg smiled.

"Bridget – there's nothing to fear but fear itself."

"–or psychobabble. You read Paulo Coelho don't you?"

"How did you know? He's such a wonderful man. Not that I've met him but – what? What are you looking at?"

Bridget had somehow managed to fix all her scorn in her eyes. They blazed out of her beautiful but frozen face.

"Spare me from New Age gurus. He's a short man with a beard and a lot of hair," she said.

"Your point being?"

I knew what her point was. It was something on which we agreed.

"The major threat to world peace?" I said. "Terrorists? Tangentially, maybe. No, it's short men. By far the biggest threat to world peace. You know it's true. Always has been. I mean they can be short al Qaeda or short North Koreans or short serial killers but what's the common factor?"

"Shortness." Bridget said.

"Damned right," I said. "True the world over."

"Our captor is tall," Cassie said.

"Well, there's tall and tall," I said stiffly.

"For anyone who's not as unfeasibly long as you, he's tall," Bridget said shortly. So to speak.

We fell silent.

I looked round the cabin.

"A laugh right now would probably cost a lot of money," I murmured.

"Bob Hope: *The Ghostbreakers*," Greg said.

I jerked round to look at him. Another film nerd? Before I could get into heavy quoting-film-lines mode, Bridget cut in.

"I'd settle for a treble g&t," she said.

I sighed.

"When wouldn't you?"

She got to her feet.

"We've still got the fridge here – let's see what drinks there are."

"Don't you think we should keep clear heads?" Cassie said.

"That would be a first," Bridget said shortly.

"Ahoy there!"

I looked up. A twitchy man in a pair of baggy shorts and a torn, faded blue linen shirt was standing on the deck just outside the cabin door.

"Permission to come aboard?"

"Everybody else has, you may as well," Bridget said, shielding her eyes with her hand to see who this man was.

He stepped gingerly down into the cabin, grimacing as he did so. His eyes were deep set and staring. He looked permanently startled and jumpy, as if he was scared someone was going to come up behind him. As it turned out, that was exactly right.

"Neill Dodds, television producer."

The name rang a bell.

"You were on the news the other day," I said. "Well, not you. News of you."

"Was there news of me?"

"Only that you were one of the recent casualties of the Yucatan Triangle."

"I was captured by pirates was what I was. Jesus Christ, in this day and age."

"What do they want with you?"

"To ransom me, of course. Didn't it say on the news?"

I shook my head.

"No mention of any ransom demand. Neither your office nor your wife has any clue what has happened to you."

"That bitch. She's so lazy that if she'd got a ransom note it would take her a week to read it. And then there's no way she'd admit it had come. She'll be too busy spending my money to want to use any of it to free me."

"Sit down," I said. Bridget had the fridge open by now. "Do you want a beer?"

"I'll take the beer." He winced. "But I'd rather stand. "

He took a long swig, nodded in thanks.

"No, it's much more likely Captain Pugwash here hasn't actually got round to sending out a ransom demand. After all, he's only had me as a captive for six fucking months. Jesus, these bloody rastas. Smoking ganja from breakfast to lights out totally fucks up their sense of time. And as for a sense of urgency – well, that's not there at all. Have you ever seen anyone play dominoes for twelve hours at a stretch? Stick around. I mean, that's no way to run an organisation. If I behaved like that in LA I'd be out of business so quickly I wouldn't have time to sit down."

He winced again.

"Supposing I wanted to."

"So have they treated you well?" I said. "You don't seem in bad shape."

That wild look came into his eyes again.

"Oh yeah? Know what a catamite is? No? Help you any if I say the Navy used to call them bum-boys?"

"Oh."

"Yeah, right. About four days in, Pugwash there decides he's going to make me his bitch. Jesus, the humiliation – the pain."

"He raped you?"

He flashed a look at me again.

"That's what I'm talking about, yes. And I don't recommend it."

Chuck looked solemn.

"He still diddling you?"

"Why do you think I'm not sitting down?"

"So are the women under similar threat?"

He looked them up and down. Shook his head.

"Not from him. English public school education, far as I can gather, and something called Balliol he goes on about. 'I'm a Balliol man' – as if that's supposed to mean something." He looked at Joseph and me. "You two might need to watch your backs though." He looked at the women. "And of course I can't vouch for his men."

"Fucking great."

"Yeah but with luck we won't be here too long."

"That's what I thought." He looked up at the sub to see if anyone was watching but the conning tower was empty. "Still, the road less-travelled eh? I used to suffer from success depression. Went to a support group for a while – there were entrepreneurial arsonists and post-Olympic depressives there – the whole shebang."

He saw my puzzled look.

"The arsonists set fire to their careers when they've been successful, just for something to do. Your post-Olympic types can't handle the down that comes after a major triumph. Success depression – sure, it's a big problem among successful people in Los Angeles. There's nothing more depressing than having all your wishes come true."

"I'll have to take your word for that," I said. "I'm more from the shoot-myself-in-the-foot school of irrational behaviour."

"Sorry to hear that," Dodds said, sounding as though he genuinely meant it. "But anyway, being here has certainly cured me of that."

"Great," I said.

"Now I'm just depressed."

"Right."

Dodds drank some more beer. After a moment, he said: "He wants to swap you for Captain Kidd's treasure – does that make sense?"

"Only as much as anything else around here," I said. "It's treasure but it's not Captain Kidd's. How do you know about the pirate's plan?"

"I hear things. He's in communication with some guy called Zane Pynchon trying to do the deal."

"Great – so we won't be here long," Cassie said.

I laughed, though there was nothing funny in our situation. "If you think for one minute that Zane Pynchon is going to give up his treasure for the sake of us, you've got another think coming."

"But I'm a movie star on the rise," Cassie said indignantly. "I'm a long-term investment. I have to be worth more than some seaweedy coins and stuff."

"An investment until the tits go," Bridget murmured.

"What has Pynchon said in reply?" I asked Dodds.

Dodds turned his hands palms up.

"He's thinking about it."

Chuck rubbed his chin.

"I guess that means he's keeping our pirate king hanging on until he's got all the treasure up," he said. "Then he's high-tailing it out of the Caribbean."

Dodds nodded.

"That's how I'd read it. I don't think your producer gives a tuppenny damn about you."

"But we had the holes in our heads drilled together," Cassie said indignantly.

Dodds couldn't think of a single thing to say either.

"So what will your man do to us if Pynchon skips with the treasure?"

"Will he kill us?" Cassie shuddered.

"I don't think he'll kill you," Dodds said.

"Great," Cassie said.

"My best guess is that he'll sell you as slaves."

"But I hate housework," Cassie protested, rather more glumly.

"That would be the least of it," Dodds said.

"We've got to get away from here, then," Chuck said. "As we are we've got no means of protecting our womenfolk." He nodded towards Joseph and me. "Or you young fellows."

"What about you?" I said to Dodds. "How were you captured?"

"Same as you. One minute I was sailing between the islands, the next I had a pirate boat alongside me. They sold my boat and kept me."

"And were you on a scouting expedition for your show or what?"

"Or what," he said, shrugging. "Definitely or what. People think I was scouting locations for *Cast Adrift*?" He shook his head. "I had the location – an uninhabited island that was just perfect for my purposes. It was photogenic, with fresh water and giant creepy crawlies. I also had the contestants."

"So why haven't we heard them kvetching in the press about their lost opportunity?" I said.

"Kvetching?" Bridget said, attempting to raise an eyebrow. Failing.

"I used to live in Golders Green." I turned back to Dodds. "Well?"

He had a weird look on his face. Sneaky, suspicious, triumphant and disappointed all at the same time.

"They aren't kvetching because I already had them on the island."

We all looked at him.

"Sure. I wanted to get everything set up so I could present the channels with a done deal. I'd shipped in enough supplies for a month. I'd advertised for participants and done the auditions. We'd landed the winners at dead of night on the island."

"How many?"

"Fifteen."

I looked at Bridget. She didn't seem to have twigged.

"There are fifteen people on this island," I said. "Now?"

He shrugged.

"I don't know about now. There were six months ago."

"With food for one month."

He nodded absently.

"My God – was there food to forage for on the island?"

He shrugged.

"Birds' eggs, coconuts. And fish in the sea, of course – if they can catch them. But on *Survivor* people lived on maggots and rats – though in the first series someone smuggled sausages onto the island up his ass."

We all took a moment to take that in.

"Were your contestants allowed luxury items?" I said quietly.

"Yeah, but it was the usual shit – nail clippers, tweezers, toothbrushes, soap. One woman took sex-shop lingerie."

"What kind of people were they?"

"Handpicked not to get on," Dodds said proudly.

"And your production company doesn't know the whereabouts of the contestants?" It was Bridget, finally catching up.

"Nobody knows," he said. "It's the best-kept secret in television."

"But that means they could have starved to death by now," I said.

He shrugged.

"Maybe." He looked into the distance. "It depends how self-sufficient they've proved to be." He looked at me intently. "Do you know that Harry Hook film starring the young Balthazar Getty – whatever happened to him? Memo to self – reality show featuring young actors who just didn't make it featuring Edward Furlong, Getty, Kulkin; maybe older actors like the other Baldwin brothers; maybe a brothers piece – the Carradines, the Keaches and so on."

"Dodds!" I said, adopting the tone Bridget uses when I'm being a movie nerd. "What about the Getty film?"

"*Lord of the Flies*?"

"Oh, you're talking about the crap remake of the Peter Brooks original based on the William Golding novel."

"Nick!" That would be Bridget, then.

"Whatever," he said. "Well, there was some talk of *Cast Adrift* trying to set up that kind of tribal thing. Hunters versus farmers."

"But people got killed in *Lord of the Flies*!" I protested.

He ignored me.

"There were certain implements left for cultivation." He thrust his hands in his pockets and did an odd little half twirl. "And others for hunting."

I looked at him appalled.

"You wanted people to kill each other?"

He looked startled and sly at the same time.

"No, of course not. But we anticipated conflict."

I heard Chuck's rumbling voice seemingly before the words emerged from his chest.

"You've set this up so that if people are to survive they need to be aggressive – and then because you've been captured by this pirate guy you've not been able to control that aggression."

Dodds shrugged.

"Bad timing."

Joseph said: "Why is it called *Cast Adrift* if they're on an island? Shouldn't it be called *Marooned*?"

I was beginning to worry about Joseph. Dodds gave him a blank look.

"Fifteen people on an island for the past six months without sufficient food. Poor sods." I looked at Dodds. "Aren't you concerned about them?"

"Of course – I'm not inhuman, you know." He looked around him. "It's just that, heck – what can I do? This whole thing is about survival of the fittest – here, on the island…in life..."

"Thanks for sharing," I said quietly. "I heard about this but I thought it was one of those urban myths. These guys are like those Japanese soldiers found on remote atolls ten years after the end of World War II who still thought it was going on."

"What's the difference between an atoll and an island?" Bridget said.

"Dunno."

"Why not just say island then?" she said impatiently.

"It's such a missed opportunity," Dodds said quietly. "If things have gone horribly, horribly wrong it's such a waste."

"Of human life, you mean?" Cassie said.

"Well, that too, naturally. But the waste I was thinking of was that I didn't get a chance to rig cameras up." He looked from face to face. "Priceless stuff will have been happening and we haven't got *any* of it on film."

"Or maybe *Castaway*?" Joseph said. "Though I think that might be taken."

Chapter Six

"Three things explain
Our Navy's triumphs
Historians often say
The lash is one
Then sodomy
And finally there's rum
Be that as it may
There is no way
That's going up my bum."

Conversation dwindled after that and ten minutes or so later Sanders went back up to the sub. We sat looking at each other.

"What do you think, Chuck?"

"I think we've got to get the hell away." He gestured with one of his big, gnarled hands. "These guys are major drug users. When it's marijuana, that's copacetic – they're going to be mellow. I remember making *The Getaway* for Sam Peckinpah with McQueen. Steve was a mean son of a bitch, actually – didn't trust anyone – but he calmed down once he'd had a few tokes. Peckinpah too – though when he was on the tequila and mescal, he was an aggressive, sadistic fucker." He tipped an imaginary hat to Bridget and Cassie. "Excuse my language, ladies."

I was thrilled to meet someone who rambled off the subject as much as me. Bridget was less thrilled.

"Your point?" she said, swigging back the gin and tonic for which she'd been pining.

Chuck picked up her impatience and looked hurt, as well a

man might who had lent a woman his handkerchief only to be abused in return.

"Well, I think there's crack and cocaine and heroin going down and that's going to make them unstable. That's a worry." He lowered his voice and looked at me. "Especially for the ladies here."

"And Nicholas and me," Joseph said, shifting uncomfortably in his seat.

I didn't like to tell Chuck Bridget could handle herself far better than I could.

"So you're saying we should take over the boat when they're in a mellow mood," I said.

Chuck nodded.

"What other choice do we have? We can't exactly swim for shore."

"Absolutely not," Cassie said. "I've never been in saltwater in my life and I don't intend to start now."

As usual she managed to throw us all.

"You've never swum in the sea?"

"I've never *been in* the sea."

"Ever? Even as a kid?"

She shook her head and caught our looks. Even Bridget with her blank face was managing to look bemused.

"What? I'm not the only one. I remember Kate Beckinsale saying when she did *Pearl Harbour* that she'd never been in seawater until then."

I recalled that too. I was riffing through my memory trying to recall what I'd read in Cassie's biog when I was sent all the background material about cast and crew for my article.

"I may be a bit slow here," I said.

"No doubt about that," Bridget chipped in.

"But weren't you born by the ocean in California?"

"Yes. Our house was almost on the beach."

"And you were a child once."

She looked at me.

"Y-e-s. Most people were. I lived by the ocean until I was fifteen."

"So why…?"

"Why what?"

"You lived a hundred yards from the beach for fifteen years of your childhood and you never *once* went into the sea."

"Your point being?"

"Is it because you were scared of water?"

"No."

I was perplexed.

"I'm perplexed. That doesn't sound normal."

"Normal?" Bridget laughed. "You're in La-La Land, among movie stars. Normal rules do not apply. Everyone in the movie business is totally fucked, surely you know that."

Cassie nodded in agreement for a moment or two. Then: "Hey, I resent that…"

"Can we get back to the business at hand?" Chuck said. "Hightailing it out of here."

"I'm not so sure we wouldn't be better waiting to see what Pynchon comes up with," Greg said. "Or maybe the hotel people will think something's amiss if we're not around."

"They know we're making a film," Chuck said. "We're not going to be missed for days. I don't think we can afford to wait that long."

"They've got guns, Chuck," Greg pointed out.

"I know that. In fact, I notice one of our guards is carrying a Colt. Fair brings a tear to my old eyes to see it. But there are only three of them. I'm fairly sure between us we can cook up a plan to distract them long enough to throw them overboard."

"Tackling armed men is all very well in the movies where they're firing blanks," Greg continued. "In real life, real guns have real bullets. Overpowering men with guns is not going to be easy."

"We'll come up with a plan," Chuck said equably.

"What about the men on the submarine's conning tower?" Greg persisted.

"We do it at night – can't think they'll have more than one guard up there."

"When?" I said.

"Sooner the better, frankly."

"What does everyone else think?"

Joseph was back to hugging himself. Cassie looked at the rest of us.

"Bridget and me walking on deck naked might be distraction enough," she said.

"For all of us, probably," Chuck said with a chuckle. "What do you think about that, Bridget?"

"I'm game," she said. She pointed at me. "As long as you don't sneak a peek, Madrid."

Chuck looked out of the porthole.

"Your gesture might have unpleasant consequences for you," he said. "Let's just remain watchful, for the time being."

Although by now it was late in the afternoon it was still fiercely hot. We stayed below decks out of the sun, portholes open, all of us sweating freely. I dozed. We all dozed. So much for remaining watchful.

I was jolted awake by another boat coming alongside. There were shouts and laughter up on deck. I peered out of the nearest porthole just in time to see something being swung on a winch from the other boat onto ours. There was a lot of clattering, then more laughter.

I went up the steps and poked my head out on deck. Our three guards all had their backs to me as they gathered around the mast. I stepped onto the deck and looked up. I thought of Mollie. Hanging upside down from the mast, twirling slowly, was a huge turtle, its flippers flapping helplessly in the air. And as I watched I saw a tear roll down its beak and drop with a tiny splat onto the deck below.

I went back into the cabin. The others were all awake and looked at me expectantly.

"What's happening, Nick?" Chuck was rolling his shoulders as he spoke.

"I think turtle soup is going to be on the pirates' menu sometime soon."

"That's a real shame," Chuck replied. "A real shame."

He stood up, went to a porthole.

"How's it looking up there?"

"Three men on the boat, about half a dozen in the conning tower. More men on the other boat."

"Seems like the sun is starting to sink," he observed.

I nodded.

"It's low enough to be hidden from us by the submarine."

"That's good," Chuck said. "Means the guys on the conning tower will be looking in the other direction."

"Maybe," Greg said. "And you've still got the men on the boat tied up to us." Chuck grimaced.

"Think I'd better scout around a little."

I followed him up on deck. All three guards were standing forward but one of them glanced back and turned to watch us, his gun loosely pointing in our direction. Chuck shook his head when he saw the turtle. He looked casually over at the boat moored beside us. The men on board stared back stony-faced.

Chuck took a deep breath and looked out across the sea.

"Let's go back down," he said quietly. "Now is not the time."

"Are we stripping?" Bridget said when we re-entered the cabin.

Chuck shook his head.

"Too many men around. I think we'd better leave it for the time being. In any case, I've been thinking that kind of distraction is going to be too hazardous."

"Hazardous?" Cassie said. "Come on, I've never had qualms about taking my clothes off if it was right for the part – you know, Bridget, if it was justified and was important for the film."

Bridget nodded soberly. I saw Greg give a little smile. I knew what he was thinking. A woman stripping off is important to a film in that it helps the box office receipts. That's the only kind of justification it ever has, despite the arguments directors put to impressionable, beautiful women.

Although there are, of course, actresses who can't wait to get their kit off – the thespian equivalent of wet T-shirt contestants or Readers' Wives entrants – and we all know who they are, don't we?

"I'm not talking about your willingness to disrobe," Chuck said. "I'm talking about the danger to you both if something goes wrong. I'm afraid that you naked will encourage these men to do just what we're trying to avoid happening."

Cassie shuddered; Bridget looked solemn. But then, given that she could scarcely move her mouth, at the moment Bridget always looked solemn.

Joseph scratched himself.

"Do you think they're going to feed us?" he said.

"There are pretzels, crisps and peanuts in that cupboard, if you're hungry," Bridget said, pointing to the cupboard beside the fridge. "If there were big chips too we could have a feast."

Bridget's idea of a healthy diet is a lot of anything but especially carbohydrates washed down with alcohol. It's remarkable she's in such good nick.

Joseph went over and rummaged in the cupboard. When he turned to face us he was holding not a bag of peanuts but a curious gun with a short wide barrel.

"What the hell kind of a pistol is that?" Chuck said.

"A flare gun," Greg said. "For sending up an SOS."

"Well, I'll be."

Chuck held his hand out and Joseph passed it to him.

"I hope you're going to tell me there's ammo in that cupboard too."

Joseph nodded.

"Half a dozen flares."

Chuck looked around the cabin.

"Ladies and gentlemen, things are definitely looking up."

"Why?" Greg said. "Those things are only any good if there are other vessels in the vicinity. We don't know where we are but as that sub is so visible it's a sure indication that we're miles from any shipping lanes. Sending a flare up, even supposing we can do it, might do nothing but bring the pirates' anger down on us."

He crossed his arms and looked defiantly round.

"I still think the best thing we can do is bide our time."

The sun went down shortly afterwards. The prospect of spending the night below decks on either the wooden floor or the thinly upholstered banquettes around the perimeter of the cabin didn't appeal to any of us, I could see, but we had little option.

I could hear the guards moving about above us, talking quietly and laughing. It seemed that the turtle was not intended for tonight's supper. It also didn't look like we were going to get *any* supper.

Bridget piled all the bags of crisps, nuts and pretzels on the little table by the fridge.

"Tuck in," she said, spraying chewed pretzels from her mouth as she spoke.

We did, all except for Cassie. She sipped mineral water instead.

"I guess if we are going to escape," Chuck said, "we should go easy on this salty fare. We don't have a lot of water on board."

Bridget, of course, took no notice, chomping her way through some 3,000 calories and probably a bowl of salt.

Around 9 a.m., the boat that had brought the turtle detached itself from our vessel and sailed away. Our boat bobbed gently in the water, occasionally knocking against the metal hull of the submarine. I went and sat on deck in the dark and heard in the still night the familiar but unlikely sound of John Humphrays on BBC Radio 4's *Today* programme announcing the time then correcting himself. And then I heard the start of *Thought For The Day*, the three minute religious slot on the programme in which various patronising folk of a religious inclination try desperately to make their archaic religious message relevant to modern times.

This was a woman with an oh-so-reasonable voice. "There's a lot of talk these days about spin doctors and spin. Well, you know, Jesus knew a lot about spin doctors. Some accused him of being a spin doctor for God…"

I bolted back down to the cabin.

Greg was bending by the fridge.

"We're down to four small bottles of mineral water," he announced.

"And one roll of paper in the bathroom," Cassie said. She looked at the men. "And somebody isn't lifting the toilet seat."

The men didn't look at each other.

"Somebody else isn't putting it back down," Bridget said firmly. "And somebody has been eating too much spicy Mexican food."

We hung our heads.

"Did you say four bottles?" Cassie said. "I need more bottles than that to wash my hair."

We all let the remark pass. After a beat Bridget said: "We're going to have to ask old Pugwash for water."

Greg shook his head.

"I don't think we should draw attention to ourselves by making demands."

"What – you think it's better to die of thirst?" Bridget said sharply.

"We can last until tomorrow. We've managed without food pretty well."

"Speak for yourself. How's the gin?"

Greg lifted out a bottle, shook it.

"Damn," Bridget said. "Give me a beer then."

Greg handed a bottle to her.

"Last but one," he said.

Chuck was sitting by a porthole craning his neck up at the submarine. I looked out too. I could just make out a guard on the conning tower but there was also a light shining down onto our boat. I could hear murmured conversation on the deck above us.

We were in a tense situation, right enough, but I was relieved that we'd had no problems with the pirates. Most especially, that they hadn't tried anything with Bridget and Cassie. I like to think I would have defended them but I know that I wouldn't have stood a chance.

Around 10 p.m. we turned out the two dim lights in the cabin and settled down as best we could. The women got the banquettes and we men lay in a row on the wooden floor. I lay on my back in the yoga corpse position, hoping it wasn't going to be any kind of presentiment for later.

Joseph was lying beside me.

"You know," he said quietly. "I don't think he should have used *sagittare* either. I think you can only use that when talking about shooting arrows."

I didn't say anything for a moment. Then: "Joseph, about this Latin thing."

"Just a throwback to my school days," he said quickly.

Joseph fell silent.

I thought about Dwight, wondering if Zane could have killed him. I thought about Larry and wondered the same. I thought about Mollie, which was a bad idea if I was hoping to get off to sleep

Although, actually, I fell asleep pretty easily. I usually do. I like to think it's because of my yoga breathing but on this occasion it was probably more to do with the amount of alcohol I'd had during a very long day.

I don't know what woke me. Perhaps it was the scuffling over my head. I sat up as the others stirred too. I headed for the stairs, banging my head in the dark in the process. Poking my head above deck I saw, in the half-light of the lamp shining down from the conning tower, Chuck struggling with one of our guards.

The guard was bulky and grizzled. Chuck was trying to wrestle him to the ground but the man looked to have a pretty solid stance.

I looked up at the conning tower. It was empty. I was momentarily distracted by the shadowy sight of the turtle still dangling from our mast.

The guard's machine pistol lay on the deck. I looked around for the other guards but I couldn't immediately see them. I moved towards the gun.

Chuck and the bulky guard separated. I saw that the guard had a knife in his left hand. I was near enough to see that his eyes were bugging out of his head. By the way Chuck was standing, he clearly knew how to handle himself in a knife-fight. However, I was conscious that he was also damned near seventy.

"Hey!" I called to the guard as I moved towards him.

He flashed a look in my direction and Chuck made a grab for the knife hand. The guy was fast. He pulled his wrist out of the way then thrust towards Chuck's body. Chuck was off-balance from his own lunge for the knife. He was unprotected. I saw the knife hit him in the ribs. I heard the dull thwack.

"Chuck–" I started to call.

Chuck doubled up. The guard withdrew his knife arm then began a slashing movement to the back of Chuck's head. But Chuck, still doubled over, ran at his opponent, catching him with his head and shoulders in the midriff. Using his momentum, Chuck barrelled the guard back to the guard-rail of the boat. The next moment the two of them went over the side.

I heard the splash as they hit the water. I rushed to the side of the boat. I leaned over looking for them struggling in the dark water. Just then, I was aware of hurried footsteps behind me. I turned to see one of the guards closing on me. He jabbed his machine gun hard into my side. I doubled over then fell to my knees, gasping for breath. I dropped my head to the deck and stayed still, trying not to throw up.

When eventually I did sit up, the guard still had his gun fixed on me and two more men were pointing their weapons down into the cabin where the others were huddled.

I was bathed in bright light for a moment. I looked up. A searchlight in the conning tower was playing across our boat and the water. I looked over the side but I could see no sign of Chuck or the guard.

Well, almost no sign. As the beam played across the water and down the length of the ship I saw something near the stern. There, bobbing on the water, was something that could have been mistaken for seaweed. It could have been mistaken for some lush, seafaring spider. But there was no doubt in my mind that it was, in fact, Chuck's toupee.

Chuck gone?

I couldn't believe it. I've lost people in my life: my mum when I was three, my dad when I was eighteen and others since. People I knew far better than Chuck. But I think Chuck had become a bit of a father figure for me. Iconic too. Not because he was a movie star. I've met a lot of movie stars through my work as a journalist and I've not been overly impressed – except when they've been beautiful, of course, shallow man that I am.

But I liked Chuck and I admired his values. I suppose he was old-fashioned in that he *had* values. Fortitude, loyalty, courtesy – okay, I'll stop, but that's the kind of thing. Values is an odd word to use these days but I aspire to have them. And as a father figure – well, my own dad was a bit of a disaster. Actually, why qualify it? A total disaster.

It was still the middle of the night. I'd been bundled back into the cabin. They'd used a long hook to lift Chuck's toupee out of the water. They threw it in the cabin after me then they barricaded us in.

One consequence of being sealed up in the cabin was that it was a furnace down there. The portholes were already open wide but the night was so still there was scarcely a breeze to shift the air.

My ribs hurt but I didn't get any sympathy from Bridget when I came back into the cabin.

"Men," she said scornfully. "Men and physical pain. You're pathetic."

"Thanks for caring," I said.

We were all shaken about Chuck. Joseph was hugging himself. Cassie was hunched up, hugging her knees. Greg was sitting on the floor, looking listlessly out of a porthole.

"I think he must have been planning to do it alone all the time," Cassie said. "The way he discouraged Bridget and me from our plan."

"He drowned?" Joseph said.

"I know" Cassie said. She looked across at the sodden pile of hair on top of the fridge. "And all that's left is his toupee? That's *so* sad."

None of us were in the mood for sleeping. We sat around talking about Chuck.

"So what do we do now?" Greg said. "They've lost a man. They are going to be so pissed off with us."

I looked uneasily at Bridget and Cassie. Greg was right and I feared that the two women would bear the brunt.

"We've got to get away in the night," I said.

"Oh what – now that they're on full alert?" Greg shook his head. "Best thing we can do is keep our heads down."

Greg's attitude had been a surprise to me. I'd always liked him but his pessimism was seriously pissing me off. Probably because a part of me agreed with him. Left to myself, my motto has usually been: when in doubt, do nothing.

One by one our little troupe dozed off. I sat with my face pressed to a porthole. I could vaguely smell marijuana drifting down from the deck above. It smelled pretty good.

I don't know why I'm such a coward. I don't mean to be. I want to be brave, valiant – pathetic, I know, as they're values instilled from a childhood watching Hollywood movies. Not that it matters because I'm not those things. I avoid physical confrontations; I avoid emotional ones, for that matter.

When everybody seemed to be asleep in the cabin I took the flare gun and four flares from the cupboard. I tiptoed over to the flimsy barricade the pirates had erected in the doorway. It wasn't secured by anything but I didn't know who was on the other side. I gave it a gentle push. It moved easily. There was a gap of a few inches between the door jamb and the barricade. I put my eye to it.

"Anybody out there?" Bridget whispered, close to my ear.

I jerked my head around.

"What?" she said. "You've suddenly turned into John Wynn?"

"Wayne," I said patiently. "His name was John Wayne."

"Even so. You don't think I'd let you do this on your own?"

I leaned over and kissed her cheek.

"Thanks, Bridget."

"Don't thank me – I just want to be sure you don't fuck it up for the rest of us. Are you going to kill them?"

She was looking at the flare gun.

"Fire one of those at them and they won't be much of a problem."

"Yes but Bridget – taking a life?"

"Well, clearly, they have to die. You've seen that turtle. I'm not Animal Lib or anything so bonkers but anyone coarse enough to be cruel to either human or animal should be dead. We have a big world population so creeps like this aren't going to leave a gap." She saw me looking at her. "What – am I missing something?"

Bridget had once killed someone, in Peru. It had upset her for a while but clearly she had come to terms with it.

We crept out on deck. The light from the conning tower was still shining down on our boat. I could see two men sitting beneath our main mast. The smoke from their spliffs drifted down the boat. I looked up at the turtle strung on the yardarm above their heads. I looked up at the conning tower. There was a man there silhouetted behind the light focused on our boat. Whether he was looking our way, I couldn't tell.

Bridget and I were squatting at the back of the boat watching the two guards when a figure loomed up over the port side of the boat. He too was in silhouette in the light from the conning tower.

I saw big shoulders and a bald head. When the figure straightened I saw that it was Chuck, *sans* toupee.

Remarkably stealthily for a man so big and old, he moved towards the two men. He looked up at the turtle then along the rope that was holding it in place. The rope was tied to a cleat at the side of the boat. Keeping a close watch on the guards, he began to untie the rope.

The two guards passed the ganja between them. The man on the conning tower didn't move.

Chuck held the weight of the turtle on the rope for a moment then played it out. I saw him settle his stance and his chest swell. Then he released the turtle. It plummeted down and landed on the heads of the two guards. It flattened them like a couple of cartoon characters.

They made no sound, but the 400lb turtle did hit them with a loud, clattering thwack. I aimed the flare gun towards the conning tower as I saw the man behind the light shift his position.

Chuck hurried over to the side of the boat where a line was holding us to the submarine. He took a knife from his belt and sawed at the line.

The man in the conning tower leaned out. I fired the flare gun at him. The flare hit the side of the conning tower with a loud clang and, fizzing red light, dropped into the water between our boat and the submarine.

The man in the conning tower jumped back. Chuck looked around then carried on sawing at the line. I fumbled to reload the flare gun. The line split and our boat immediately started to drift. The man on the conning tower reappeared. I fired the second flare.

It whooshed straight towards him. He ducked down and the flare whizzed past. I followed its trajectory low across the sky before it burst in a flamboyant red umbrella of light.

As it hung there in the sky Chuck turned and waved.

"Time to go," he said, striding across the deck. "Anybody know how to turn this engine on?"

Bridget was already at the wheel, pressing every button she could see, pulling on knobs, twiddling dials. The engine caught fire.

"Go!" Chuck said.

And we did. As we passed the conning tower I kept the flare gun pointed towards it. Our boat scooted out past the tail end of the sub. The flare's light faded and I saw the man on the conning tower again. I fired the third flare back at him.

This one smacked against the top of the conning tower, did

a little flip and fell inside. As we were heading off into the night I saw the man leap overboard, then I could see this incredible shower of light filling the bowl of the conning tower, fizzing up orange and yellow sparks that fell in molten drops down the side of the submarine.

Chuck had gone back to the middle of our boat. The turtle was moving slowly across the deck. Chuck grabbed one of the men and hauled him over to the side of the boat. He threw him in the water. He did the same with the second man, then stood beneath the mast, sucking in air.

I watched the submarine behind us as we headed off into the pitch-black night. Aside from the cauldron of spitting red fire I could see no movement behind us. Then the light of the flare dwindled and I could see nothing at all.

The others crowded onto the deck.

"Chuck!" Joseph offered him his hand.

Greg nodded.

Cassie gave Chuck a big hug, looked up at his bald pate.

"Hey, sexy," she said.

Then, in the light on the mainmast she caught sight of the turtle moving slowly around the middle of the deck and hurried over to it.

"I've switched the lights off below," Joseph said. "The darker the better, I assume?"

"Even if they can't see us, they'll be able to hear us," I said. "And they'll have radar."

"They're not following us for a little while," Chuck said. "Unless they come after us in the sub. I demobilised their speedboats."

"Suddenly you're a man of the sea?" I said. "How?"

Chuck reached into his pocket and pulled out two sets of keys. He grinned then tossed the keys overboard.

"It will slow them down," he said.

I shook my head, put my hand on Chuck's shoulder.

"Chuck, are you okay? I saw you stabbed."

He laughed, a big, unfettered laugh. With the accent on unfettered. I looked at his belly hanging over his pants.

The corset was gone.

Chuck saw me looking. Nodded.

"Damned corset deflected the knife. Don't know what it was made of but I'm going to give the makers a testimonial, you can bet on that."

"Where is it?"

Chuck rubbed his belly.

"Decided I didn't need it. Besides – you ever tried to breathe underwater in one of those things?"

Joseph had taken over at the wheel. I'd noticed that since we'd been kidnapped he hadn't actually been seasick. And I remembered the way he'd stood in front of the women. There were hidden depths to the man, if you could ignore the Latin thing.

I walked over to him.

"What do you think, Joseph?"

"Nicholas, I think that film-making is a strange world."

I laughed.

"You have that right."

"I think I'll stick to theatre."

Bridget had joined Cassie and Bridget by the turtle.

"We've got to get him back into the sea," Cassie said, stroking the beak.

"Is he in good enough nick?" Bridget said.

"Good enough what?" Cassie said.

"Not that Nick," Bridget said, flicking a finger at me. "Colloquial nick."

Cassie frowned.

"Colloquial Nick?"

"Forget it."

Cassie shrugged.

"So how do we do this?" she said.

"In the old days," I said. "Sailors used to lug them up on their backs and carry them aboard ship."

Chuck looked back in the direction of the submarine.

"We shouldn't do anything until we're further away from the pirates. Maybe we can wait until morning."

Greg had ducked down below. Now he came back up and handed Chuck his wig. Chuck looked at it, weighed it in his hand. He walked over to the side of the boat and dropped the wig overboard.

Cassie and Bridget had been watching.

"Empowerment," Cassie whispered to Bridget. "Chuck's empowered."

Chuck turned – from the waist, for the first time since I'd met him – and winked.

"Darned if I'm not."

We weren't followed so far as we could tell. However, our main problem became apparent over the next half hour. None of us knew where the hell we were or where we were headed.

It was a beautiful night. The pitch black water was still, a light breeze soughed around us. The stars were bright as could be. We all knew that at night sailors steer by the stars. But none of us were sailors.

My knowledge was limited to a little cluster of stars that form a question mark. And all I knew about them was that I seem to have looked up at them in the middle of all kinds of entanglements across my life.

Chuck, whilst we all looked to him as our leader, was, well, all at sea out here.

"Anybody know anything about stars?" I called.

"They look pretty over the prairie at night," Chuck said. "That's about the extent of it for me."

"I do," Cassie said.

"Steering by them?"

"Well, I'm Pisces, which is dreamy and loving. I know Gemini is untrustworthy…"

Okay, all except Chuck and Cassie knew that sailors used the stars to steer by night.

We chugged on.

"Are there no instruments we can use?" Chuck said.

"It's a basic boat," Joseph said. "There's no directional navigation equipment on here. Unless we can read the stars we don't know where we're going."

In other words, we were absolutely, totally, utterly and completely lost.

"We've been going for an hour or so," Greg said. "I don't think the pirates will be able to find us. Since we don't know where we're going, maybe we should stop and wait until daylight. When the sun rises at least we'll know what direction we're heading in."

It seemed like a good idea. We cut the motor. All of us sat on deck, listening to the water slapping against the side of the boat, listening for any distant sound of motors and engines. There was none.

Dawn came quickly, or at least an indication where the sun was rising in the east.

"Okay," Greg said. "Now we know to head in the opposite direction. Avast ye, Joseph – to the wheel."

"Aye, aye cap'n," Joseph said, remarkably chirpily.

"What about the turtle?" Cassie said. "Can't we put it back in the sea?"

The turtle seemed to have suffered little damage from its experiences with the pirates. But then, how could we tell since it was essentially a shell with flippers and a head.

We found a plank of wood and lay it down over the side into the slow swell of water. It was hard to hold steady but the men did that whilst the women coaxed the turtle onto it. It was too wide to be able to use its flippers so it sat there, on the top of the plank, moving its flippers helplessly.

"It's going to have to slide," I said. I saw Cassie's look. "It's got a shell and it's only a few yards."

We gave the turtle a push. The turtle scudded down the plank and hit the water with a big splash. It floundered on the surface for a moment or two then dove down into the water. One for Mollie.

The sun rose. We all stood on deck, munching our breakfast – peanuts and pretzels – looking towards the sun. We looked at each other.

"Okay, can I ask a practical question?" Bridget said.

"There's nothing we can do about the toilet until we get back to land," I said.

She threw me a foul look. I was grateful her face couldn't chuck in the other half of the look.

"How does knowing where the sun is rising help us, since we don't know which direction we've come from?"

We looked at each other.

"Darn good question," Chuck said. He stroked his bare pate. "Wish I had the answer."

"No, no," Joseph said. "We know that the Yucatan must be west of here. So let's just head west and see what happens."

We all nodded. None of us had a fucking clue.

"I can't wait to get into a bath," Cassie said. "How long until we get back?"

"If Joseph's right – and he must be," I said, "two or three hours before we hit land."

It quickly became apparent none of us had a clue, either, about how the boat worked. Just after ten in the morning we ran out of fuel.

The Caribbean and the Gulf of Mexico are interesting stretches of water. The Caribbean side of the Yucatan peninsula is hedged, eventually, by Cuba on the north side. If you go through the Yucatan channel to the Gulf of Mexico then you have a ring of ports in Mexico but the current will most likely take you to Galveston, Texas. That's partly because, contrary to our normal assumption, the Gulf Stream heads north not south, into the Gulf rather than out into the ocean.

There are strong and dangerous currents in this area. There are a large number of sunken ships here because of these very currents. So when we started to drift, I started to worry. Especially as we were drifting not west but north-east.

"God, I'd kill for a drink," Bridget said.

We were all lying half in, half out of the cabin.

"You know we're out of water so why torture us all by reminding us?"

"Who's talking about water? I want a large g&t." She gestured up at the sun, shining horribly brightly down upon us. "And don't tell me the sun's not over the bloody yardarm."

I sighed.

"Bridget, I don't think you fully realise the severity of our situation. We're adrift on a vast ocean beneath a pitiless sun with neither food nor drink. Two options face us – either starvation or death from lack of water or insanity by virtue of the sun's rays beating mercilessly down on us."

"That's three options," Chuck said.

"I was counting starvation and death by lack of water as one."

"I think you're overestimating our problems," Chuck said. "All else fails we can drink our own urine."

"Ugh!" Bridget said. "How disgusting. That's the kind of thing Nick might do but I think the rest of us might have something to say about that."

"Well if the idea of drinking your own is abhorrent perhaps we could drink each other's …?" This from Joseph, looking thoughtful. "Maybe mix a cocktail"

"Enough," Bridget screeched. "Forget I mentioned the g&t. But what about food – shouldn't you guys be baiting lines and catching fish for a barbecue or something?"

"Did you ever read that book about the sinking of the whaleship Essex by a sperm whale?" Joseph asked.

"A whale wrote a book?" Cassie said.

I looked uneasily out to sea.

"Glad you brought that book up."

"The crew were cast adrift in three boats, 2,000 miles from the nearest landfall," Joseph said. "Ended up eating each other."

"Eating each other?" Bridget said. "What, you mean I'm tucking into your arm whilst you're slicing off cuts from my leg?"

"You know what I mean," Joseph said impatiently. "When the food ran out. First they ate people as they died, then they drew lots for who they were going to kill to eat."

"I couldn't eat anybody," Bridget said. "And certainly not you, Joseph, you're far too stringy."

"I wouldn't know where to begin," Cassie said. "I simply couldn't eat another person."

"Maybe if they were family?"

Joseph wagged his finger.

"Cannibalism is already a cultural embarrassment but gastronomic incest is a definite taboo."

"Gastronomic incest?"

"So are we going to wait for someone to die or are we going to draw lots?" Cassie said. My God, she was getting into the spirit of this pretty quickly.

"Draw lots – I've always been lucky at cards," Bridget said. "And concomitantly unlucky in love."

"Concomitantly?"

"Yeah, I went to university." I glanced at her. She raised a hand in warning. "So what if it was once a poly? It's a university now."

Cassie looked around.

"Actually, I'd rather starve than eat one of you."

Joseph nodded.

"It's a no win situation," she continued. "You're not going to want to eat a friend and quite frankly eating someone you can't stand – well, it's worse than doing a love scene with them. It's bad enough them trying to stick their tongue down your throat. Suggesting the rest of them goes down your throat too – ugh."

"Hear, hear," Greg said.

"You won't say that when you're starving," Joseph said.

"I am bloody starving," Bridget said. "God, what I could do to a lobster–"

Bad memories of lobsters popped into my head.

"When you're really starving, you'll know it," Joseph said. "Starvation victims have about half the normal edible meat.

Muscle tone atrophies and fat goes. The internal organs shrink."

"Sounds like some diets I've been on," Bridget said. "What's the downside?"

"This isn't funny," Joseph said. "Once a starving body exhausts its reserves of fat, it begins consuming muscle. That process results in the deterioration of the internal organs and, eventually, death."

"I've read that women tend to outlast men because they have ten per cent more body fat," I said. "You should be okay, Bridget."

Bridget whacked me.

"What was that for?" I said indignantly. "You're always saying you could lose a few pounds."

"Yes – I say it. I'm allowed to. You, on the other hand..."

Joseph hadn't finished.

"When you're really starving boils break out on your skin."

"Ugh." Cassie glanced at her beautiful, unblemished arms.

"Look we don't need to resort to cannibalism," Greg said.

"Thank Christ. What do we do then?"

"First one that dies we chop them up and then trail bits of them in the water as bait for sharks. Then we kill the sharks and live off their meat."

We all slowly turned to look at Greg. I thought I'd be even more practical.

"We kill the sharks? How, exactly?"

"There are ways," he said.

"Do you know what they are?" I said.

"Well..."

"Sailors have been surviving on the remains of dead shipmates for centuries," I said. "It was so widespread in the early nineteenth century sailors who survived shipwreck made a point of telling their rescuers if they hadn't eaten anyone."

"On the Essex they ate the black people first," Joseph said.

"Wouldn't share a table with them at dinner except when they were dinner," I said.

"Don't worry about the starvation," Joseph continued. "The thirst will kill you first. It will be horrible to see."

"I'm sure," I said.

"When a mouth stops generating saliva, the tongue becomes this swollen, heavy thing, swinging on its root. You can't speak. As your body starts to mummify your tongue swells and forces its way past the jaws. Your throat closes up so you can't swallow. Your eyeballs bleed."

"I get the picture," Bridget said weakly.

We'd been adrift for three hours.

Chapter Seven

"I tore the hearts of victims out
And ate them for my dinner
With fava beans and Chianti
This marked me as a sinner
But truth to tell, I here confess,
I did it just for show
My own heart wasn't in it –
I'm vegetarian you know."

We were a cast adrift in so many ways. All of us on deck, keeping an eye out for land or pirates – or worse.

"Are there sharks in these waters?" Cassie said at one stage.

"I'm sure there are," I said without thinking.

"But they don't attack boats do they?" she said.

"You never seen *Jaws?*"

She moved away from the side of the boat.

"Well, eventually we'll hit Cuba," I said, trying to be cheery. "I've always fancied going there."

"When you say eventually, Nick, how eventual is that?" This was Chuck.

"Drifting? I have no idea. Maybe a couple of weeks."

"A couple of weeks?" Bridget said. "But we're out of booze."

"More to the point we're out of water," Greg said. "And as food, pretzels and peanuts can only go so far."

"And I need to wash my hair," Cassie said, almost to herself.

We drifted. For a while we tried to remain jolly. After all, a friendly skipper was bound to come upon us. We chatted about this and that.

Bridget's contribution was a rant about baseball caps.

"One of my biggest regrets is living through the period when the baseball cap colonised the world," she said. "Cassie, you're a woman of taste –" I raised an eyebrow – "Would you ever sleep with someone who wore a baseball cap?"

Cassie thought for a moment.

"You mean who wore it in bed?"

"No," Bridget said patiently. "In general."

Cassie frowned.

"Brad Pitt."

Bridget sighed.

"Good point."

"But actually," Cassie said, "I wouldn't sleep with him."

"You wouldn't sleep with Brad Pitt? Are you mad?"

"No," Cassie said. She seemed to take a deep breath. "I'm a lesbian," she blurted out.

All the men looked at me rather than her. Cassie saw the look.

"Nick was just my beard. My lavender marriage."

"Thank God," Greg said. "I couldn't make sense of the world when you seemed to have fallen for Nick." He saw my look. "Oh, no offence, Nick."

"Sure," I said.

"This doesn't seem the time for lying," Cassie said. "I think it would be good for all of us to come clean."

"About what?" Bridget said.

"Stuff."

Nobody said a word until eventually Chuck piped up.

"I appreciate what you've said, Cassie, and I think we should all be proud of what we are. We shouldn't have to hide our real selves."

"Thank you, Chuck," Cassie said.

"I'd like to add, on behalf of all the men here, with regard to your admission," Chuck said, "– what a damned shame."

And so it went. I did a little rant about organized crime.

"Organised crime has taken over the world," I said. "Smuggling caviar out of Russia; the trade in turtles here. Try fishing for stickleback back in England. The Lancashire crime families – the Congleton mafia – if you haven't got the right look when you're in Congleton, forget it. There are some tough types around Parbold too I hear."

Joseph, Greg and Cassie stared blankly at me.

"Nick," Chuck said. "Half the time I can't understand a word you're saying."

The others nodded.

"And the other half isn't worth listening to," Bridget said.

It was around then we sighted land. It was off to the north-east of us – two low conical hills a couple of miles apart and rising behind them a third and higher hill, also conical.

"Land!" Bridget cried. "Land! We're saved, we're saved!"

"Bridget, we haven't even been adrift a day yet," I said. "What's with the high emotion?"

She gave me what I could tell was intended to be a disdainful look but her frozen features let her down. Her ears shifted a little.

"I'm an ac-tor, darling, my emotions run near to the surface. Plus, I'm practising my range."

"Maybe we'll see another boat and it will tow us in," Greg said.

"Maybe there's an ayurvedic centre here," Cassie said. "Reiki, aromatherapy..."

"If the island is inhabited," Joseph said.

We slowly drew nearer to the island. We had no paddles and although we could steer a little with the rudder we were pretty much at the mercy of the tides. We had toyed a few hours earlier with the idea of rigging up a sail but there were no sails on board and since we were all dressed in T-shirts and shorts we didn't have the material to make one either.

We could make out a line of surf some way from the island. As we approached we could hear a loud booming. We'd all seen enough movies to know what it was.

"A coral reef," Joseph said.

"Isn't this where usually the boat gets wrecked on the reef and everyone has to swim for shore?" Bridget said.

I nodded glumly.

"Shit," Greg said.

The closer we got, the louder the booming became. The waves were crashing against the reef then rolling back causing a high swell.

"What are we going to do?" Cassie said, panic back in her voice.

"Hope that the swell will take us over," I said.

"And if it doesn't?"

"This may be your opportunity to discover the delights of seawater," I said. "Can everyone swim?"

"In that?" Greg said.

"Won't this boat have lifejackets?"

"And there's a lifebelt," I said, yanking it off the outside wall of the cabin. "Who wants it?"

Greg went below decks and came back up with two lifejackets.

"All I could find." He handed one to Cassie. When he offered the other to Bridget she shook her head.

"Bridget's a great swimmer," I said. "And I'll be fine too."

Famous last words.

"I was a surfer. I've been on, in and under water most of my life," Greg said. "I'll manage. Chuck?"

"Swimming is not exactly my favourite occupation," he said slowly. "Though I do it if I have to."

Greg pressed the jacket on him. Joseph took the lifebelt.

When the swell lifted us up I could see more of the island. It was mostly wooded but the three cones of rock stuck out above the treeline. I could also see that beyond the reef was a calm lagoon.

"We just have to get over the reef and then we're in calmer waters. It's not far to the shore."

"Do we try to stick together?"

"If we can," I said, sounding far more confident than I felt. I'd had close encounters with coral before – it is sharp as razor blades. I didn't fancy us being dashed against a reef of it by these waves – we'd be cut to shreds.

"Can't we surf in?" Cassie said.

"You can surf too?" Greg said.

"Well, no, not actually," Cassie said. "I've seen photos of Cameron Diaz doing it and she looks great. Anyway, I don't mean proper surfing, I mean body-boarding."

By now we were about three hundred yards away from the reef. The swell was drawing us nearer.

I looked around.

"What do you think?"

Greg stated the obvious.

"We don't have any surfboards."

"The whole boat is wood," Cassie said. "We just need planks."

We all looked from Cassie to the surf. Cassie with a halfway sensible idea.

"We'd better hurry."

The benches around the cabin were the readiest source of planks, each about two foot wide and five feet long. Chuck and Greg prised them loose and we carried them back on deck.

By now the boat was in a trough with the swell rising up in front of us, obscuring totally our view of the island. The sound of the surf was deafening.

"How do we do this?" I said.

"We wait to see if the boat is going to get over the reef," Greg said. "If it does we're fine. The minute we hit something, we go over the side with our planks."

We each looked at the wall of water rising above us then at the puny planks.

"Group hug!" Cassie suddenly declared, and we quickly gathered and rather awkwardly squeezed each other whilst holding on to our planks. I squeezed Bridget's hand.

We separated as the boat started to rise on the swell. We were sideways on to the reef, which wasn't good.

"Hang on to something!" Greg yelled. "And grip your boards tightly."

We reached the top of the swell then the water dropped away from us. I swear that for a moment we were suspended in the air, hanging motionless, before the boat dropped like a rock into a great wave of surf.

Water, hissing and pounding, rose up all around us. A wall of water rose up in front of us then broke over the boat. I knew from a horrible ride on the rapids of the St Lawrence waterway a few years earlier how powerful a surge of water can be. Since a friend had been drowned there I'd tried not to dwell on that experience as we approached the reef.

Now there was no time to dwell on anything.

The water hit like a huge slab of concrete. It knocked the air out of me, lifted me off my feet and threw me out of the boat.

I hit the water, clutching my plank and was whirled head

over heels beneath the water. I was desperate to kick for the surface but I was so dazed by the force of the water hitting me I didn't know which way was up. I gripped the plank to me with all my strength. It rolled so that I was hanging underneath it and I felt a sharp blow to my back as the surf dragged me across the reef.

I had water in my mouth and no air in my lungs. There was enormous pressure in my ears and it felt like my eyes were popping out of my head. Then in another surge of water I broke the surface. I gasped for breath as a wave lifted me high into the air. I had a mad kaleidoscopic vision of blue sky, tufts of cloud, trees, another body flung high in the air somewhere nearby then the wave dashed me down again.

My face smacked hard against the plank as I hit the water. My grip loosened and the plank was swept away. I rolled over and over, carried by the fury of the water. Something bulky banged into me.

I rolled again but more slowly. Then I realised, probably only seconds later though it seemed an age, that the water wasn't buffeting me anymore.

I was being pulled by the water, sure, but it wasn't tossing me around like a rag doll. That's good to know, I thought, as the undertow sucked me under and consciousness left me.

I woke up vomiting water. There was a heavy weight pressing down on my back. My face, turned to one side, was squashed into wet sand. My ribs were aching and pain ripped through my chest with each surge of water out of my mouth and nose.

"He's coming round," I heard a voice say somewhere above me. Hands grabbed my arms and I was pulled over and up into a sitting position. I spluttered. Water seemed to be streaming out of every orifice – my eyes, my ears, my nose and mouth.

Blearily I looked around. Cassie was kneeling in the sand in front of me in a life jacket and a thong. To her left Bridget was also kneeling, bare-breasted. They both had concerned expressions on their faces.

I looked at Bridget's breasts.

"Yeah, yeah, get a good look you pervert," she said. "The surf tore our clothes off."

I looked back at Cassie's thong.

"Took my shorts right off me," she said with a shrug.

I nodded slowly and as I did so realised I was stark naked. I clamped a hand over my privates.

"Bit late for that, sweetheart," Bridget said. "Besides, we've both seen it before – though I've never seen it angry. Does it look much different then, Cassie?"

She shook her head.

"Not noticeably."

I lay back in the sand.

My sinuses were in agony from the water that had been forced into them.

"I thought I'd drowned."

"You would have done if Cassie here hadn't brought you ashore," Bridget said.

Casssie looked embarrassed.

"It was only by chance. We collided in the water and I just grabbed you, that's all."

"What happened to you two?"

"That big wave knocked me out of the boat," Bridget said. "My plank went west the minute I hit the water." She indicated gashes on her arms and belly. "The coral caught me a bit but I managed to get into the lagoon without much difficulty. You've got a nasty cut on your back, by the way, that will need seeing too."

"I saw you two go over but I managed to hang on in the boat," Cassie said. "We came back up another wave and that's when the boat and me parted company. But my plank actually worked – I slid down the wave, rode a couple more and I was in the calmer waters when I collided with you." Cassie's eyes were shining. "It was great."

"Welcome to the sea," I croaked.

"Look what I've been missing all these years."

I sat up again.

"The others?"

Bridget turned her hands palms up.

"They were still in the boat when I came out," Cassie said.

"Hope they're okay," I said.

"We can check down the beach when you feel well enough to walk," Bridget said.

I struggled to my feet.

"I'll be okay. How come you two aren't hurting as much as me?"

"We're women," Bridget said, patting me on the shoulder.

I looked around us. The reef of jagged rocks and coral was about a quarter of a mile out. The surf continued to boom and I watched the high swell of the water crashing against the reef and the white plumes flying into the air above it. The lagoon was in the shape of an amphitheatre with headlands about a mile from each other. The water was clear, turquoise. Behind us, the trees came right down to the high water mark, vivid green. I could see about fifty yards away a river running down into the lagoon.

We set off down the beach in loose formation. The sand was coarse and dark. I think it was coral sand – I'd experienced it before.

"Watch out for bits of coral in this sand," I said. "It will cut your feet."

"Thank you, darling," Bridget said.

About a hundred yards along I stopped and peered at the sand in front of me. I fluttered my hands.

"What?" The others walked over.

I pointed at the single, perfectly formed footprint.

"A one-legged man?" Cassie said, fiddling with her hair, which was matted from the seawater.

"With a very long hop," Bridget said, "since it's the only print around here."

"Someone's taking the piss," I said.

"Is it one of our three men?" Cassie said.

"It's someone who's read his *Robinson Crusoe*," I said. They both looked at me blankly, though in fairness Bridget couldn't help it given her facial condition.

"That's how he comes upon Man Friday." I looked round nervously. "I can't remember if that's before or after the cannibals attack him."

We kept walking, although now I kept a close eye on the undergrowth. Mind you, the way the tree canopy filtered the sun, creating areas of deep shadow, an army could have been hiding in there and I wouldn't have seen it.

We were approaching another shallow river which ran across the sand from the trees to empty into the lagoon. The air round here seemed to hang heavy – there was the odour of rotting things. When we were about ten yards from the river something long and straight flashed by in front of my face. I jerked back and looked to where the object had fallen onto the sand.

It was a length of wood crudely sharpened at one end to make a spear. My God, we *were* going to be attacked by cannibals. I picked it up and turned to warn the women but then caught sight of a white man crouching at the edge of the wood by the river, a frightened look on his face.

"Hey you!" I said. "What d'you think you're doing?"

I started up the beach towards him but he backed into the trees.

"Don't make me come after you," I called, in a frankly foolhardy manner.

He poked his head through the foliage. He was a white man but his skin was very dark – even his lips were black. The darkness of his face made his pale blue eyes stand out the more. His blonde hair was long and unkempt, as was his beard.

"You're not meant to be here. This is a private island." His voice sounded hoarse and awkward, like a rusty lock. His eyes were not, however, on me. They had been, for a moment, examining my nakedness then giving a little smile as he focused on my genitalia. But now his eyes were flicking from Bridget's naked breasts to Cassie's near-naked nether regions.

A private island? I looked more closely. No, Richard Branson would never let his beard get so untidy.

"Well, we didn't intend to be here," I said cheerily. "We're sort of shipwrecked."

He thrust his head forward.

"Sort of shipwrecked? Either you are or you aren't."

He wasn't looking at me when he said this.

"Clever dick," I muttered, then more loudly: "Right, well, we are then."

"You are what?" he said, his attention on the women, his eyes almost out of their sockets.

"Shipwrecked. What about you?"

His head disappeared for a moment then he stepped out of the shadows onto the beach. He was holding another spear. He was thin, sinewy, clothed in tattered shorts and sleeveless T-shirt. He had two legs. So much for Cassie's theory.

He took a step forward. Bridget and Cassie both took a step back. Bridget crossed her arms over her breasts.

"I know they're nice but they're not exactly rare," she said, remarkably mildly for her.

The man leered.

"They're rare on this island. I haven't touched a woman's breasts since I can't remember when."

"Were you shipwrecked too?' I said quickly.

"Marooned," he said, licking his lips and moving a step closer. "I haven't spoke with a Christian these three years."

"Oh God, a religious nut," Bridget murmured.

"Really?" I said suspiciously. "What's the name of this island?"

"This be Skeleton Island," he said, with a wink at Cassie and Bridget.

I nodded.

"You'll be Ben Gunn then," I said.

He jerked his head back and looked back at me. He tightened his grip on the spear.

"I am poor Ben Gunn, I am – but how be you knowing that?"

"Because I've read *Treasure Island*. And *Robinson Crusoe*. How did you do the footprint, by the way?"

A look of cunning crossed his face.

"That'd be telling." He looked back at Bridget and Cassie. "These women both yours?"

"No, of course not."

"Good – because it's share and share alike around here, matey. You got anything else. Any food?"

I shook my head.

"My heart is sore for a Christian diet. You mightn't happen to have a piece of cheese about you now? Many's the long night I've dreamed of cheese." He put his hand out towards Bridget. I've never actually seen a man drool before but I guess that's what he was doing now. "But even more I've dreamed of a woman. And the sea coughs up two."

He made a grab for Bridget's breast.

I should have warned him, I suppose. You mess with Bridget at your peril. She grabbed his wrist with one hand, swept her other up abehind his outstretched arm and bent his arm the way his arm didn't naturally bend, using her forearm as a fulcrum.

He screamed but the scream changed pitch as she turned at the hip, stuck her right leg behind his leg and slammed him into the sand. The scream was replaced by a whimper when she then stood on his groin and ground her heel into his testicles.

She let go of his arm and stepped down.

"Way to go, girl!" Cassie said, gazing at Bridget in wide-eyed admiration.

The man curled into a ball and lay hugging himself. Bridget picked up the spear that he'd dropped when first he hit the sand.

"What's all this weird language he's using?" Bridget said to me. "Have we stepped back in time?"

I shook my head.

"He's speaking Ben Gunn's dialogue from *Treasure Island.* He must not have had anything else to read for however long he's been here."

"If he's been stranded for three years, that's not good news for us," Cassie said.

"That was Ben Gunn in the book."

I looked into the trees beside the river.

"He must have some kind of home back up there." I reached

down and took his arm. "Come on, poor Ben Gunn, aren't you going to invite us in?"

"God, it stinks," Bridget said when we entered the rough hut that the man directed us to. It was not much more than a lean-to with roof and walls of fronds from some of the bigger trees around. There was a hammock strung up at the back of the hut. Clothes were piled in one corner. There was a box about a foot square by the bed and two or three books beside it. The top one was a tattered copy of Stevenson's *Treasure Island.*

She was right about the smell but it seemed to pervade the whole clearing where his shelter was. That same smell of rot and decay I'd got a snatch of on the beach.

"This is my summer residence," he said in what I presumed to be his normal voice. He gave me a sly look. "In the rainy season I was holed up in a cave a little further inland. I use that for my larder and my weapons store now."

"Weapons?"

"Spears and one or two other things."

"Are you under threat here?"

Again the sly look.

"Not any more."

"How long have you been here?"

"I gave up counting the days after the first three months. Maybe six months, maybe a year."

"How did you get here?"

He was looking hungrily at Bridget and Cassie again. We all noticed at the same time that his hand was making movements in the pocket of his shorts.

"Quit with the pocket billiards," Bridget warned, jabbing him lightly in the chest with the spear.

"Just seeing if everything is okay after you attacked me," he said with a simper.

"What a creep," Bridget said under her breath.

He gestured to the pile of clothes in the corner.

"There are garments there if you want to put them on – though, of course, I'd rather you didn't."

Cassie looked from him to the pile and back. Sniffed the air.

"I'd rather we didn't too."

I was conscious of my nakedness but the idea didn't much appeal to me either. A couple of fronds might do the job instead.

"I have some other clothes – women's clothes – that have never been worn," he said in sudden animation. "They're in a private place but I'll take you there."

The women looked at each other.

"I do feel a bit exposed," Bridget said.

Cassie nodded.

"Aside from anything else," she said, "my butt is being bitten to death."

"Like me to scratch it?" Gunn said, in a pleading voice.

"Lead on, Ben Gunn," I said. "What's your real name anyway?"

"I'm poor Ben Gunn, I am."

As he took us along a narrow track Cassie said:

"Guess you can't blame the guy for being horny if he's been on his own for all this time. You know in that film *Castaway* where Tom Hanks was on his own on that island for four years. Don't you think it strange he never had sexual urges?"

"I know what you mean," Bridget said. "Four days and I'm going up the wall. What did he do for four years aside from talk to that damned volleyball?"

"Nothing," I said. "No stimuli, you see. You lose the sex urge."

"I saw that film," Gunn called back. "Sure he had sexual urges – how do you think that volleyball got punctured?" He looked back over his shoulder, sly once more. "You adjust."

He walked into another clearing and stopped. He looked back over his shoulder and beckoned to us. We joined him and he stepped to one side. We saw the pile of sex-shop lingerie first, laid out neatly on a rock. Then beside that we saw a single half-cup, push-up bra, some kind of corset/basque thing, a pair of crotchless knickers, a suspender belt, and a badly laddered pair of fishnet stockings.

But then they would be badly laddered because they were pulled over two logs of wood.

Actually, it was one forked piece. The crotch of the knickers – lack of crotch I suppose – drawn tight over a knot-hole in the wood. The basque encased the rest of the trunk. In the push up bra were two half coconuts.

Cassie, Bridget and I looked at each other. Then Cassie pointed to the top part of the trunk of wood where two outstretched branches looked vaguely like arms. Both branches were tied by knotted underwear to a crossbar of wood.

"Jesus," I said. "The guy's into bondage."

Bridget gave me a long look.

"Nick, he's dressed a lump of wood in women's underwear and you're–"

"You're shocked because of the bondage?" the man said. "Broaden your horizons."

"Just surprised at the need for it," Bridget said. "This is a tree trunk you're having sex with. I assume it's consensual."

"Damned sensual."

It was difficult to respond to this bizarre scene. I could think of just one thing: splinters.

The women turned down the sex-shop underwear.

"Where did you get the lingerie from, Ben?" I said as we walked back to the hut, wondering if *Through The Looking Glass* was also on his reading list.

He came over very coy but ignored my question.

"I suppose they all cheered our first kiss?"

"Who? What first kiss?"

"Mine and my special friend. Didn't she look sexy?"

"As wood goes, she looked terrific," Bridget said.

"Oh not as lovely as you two beauties." He was back in lascivious mode. "There's nothing like the real thing."

Bridget poked him in the bum with her spear.

"Down, buster."

"Who cheered your first kiss?" said Cassie.

What was this? A conversation going over Cassie's head and she tries to make sense of it? Was this evolution in action?

He looked wary now.

"I shouldn't have mentioned it. Nobody."

Bridget poked him with the spear again.

"Spill, babe."

"The audience," he said as we reached his hut. He swung round:

"You're not part of the show are you?"

"Show?" Cassie said.

"Not contestants?"

Bridget and I twigged at the same time.

"You're one of the contestants in *Cast Adrift*," Bridget said.

"I thought you might have recognised me earlier," he said. "What were our ratings?"

"I've never seen the show," I said.

He frowned.

"How'd you know who I was then?"

"We've been with the creator."

A suspicious look came into his eyes.

"God?"

"No, not that one. The creator of this show."

"Oh, him." Gunn scratched his beard. "Haven't seen hide nor hair of him since he dropped us off here goodness knows how long ago."

"How many of you are there?" He tossed his head back.

"I think I'm the sole survivor. Think the rest have all been voted off. Think I'm the winner."

"Congratulations," I said, wondering how to break the news to him.

"So the others – what – left by boat?" Bridget said.

He looked shifty.

"It's reality television – you know. People get voted off."

"But when they were voted off, what did that mean?"

He grinned.

"Off meant off – they were never coming back."

I was having bad thoughts.

"They left you enough food for a month. What did everyone live off – or is that on? – after that?"

"That ran out pretty quickly. After that, we foraged."

"And when the other participants got voted off, how did they leave?"

He was giving me an up from under look.

"Oh, they didn't leave. They were marooned here."

"So what–?" Bridget started to say but I squeezed her arm.

He walked into his den.

"Do you know when the game is officially over?" he said.

"I don't know for sure but I would imagine around now as you're the sole survivor. You're sure you're the only one left – you've looked all over the island to see if anyone else is around?"

I sat on his hammock and set it swaying.

"Well, not over all the island, obviously."

"Obviously," I said. Then: "Why obviously?"

"Well, I don't want to annoy the drug dealers."

"Of course not," Bridget said in her best treat-this-moron-gently voice. "Just out of interest – what drug dealers would they be?"

"The drug dealers on the other side of the island."

"Oh those drug dealers. And do they know you're here?"

"Not me. They got a few of the others though."

"When you say got…?"

"Killed them." We must have looked shocked. "Well, it's only reasonable if you're trying to run a multi-million dollar operation under strictest security and someone blunders in on you uninvited."

"Is that what happened?"

"When we hadn't had contact with anyone from the TV company for a couple of weeks some of the contestants decided the game hadn't started yet and that there was a problem. We'd been told that we weren't supposed to use the whole island, just our side – something to do with how many cameras could be deployed. But now we went all over it. We found this operation going on across the other side. Some of the others thought it was the HQ for the TV company. They went in to talk to them about how we'd been left to fend for ourselves."

"But you didn't go in."

"Of course not – fending for ourselves was the whole point of the operation. Besides, I'd been playing the game from day one and I play to win." He looked sly again. "I didn't think they were TV people. I've been around."

"I'm sure you have," Bridget said. "So the drug dealers killed them."

"Pretty much."

"Pretty much? Either they did or they didn't."

"Well, okay. Then, yes, they killed them."

"How many?"

"About six."

Bridget and I looked at each other for a moment.

"So what did you do?" Cassie was trying gamely to keep up.

"When we saw what had happened to the others we came back over to this side of the island. It's a tough hike to get here if you go cross-country so they never followed. Every so often their boats go by on the lookout for anything here but they can't easily get over the surf. That's why I'm dug in so far back from the treeline."

"And the others?"

He looked at his hands. Clasped them.

"They'll never find them."

I looked at the pile of clothes in the corner. Then at the books. I was remembering something Neill Sanders had said to me.

"What was your luxury item?" I said idly.

"A book."

"*Treasure Island*?"

"No, not that one."

"*Robinson Crusoe*?"

"No. Another one."

I nodded.

"Did one of the women bring the sexy lingerie as her luxury item?"

"Man she looked hot in them too."

He stopped abruptly.

"She get voted off too?"

He nodded.

It was as if a light had suddenly come on in Cassie's head. She suddenly let out a cry.

"My God – you know what I think? I think you killed those other contestants, you vile man." She pointed at the pile of clothes. "I think those are their clothes right there."

She'd finally caught up.

"Not all of them," he protested. "There were the ones the drug people killed, then the contestants started killing each other."

"You know what I think?" I said, bending down to pick up the third book on Gunn's pile. "I think killing was the least of it."

I read the title out loud: "*Contingency Cannibalism: Superhardcore Survivalism's Dirty Little Secret.* By Shiguro Tikada".

I looked at Gunn.

"Does this have recipes?"

He reached for the book.

"As a matter of fact, it does. Cook books are the most popular genre in publishing you know. There's a list of recipes and a diagram indicating the preferred cuts of meat."

"What?" Bridget grabbed for the book.

"As the title indicates," I said, "it's a survivalist's guide to cannibalism."

"The first thing you do is you chop off the bits that make them appear human – the head, feet and hands," Gunn said, looking earnestly from one to another of us. "Then you skin them. Take out the heart, liver and kidneys. Then set to on the meat around the backbone, ribs and pelvis. That's where the best stuff is." He sighed. "The problem was wastage. The average human being provides about 66lbs of edible meat." He waved his arm round the hut. "Well, I have no refrigeration here. It's hot. It's humid. I tried using the cave as a cold store and that helped a bit."

"When did you start eating the other contestants?" Bridget said – a question I never imagined I would ever hear.

"Not for ages! What do you think I am – some kind of animal? But I was starving. I've got the wrong metabolism. People who survive best have either a higher percentage of body fat to feed off or more efficient metabolisms. It means they can live longer on less food than thin people like me.

"And do you know the strange thing? When you're starving, instead of easing the hunger pangs the first taste of meat only intensifies the urge to eat. The more you eat, the hungrier you become. I made a glutton of myself, I can tell you."

"Is that right?" I said.

Bridget and I looked at each other.

We cocooned him in his hammock, wrapped it tight around him. Only his head remained free. He didn't complain but then he was mad as a bag of snakes, if you'll excuse the technical expression.

"Well, okay," I said, standing over him. "We're going to have to see if we can find any other survivors of our own shipwreck. Then we'll come back."

"Good luck to you," he said, smiling a crazy smile. "You find them, you bring them to dinner. Eight sharp. We'd love to have you join us."

"Thank you kindly," I said.

As we walked away, Bridget hissed at me: "Thank you kindly?"

"We seemed to be in Southern hospitality mode."

Cassie was on the other side of me.

"That man killed and ate human beings?"

"He cooked them first," I said. "That shows some civilizing influence."

I put one arm round Cassie's shoulders and the other round Bridget's and gave them both a little squeeze.

"But, let's just say I don't think we should take him up on that dinner invite. I guess we shouldn't judge him too harshly. Marooned on an island for six months with one month's supply of food. What else is there to eat?"

"Would you eat me?" Bridget said, shrugging my arm off her.

"No – I'd let you eat me," I said, which was a pretty generous offer, even if it was within a rather unusual context.

"No thanks very much. I know where you've been."

So much for generous offers. But this was no time to be hurt.

"Do you think his invitation to come to dinner was to eat with him or be eaten by him?" Cassie said.

"Moot point."

We reached the headland.

"Do we have a plan?" I said.

"Do we ever?" Bridget said. "I guess we walk around in circles until we find them."

"Walk around in circles – story of my life." We plodded on over the soft sand and struggled up onto the headland.

"Bridget," Cassie said. "How are you feeling about Dwight?"

"I'm hoping he's alive," she said simply. "And if he isn't, well, I'm going to make Pynchon pay."

"Right," I said. Thinking to myself: "Assuming we get off the island."

From the headland we could see down into the next bay. Our boat was lying waterlogged in the lagoon and three figures were sitting on the sand.

Chapter Eight

"Weevils in my biscuits
But love in my heart."

I went ahead of Cassie and Bridget onto the next beach. I was pleased to see Chuck, Greg and Joseph safe and sound. They were pleased to see me too, judging by the way they were laughing as I strode towards them They had risen to greet me but when Greg fell back to his knees I wasn't so sure. Especially when he seemed to be pointing to my crotch.

It's not easy being naked. Especially when you're me.

"Nick, you made it," Chuck said, putting a hand over his mouth.

Joseph tittered. I looked sharply at him. *Et tu* Joseph?

"What happened to your clothes?" Greg asked in a strangled voice.

"Undertow," I said sourly.

Bridget and Cassie joined us.

The men didn't speak for a good minute and a half, trying not to be obvious about looking at Bridget's breasts and Cassie's bum. Then Chuck whipped off his shirt and offered it to Bridget and Joseph proffered a towel to Cassie. Me they were happy to leave naked.

"What happened?" I said, indicating the boat with one hand. The other hand was acting as a fig leaf – a man can only take so much.

"Darndest thing," Chuck said. "I think I'm right in saying that all three of us clung tight to that boat. In my case it was because I can't swim worth a damn. And the boat bucked those waves and brought us up here." He waved around. "Wherever the hell here is."

"The boat looks a little the worse for wear."

"It took a battering on the reef. Got into the lagoon and ran out of steam."

"Anything salvageable?"

Greg pointed at a pile of things in the sand some yards away.

"We still have the flare gun and two flares. One packet of peanuts. Some towels. Four empty plastic water bottles."

I walked over and grabbed one of the towels, wrapped it round my midriff.

"Ah – shame," Greg said.

Bridget walked over and grabbed the peanuts. Emptied the packet into her mouth.

"We thought of dragging the boat out to make a shelter," Joseph said.

"The first thing we need is water," Chuck said. "Have you located any?"

"Over in the next bay," Bridget said, through a mouthful of nuts.

"Food?"

"Oh there are all kinds of things in the next bay," Bridget said. "How do you feel about cannibals?"

"What?" Joseph said, visibly shrinking. "There are cannibals on the island?"

"Just the one. He's a multiple murderer too."

"I suppose the two things go together," Cassie said. "It would be disgusting if he ate people alive."

"Good point," Bridget said, flashing her a quick look.

Bridget explained about Ben Gunn.

"He killed his fellow contestants to eat them?" Joseph said.

"I know it's hard to swallow," I said. Well, I couldn't resist.

"Nick!" Bridget warned.

"But in fairness some he just ate – they were already dead."

Bridget did her best to give me a dirty look.

"Oh, that's all right then," she said.

"What are we going to do?" Greg said.

"We're going to survive," I said.

"How exactly?"

"There are drug smugglers based on the other side of the island. They'll have boats."

"They'll have guns too."

"They killed some of the contestants who went over there to say hello and ask for help," Bridget said.

"I'm not suggesting we go over and say 'hello'," I said. "I'm suggesting we go over and steal a boat."

Bridget looked up and snorted.

"Listen Einstein. You four stooges here steal a boat from drug dealers? I think the drug dealers might have something to say about that."

"Excuse me?" Greg said. "Four stooges?"

"No offence," Bridget said, waving him away.

"Oh, none taken," Greg said, bristling. "I like being called an idiot."

"I don't," I said, "but I've got used to it."

"*That* I understand," Greg said. "You're the guy who wants to steal a boat from drug dealers."

"If we're careful we'll be fine."

Bridget looked me up and down.

"Nick being careful. Right. Why aren't I persuaded?"

"Because you know me," I muttered.

"From criminals with guns," Greg said. "Good thinking."

"Hey, we're the guys who got away from bloodthirsty pirates," I said. "And what's the alternative anyway? Make a boat out of coconut fronds? Live a Swiss Family Robinson existence on birds' eggs, which we probably can't find; and fish – which we probably won't be able to catch?"

"Swiss Family Robinson sounded so romantic when I was a kid," Bridget said. "This idyllic island – all sun and sand. Now I realise there would have been sex too: the father would have been chasing his daughters all over the island."

"Sounds like parts of Yorkshire," I said. "Apart from the island and the sun, of course."

"Incest," Bridget said. "At least it saves on fares."

Chuck got to his feet.

"Nick's right. We have no alternative but to go and steal a boat."

"What about this cannibal guy?" Greg said.

"We can't take him with us," Chuck said. "But he's not going anywhere. When we hit civilization we'll inform the authorities and they can pick him up."

"Yeah, but he's a mass murderer."

"We think," Chuck said. "We don't know for sure."

"How else do you explain the disappearance of seven or eight contestants?"

Greg was getting agitated. Chuck looked at him.

"I don't try to," he said quietly. "That's not relevant to us here. What's relevant to us here is how we get off the island."

"Do we all go?" Joseph said.

"I expect you're thinking of leaving the *ladies* behind with Hannibal Lecter?" Bridget again.

"It's safest if we all go over to the other side of the island," I said. "I wouldn't want to leave any of us within reach of poor Ben Gunn. And then a couple of us can steal the boat."

Language is a remarkable thing. You can say anything. You can make it sound convincing, authoritative even, whilst inside you're shrinking into a tiny, tiny ball. I was that person at the thought of taking on the drug smugglers. There are degrees of ruthlessness among criminals but drug folk, especially in the Caribbean, seem to strive to outdo each other in brutality and viciousness.

I looked at Bridget.

"Bridget – you up for this?"

She sighed.

"What the hell. You betcha, Nick Madrid."

Bridget and I have this curious relationship. She's horrible pretty much all the time but we're closer than brother and sister, closer than lovers in many ways. It remains unspoken, however. Well, by Bridget. I've tried to talk to her about our relationship many a time but she doesn't do that kind of conversation. Frocks: yes. Shoes: definitely. Gossip: stop her if you can. Relationships of any sort: forget it.

"Come on, darling," she said, hooking her arm into mine. "Let's get off this ruddy…*atoll.*"

It took five hours to walk across the island. We were all barefoot so we had to be cautious once we got into the undergrowth. From the bay the first thing we came to was a marshy tract full of swampy trees. We men were tiptoeing pretty gingerly but Cassie and Bridget just waded in.

Most of our journey was through undulating, sandy country, dotted with trees whose branches contorted in extraordinary ways. I was concerned that we were going to have to climb one of the hills but there was a wide valley that bisected the island. We found water and drank then filled up the bottles.

It was dark by the time we reached the other side. We scrambled as carefully as we could down to the shoreline. About a quarter of a mile off to the east we could see half a dozen boats bobbing on a spotlit stretch of water. There were buildings in a large clearing near the shoreline, also brightly lit.

We decided it would be safest, on the whole, if we all went to steal the boat. It would mean a fast getaway.

"Stealing boats – I seem to have been here before," Chuck said.

We crept down the shoreline until we got near to where the lights would illuminate us.

There were six boats at anchor. Five were whizzy-looking speedboats. The sixth was much bigger, a cruiser of some sort. All its lights were on and through its windows we could see people moving about below decks.

"I don't understand why there are no guards," Chuck whispered.

We were on hands and knees by now, crawling cautiously along the water's edge. It was a humid night and very still. As we neared the compound I became aware of voices and dramatic music. Then, in a dislocated way we heard gunfire and explosions.

"Well, well," Chuck murmured. "They're watching a film."

It was a DVD, actually, on a giant plasma screen.

I peered in through the window of the long, low building. At the near end, half a dozen men were lounging in chairs gazing up at the plasma screen. They had guns lying either by their sides or in their laps. Beyond them I could see a couple of dozen benches. On each of the benches were identical machines, lights winking. DVD and CD burning machines. Around the walls were shelving containing rack after rack of DVDs and CDs.

These people weren't just dealing drugs. Like any good entrepreneurial crime gang, they were pirating films and music too.

What surprised me, however, was the fact that the men watching the film were not Jamaican or Mexican, as I had expected, but – judging by their features – Slavic. I thought of the Pirate King's submarine. These men were the Russian mafia.

This made me feel queasy quite aside from the immediate danger. I'd unwittingly got involved with the Russian mafia in New York a couple of months earlier and their friends in London had trashed my flat when they didn't find me there. If we tangled with these guys, I didn't want to find I was the target of a worldwide vendetta.

About ten minutes later I was still standing by the window, peering in. I started when somebody grabbed my leg.

I managed not to cry out. I looked down, my heart yabbering in my chest. It was Bridget, kneeling below the window. I crouched down beside her.

"What the fuck are you doing?" she hissed.

I flushed.

"Nothing."

"Are the guards in there?"

I nodded.

"What are they doing?"

"They're pirating CDs and DVDs in there."

"More fucking pirates? But what are the guards doing?"

"Watching a film."

She dug her nails into my leg.

"You were watching the bloody thing too, weren't you?"

"Only for a minute," I said.

"Ten bloody minutes we've been waiting for you." She slapped my leg. "Jesus, Nick, we thought they'd got you."

"Sorry," I said, as we crawled away from the window. "It was *Spiderman 3* – it's not released yet."

The others were waiting by the water's edge.

"What's happening?" Chuck said.

"Spiderman's battling with Doc Ock," Bridget said.

"That was *Spiderman 2*," I said.

"I'm afraid you two have lost me entirely," Chuck said. "Not for the first time."

"Don't worry about it," I said. "The guards are otherwise engaged."

"No way to run a business," Greg said. Tutted actually.

We looked out at the boats bobbing at anchor.

"Which one?" Joseph said.

My eyes were drawn to the cruiser with all its lights blazing.

"I wonder what's going on in there?"

"None of our business, Nick," Chuck said. "Our business is to get back to Fuentes."

"I know, I know."

Joseph pointed to a boat with two masts and furled sails.

"Why don't we get the boat with the sails as well as a motor. That way if we run out of fuel we can sail back."

"Good idea," Cassie said.

Greg agreed.

"Which of you knows how to sail then?" Bridget said. Nobody spoke. "Typical."

"I'm sure we could work it out," Joseph said quietly.

"Before or after the boat capsized?"

"Let's move," Chuck said and he waded into the water. The rest of us followed and made our way as quietly as possible to the boat Joseph had pointed out. It was moored near to the cruiser.

Bridget and Cassie went aboard first because, frankly, they were the fittest. I followed and helped Chuck and Joseph clamber aboard. Greg climbed up on the other side. We crouched low in the small cabin at the back of the boat.

Chuck went to the wheel.

"There's a key in the ignition. Nick?"

"Good," I said but my attention was on the cruiser. Half a dozen people had just come up on deck. A heavily accented voice drifted across the water.

"But I am telling you, if anyone is better than Tarkovsky I want to meet him. You talk about Kubrick and *2001* – well, look at Tarkovsky's *Solaris.*"

"I saw that," Cassie whispered. "George Clooney – what a dish. Even I'm tempted. But I thought it was directed by Stephen Sondheim."

"Soderbergh. That was the remake. Didn't compare."

"And you might talk about Hollywood," the man continued. "But where did it all start? Eisenstein, my friend, Eisenstein. A Russian. He introduced cutting and montage – the whole language of film – to the world."

He was right. I could see the man, medium height, chunky, in a white shirt and black trousers. I couldn't see who he was talking to.

"Brian De Palma did a nice reworking of some famous Eisenstein scene in *The Untouchables*," the man he was talking to replied.

I was dying to join in the conversation … I *know* I'm a film nerd. But I recognised the voice. Then the man who went with the voice stepped out of the shadows into the light. Zane Pynchon.

"I know that guy," Chuck said.

"What the hell is Pynchon doing here?" Greg whispered.

"Arranging to smuggle the treasure into America?" I said.

"Captain Kidd's treasure?"

"It's not Captain Kidd's," I growled.

The other men on the deck were guards. They stood patiently, occasionally looking around. We all remained crouching at the back of the speedboat.

"Not many laughs in your man Tarkovsky's films," Pynchon said.

"Life is not a lot of laughs," the Russian said.

"What's with Russians and gloom? You ever read Dostoyevsky? Jesus – get a life, Fyodor."

This not from Pynchon but, astoundingly, from Cassie.

"A dog wrote a book?" Greg said.

"Fyodor, not Fido," I said absently. I was still digesting the fact that Cassie had read Dostoyevsky. Greg read my mind.

"It's a lesson to us all," he said in my ear. "Don't judge people by their looks. We see a beautiful blonde and we assume she's a bimbo. Turns out she's read a book. A Russian book, yet."

"But she's also chosen to have a hole drilled in her head to release her creativity," I said back into his ear. "Don't you find that…quirky?"

"It's a judgement call, sure enough," Greg said.

I love understatement.

I felt hot breath on my other ear.

"Why are you talking about me as if I'm not here and can't hear you?" Cassie said.

I immediately lapsed into playground mode.

"He started it."

At that moment a seventh person came out on the deck of the other vessel. Probably the last person in the world I expected to see there. My stomach did a little somersault.

"Oh shit," I said. "Oh shit."

It was Mollie.

"Isn't that your friend, Nick?" Greg said.

"It is."

"What's she doing there?" Bridget hissed.

"I should know?"

A man behind her pushed her forward.

"What's going on?" Chuck said from behind us. "I can't see a damned thing back here."

"We've got trouble," Bridget said sourly.

"What kind of trouble?"

"Girl trouble."

Bridget and I looked at each other.

"We need to get out of here but I think I know what you're going to say next," she said.

"I've got to rescue Mollie."

"Why am I right all the time?"

"You wouldn't leave her there would you?" I said.

"Honey, any girl with legs that long is on her own as far as I'm concerned."

The Russian stepped across to Mollie and cupped her chin in his hand.

"Are you sure we cannot make this beautiful lady part of our deal?"

Mollie jerked her head away and he laughed.

"I need her to keep this Martini guy in line," Pynchon said. "I don't want him saying anything to the authorities until we're out of here."

"Tomorrow, then."

"The sooner the better. The pirate guy is waiting for me to do a deal with him but he's not going to wait very long before he gets suspicious. My men are guarding the treasure but we don't want another gun battle at sea."

"Don't worry about Cecil," the Russian said. "I've had dealings with him before. I sold him a submarine."

"That's not a line you hear much in day to day conversation," I said.

"It's kind of them to fill us in on some back-story," Bridget said.

"Just like in the movies," Cassie said.

The Russian and his men went down the ladder on the far side of the cruiser. A moment later a boat with an outboard motor headed for shore with them aboard. We watched them step onto a short jetty and go into the long building.

"Can we go now?" Chuck said, reaching for the key.

I grasped his wrist.

"Not yet."

"What's going on?" Chuck said.

"Nick's got something to do," Bridget said.

"Can't you hold on a bit?" Cassie said. "I've been dying for a pee-pee all day but I've been holding it in."

Pee-pee and Dostoyevsky didn't quite go together but I had no time to contemplate that now.

"Not that," I said. "There's someone on the other boat who needs my help."

I looked across at the cruiser.

"Maybe we can even take that boat instead."

"Nick, you don't know how many bad guys are down below. Pynchon will have his own men."

"How do you know? You heard him say his men were guarding the treasure."

"It looks like a nice boat," Cassie said. "I bet it's got a neat bathroom."

I glanced at Cassie.

"Did you really read Dostoyevsky?" I said.

"Sure," she said indignantly. "It was this treatment my agent sent me. She thought there might be a part for me."

A treatment. That made more sense. Treatments are one, maybe two page outlines. There's a truism in Hollywood that above a certain level nobody actually reads *anything*. Heads of studios give the green light to $100 million dollar projects based on novels or original scripts they've never read. They make those decisions based on the aforementioned treatments.

"Look, just give me ten minutes to get her off the boat. If I'm not back by then you take off."

"Has anybody got a watch that's still working?" Greg said. "Mine's fucked."

Not a watch between us.

"Leave you behind?" Chuck said.

"If need be."

Chuck shook his head.

"I don't think so. Don't we need to talk to that guy Pynchon about Dwight? We should all go."

I shook my head.

"If we're heard there could be a bloodbath. These are bad people with a lot to protect."

"Nobody's got killed so far in our little adventure," Chuck said.

"Aside from Larry and possibly Dwight," Greg said.

"Don't," Bridget said. "We don't know yet about Dwight."

"And Larry was killed before our adventure really started," Joseph said.

"Yeah," Greg said. "We're not in that kind of story. This is a PG."

Cassie cleared her throat.

"What about the cannibal on the other side of the island? All the people he's killed."

We looked at each other.

"Shit, you're right," I said. "There's no way this would get a PG rating." I shivered. "In that case, things could very well get nasty. Even more reason that I go over alone."

Before they could argue further I stepped over the side of the boat and slid down into the water. As I did so the towel slipped from my waist. I grabbed for it but it drifted away. I ducked under the water and swam towards the cruiser.

I swam round to the portside and came up beside the ladder. I was halfway up it when something tugged at my leg. I looked behind me. Bridget was in the water at the bottom of the ladder. I smiled.

"You couldn't let me do it alone again," I whispered.

"I told you before I couldn't let you do it alone because you'd fuck it up and get us all killed."

A bald pate came up in the water beside Bridget. Chuck emerged beside her.

"Amen to that," he said.

Hmm.

"But the ten minute rule still applies."

"More or less," Bridget said. "Given that nobody knows what day it is, never mind the time."

I went up the ladder first. There was nobody on the deck by the wheel. I ducked down and looked into the cabin.

It was a long room with two doors at the far end on either side of a mahogany bar. A thick set man was standing behind the bar holding a drink.

There were banquettes either side of the room running its length. Mollie was sitting on one, Pynchon on the other. I couldn't see anyone else in the cabin.

The man behind the bar was the problem. He would undoubtedly be armed. I had the flare gun but didn't know if I would be able to fire it at someone. I know enough about guns to know two things: if you point one at someone you have to be prepared to use it; and to be sure of hitting somebody you need to aim at the body. Firing a flare into the chest of the bodyguard would definitely bugger my PG rating.

As I've said, Bridget had once killed someone, in self-defence, on the bank of a river in Peru. She didn't like to talk about it much but I knew it had messed her up for quite some time. And I know my grandfather had killed two men in Burnley before the war. For him it was justified. But it's a massive thing taking someone's life and I didn't think I could do it.

Chuck and Bridget were behind me.

"Is there a plan?" Chuck said. Bridget gave him one of her looks.

"That would be a first."

I took a calming breath. Well, theoretically calming.

"Follow me."

I plunged down the stairs into the cabin, my arm stretched out in front of me pointing the flare gun at the man behind the bar. I ran towards him, ignoring Pynchon and Mollie. The man was slow to react. By the time he'd started to reach for something under the bar I had the flare gun pushed into his chest.

"Lean over and drop your arms over the bar," I said. I was slightly distracted by giggling from the sofas.

He had angry eyes. I almost flinched from his look.

"Do it!" I said, stepping back. Slowly he leaned forward and unwillingly lowered his arms over the front of the bar. I swung round and the sniggering got louder.

Pynchon spoke.

"Know why nude ballet is always such a hoot?" he said. "Because not every part of the male body can keep time to the music."

"Just sit on your banquette and keep quiet," I said. I looked at Mollie. Given that I was saving her life I was rather disappointed that she too was tittering on her banquette. Although it was nice to hear someone titter – I'd often wondered what a titter sounded like. I remember how pleased I was the first time I heard a guffaw – made my day.

"Are you alright?"

She dragged her attention away from my penis and looked at my face. She nodded.

To be honest I was tired of people laughing at my penis. I was fed up with it. Not my penis – that is what it is. And then I realised. That was exactly it. Cue solemn music. My penis is what it is.

Tiny.

There, I've said it. And I feel better for it. Empowered if you will.

Bridget was standing in the doorway keeping an eye out for the drug dealers. Chuck walked by me, patting me on my shoulder as he passed. He reached the bodyguard stretched out over the bar, whacked him at the base of his skull with a paddle he'd picked up on deck. We heard an ouf and the guy slumped.

"That's better," Chuck said, turning back to the rest of the cabin. "Carry on, Nick."

Since Chuck had ditched the rug and corset, he looked more impressive. A Gerard Depardieu sans hair kind of look.

"Okay shitheel," I said to Pynchon. "We need to talk."

"What is there to talk about, Mr Martini?"

"Murder and kidnapping spring immediately to mind."

"Who have I murdered?"

"Larry the stuntman, for one. And where's Dwight?"

"I don't think I've ever met this stuntman."

"He came to see you at your hotel the night he disappeared."

"As I told the police, nobody came to see me that night. And nobody at the hotel saw your stuntman either."

Bridget came over from the door and stood above Pynchon.

"Where the fuck is Dwight?"

"Back in LA by now I suppose."

"I don't believe you."

Pynchon looked up at Bridget and shrugged. His first mistake. He sneered. His second mistake.

"I should care whether Dwight's cooze believes me?" His final mistake.

I still retain my sense of wonder that Bridget can live such a debauched life and yet be an Olympian when it comes to physical stuff. I saw a blur as she launched herself at Pynchon.

It was brief.

"Let's just take this asshole with us and deep six him out at sea," she said, standing up.

The asshole in question was slumped against the window, blood streaming from his busted nose and mouth, clutching his genitals.

I looked back at Mollie. She was still sitting, gazing blankly at Bridget.

"You sure you're okay?"

Mollie turned to me.

"Yes, I love being kidnapped."

"Don't we all. What happened?"

"I went to your hotel. You weren't there." She gestured towards Pynchon. "This creep and his – what's the right word – *henchmen* were there."

"Henchman. Yeah. Interesting the way that has changed meaning over time. In Anglo-Saxon days it meant something different."

"Nick – can we go please."

That was Bridget, with an edge in her voice, cutting to the chase as usual.

"Sounds good to me," Chuck said.

I raised my chin at Pynchon.

"What are we going to do with him? Take him with us?"

"I told you – drop him in the middle of the ocean to be with the other sharks."

Pynchon was dabbing his mouth with a handkerchief.

"I only have to call out and you're all dead," he said. "My friends on shore don't welcome uninvited guests."

"So we've heard."

Bridget moved back over to him. He flinched. Wise man.

"What are through those doors?" I said to Mollie.

"Bedrooms."

"There's nobody in them is there?" I said, suddenly panicked.

"No one else. The man lying over the bar is the only crew." "Would you go and find something to tie Pynchon up with."

She walked over to me and gave me a kiss on the cheek.

"Sir Galahad," she said.

I blushed then jumped a foot in the air. She'd pinched my bum on her way to the bedroom.

"You need your nails cutting," I called after her.

She returned a couple of minutes later with cord from a dressing gown and a pair of boxer shorts. She also had a pair of trousers and a shirt. She handed these last items to me.

"Thought you might want to get dressed."

She walked past me and stood beside Bridget.

"Open wide," she said to Pynchon.

He looked up at her. Bridget moved towards him. He moved the handkerchief away and opened his mouth. Mollie stuffed the boxer shorts into it, none too gently.

"So is he going with us?" Chuck said.

"I'm not sure there will be room on the boat."

"Why don't you take this boat?" Mollie said.

I shook my head.

"The guys on shore would wonder where Pynchon was off to before we could get out of the bay. Plus it's not very easy to miss. We're better on a small boat."

"We can't go yet," Bridget said. "He hasn't told us what he's done with Dwight."

"I can tell you that," Mollie said. "He killed him." She looked at Bridget. "I'm sorry. I heard him bragging about it to that creepy Russian."

"Give me that flare gun, Nick," Bridget said coldly.

"Bridget, you can't–"

"Give it to me," she snapped. I walked over and put it in the palm of her hand. She knelt on the cushion beside Pynchon and put the barrel of the gun to his left eye. He tried to squirm away but she held it there.

"I have a bad temper," she said. "And I sometimes do things I regret later. This, I don't think I would regret. Tell us what happened or I fire this thing."

I didn't for a moment think she'd do that but Pynchon didn't know her as well as I did. He grunted and gestured towards the boxer shorts. With her other hand Bridget drew them out of his mouth and dropped them in his lap. He began babbling immediately.

"It was an accident, I didn't mean to do it. We argued. We got into a pushing thing. We were standing, he had hold of my arms. He was shaking me and saying he was going to tell the authorities about salvaging the treasure."

He went quiet.

"Then what happened?"

"He let go of me and turned to go. I pushed him in the back

because I was angry. He fell over the coffee table and banged his head. I wasn't trying to kill him."

I was keeping a close watch on Bridget as he was confessing. I still didn't think she'd pull the trigger. She was fond of Dwight but he wasn't the love of her life. Even so, she does have a temper.

She lowered the gun and stood up.

"What did you do with Dwight's body?"

"Took it out to the second unit's boat."

"Then dumped it at sea?" Bridget said fiercely.

"No, no – put him in the freezer until I could figure out what to do."

"What about the stuntman?" I said again.

"I keep telling you – I never met the man."

"Okay," Bridget said, ramming the boxer shorts back in his mouth. "Up you get."

"We're taking him?"

"We have to – he's confessed to a murder. Can't risk him getting away."

She handed Mollie the flare gun and tied Pynchon's hands behind his back. I put on the clothes Mollie had brought me. Chuck was crouching to look at the unconscious man's face.

"He'll be out for a while," he said, straightening.

Bridget took the gun back from Mollie and put it to Pynchon's eye again.

"Now, you listen to me. If you do anything to draw the attention of those on the island to us I will use this on you, have no doubts on that score."

He nodded energetically.

"Let's move," Chuck said. He looked at the trousers I'd put on. They were about six inches too short for me. "I hear cut-offs are the fashion at the moment."

"I heard that too," Mollie said, helping Bridget lead Pynchon out.

We could hear that the film was still playing on the beach. None of us could see a single guard. Chuck got in the water first then we handed Pynchon down. Bridget used to be a lifeguard during the summers of her late teens. When we were all in the water Bridget grabbed Pynchon, turned him on his back and swam to the motorboat pulling him with her as he floundered weakly.

"About time!" Greg said.

"Help us get this creep in the boat," Bridget said.

Pynchon weighed a ton but here at least we could stand on the sea bottom. The powerboat listed alarmingly as Greg, Cassie and Joseph pulled and Chuck and I pushed at Pynchon.

Once he was in the boat, the rest of us hauled ourselves on board. It was a tight fit.

"Hey, cut-offs are in this year," Cassie said to me.

"Can we go now?" Greg said patiently.

"Do you know how this boat works?" I said.

"I've had plenty of time to figure it out. Hang on."

He twisted the key in the ignition and the engine rumbled immediately into life. It sounded deafening in the quiet of the night. Greg pushed a lever down and the boat shot forward so suddenly we all tumbled against each other. About ten seconds later its nose came up and the boat seemed about to take off into the sky at the same time as our forward motion came to an abrupt halt with a frantic whirring of the engine. We all tumbled backwards. There was a loud splash in the water behind us.

"Raising the anchor would probably have been a good idea," Bridget said drily, pointing to the taut line which ran about twenty yards from the back of the boat before it disappeared into the water.

Greg revved the boat. I was looking over the side to see what had caused the big splash. There was a loud twang, the line parted and half of it whipped through the air back towards the boat. The boat, suddenly released, darted forward, its nose slapping back down on the water.

I looked round the cramped cabin.

"Shit – where's Pynchon?"

Joseph pointed behind us.

"He fell in the water," Joseph said.

"We've got to go back," Bridget said.

Chuck was standing looking back at the island.

"I don't think so," he said.

We all looked. The door of the low building was wide open and men with guns were running out and down to the shoreline.

"I don't think so either," I said as Greg steered us out of the bay. "With luck he's hit his head and drowned."

"I somehow doubt it," Bridget said.

So did I.

The motorboat had a compass so we were able to steer in the right direction – a major step forward for us. We knew we'd hit the Yucatan coast somewhere and that was good enough for us. Once clear of the island we slowed down and pottered through the night. There was no indication that we were being followed but it was a pitch black night so we probably wouldn't have seen if there was.

Unusually there was a lot of cloud in the sky and a stiff wind was blowing. We tried to doze, wedged tightly together. Chuck and I spelled Greg at the wheel through the night.

Dawn came early in a mackerel sky. The wind picked up but we could still feel the humidity. We woke up one by one. Cassie immediately started scanning the ocean for dolphins.

Mollie sat cross-legged looking down at her hands. Bridget too was withdrawn.

Chuck looked over the back of the boat and saw the line that had secured the anchor trailing in the water behind us. He hauled it in and unhooked the other end from the boat. He spent ten minutes fiddling with it. Then, with a smile on his face that made him look twenty years younger, he displayed the lasso he'd made.

"I wish we could find you a horse."

"Oh, I don't know, Nick, I'm getting used to this life on the ocean waves. And I'm getting a bit old for saddle-sores. Mind you I haven't had such a painful time making a film since my stunt-work days. When I was starting out I was green and ambitious. I'd volunteer for stunts none of the more experienced stuntmen would do. Didn't occur to me there were very good reasons why they wouldn't do them."

He was coiling and uncoiling the lasso in his hand as he talked.

"I remember once making a cheap oater in the late sixties and the director needed a stunt double to jump from a first floor balcony into the saddle of a horse below and gallop off. You can picture the scene – you've seen it a hundred times. None of the other stuntmen came forward. Didn't look hard to me so I volunteered."

He smiled to himself.

"And?"

"Nothing to it, right?"

"Seems straightforward enough."

"Wrong."

"The horse moved?"

He shook his head.

"That horse was trained to stand on its mark all day if need be."

"Then it wouldn't move when you got in the saddle?"

"Oh it moved alright."

"You fell off?"

"Clung on for dear life actually."

I shook my head.

"You got me then."

"This is what it was. Think about it – you're jumping from a decent height with your legs apart to land on this leather saddle. You're going to land hard. And what bit of you is going to hit that saddle first, given that your legs are wide open?"

I got there.

"Ouch," I said, laughing and wincing at the same time.

"Ouch indeed. Damn near crushed my cojones I hit that saddle so hard. Excuse my language, ladies."

He shook his head.

"I tell you, it hurts just thinking about it."

We all laughed, including, I was relieved to see, Mollie and Bridget. Mollie didn't look physically much the worse for her ordeal but I sensed there was something she was keeping hidden. She seemed closed. I noticed Cassie giving her looks from time to time.

"Do we have a plan?" Greg said.

I looked over at Bridget but she made no sarcastic comment. Not fully recovered then.

"Hit the mainland, get to the cops."

"Get to a bath," Cassie said. "And a mirror, see what state the salt and the sun have left my complexion in."

The sea was getting increasingly choppy. Large clouds were scudding across the sky and the light had turned a curious gun-metal grey.

"I think we're going to have a storm," I said.

"Perfect," Bridget said. "I knew we'd missed something out of our seafaring itinerary."

"I can see land," Joseph announced.

"There is a God," Bridget said, looking up at the sky.

As we drew nearer, Greg said: "I recognise this coastline from when we came scouting for locations. Damn if we're not almost dead on target."

Twenty minutes later we were approaching Fuentes and the false harbour front the film production had constructed in the little bay a mile to the east of the village.

"The galleon's moored on the waterfront," Cassie said.

Indeed it was, moored right next to the half galleon. And on the deck we could make out two figures.

We came alongside the galleon. Well, to be accurate, we collided with it.

"Sorry," Greg said. "I'm better at starting than stopping."

"Men the world over. With sex they think that if they keep going for a long time it's the same as being good at it."

Bridget was back.

"I've never had that problem," I said.

We climbed up the ladder hanging down the side of the galleon one by one. The two figures were waiting to hand us aboard.

"The wanderers return," Yves shouted.

"About bleeding time," Stacey added.

Chapter Nine

"Is that a cannon I'm hearing
Or my heart that goes boom-boom?"

Mollie, clumsy as ever, fell off the ladder and into the bay. It could have been dangerous as the water was getting choppier by the minute and our boat was banging against the galleon's wooden hull. I reached down and grabbed her wrist and between us Greg and I pulled her back onto the motorboat. Her wet dress had become see-through and clung to her tightly. We said nothing.

By the time we got on board the galleon, Stacey and Joseph were having a reunion at the other end of the deck. Yves looked Mollie up and down. Then he actually said '*Oo la la*,' the fat piece of Gallic ham, and kissed her hand when he introduced himself.

"Where have you been?" Yves said. "I come back from the hospital and there is no film. Technicians sitting around the hotel. The beautiful Stacey with no make-up to make-up. Extras loitering on the dock. But none of my fellow actors. No director."

He did the Gallic shrug with the addition of the hand gesture – arms out, palms upward, "What am I to do?"

"So what did you do?"

"Went to see the producer. He too has gone up in a *perff* of smoke. Then Stacey and I get this little boat and we go out to the galleon. It is like the *Marie Celeste*. We go over to the second unit. And, *quelle surprise*, that vessel has gone."

You will have noticed that I've gone for a bit of the patois above. Well, the man temporarily wore me down.

"It wasn't there?" I said.

There was more Gallic shruggery.

"There is no longer a second unit."

"Who brought this galleon back into harbour?"

"It was here when Stacey and I came down to the dock just now. We thought you might be aboard."

If the second unit vessel had gone did that mean the Russian Mafia had already got the treasure? The simplest way to do the transfer would have been for Pynchon's men to sail over to the island and do it there. But from the conversation between Pynchon and the Russian I'd inferred the transfer would take place at the site of the wreck. Perhaps Cecil and his men had already come back and this time they'd succeeded in taking the ship and the treasure? Or perhaps Pynchon's men had moved the boat and/or treasure for safekeeping.

Bridget took Yves's arm and began to explain what had been happening. Greg and Chuck offered to show Mollie over the boat and led her away aft. There suddenly seemed to be a remarkable lack of urgency.

I looked up at the rigging. The increasingly fierce wind was rattling the spars and tugging at the lines. The galleon was hitched to the dock by two lines fore and aft but the deck was shifting noticeably as the boat rode at anchor.

"Where do you think the treasure is, Nick?" Cassie said.

She fell into step beside me as I walked forward. Stacey and Joseph had been taking turns at doing the bit in the *Titanic* where the young lovers lean out over the sea. Now they were innocently canoodling. I never thought I'd put "innocence" and "Stacey" in the same sentence. Actually, that's unfair. There had always been something innocent in the way Stacey approached sex in her healthy, open way.

Unusually the hatch over the front hold of the galleon was

closed. There was a new padlock on the latch. I squatted down to take a closer look.

"What is it?" Cassie said.

I looked around. A prop cutlass lay beside a barrel a few yards away. I reached for it and inserted it between the latch and the hatch. I stood and strained to wrench the latch open.

"If you had to hide pirate treasure where would you hide it?"

"Didn't they bury it on desert islands and draw silly maps?"

"I'm talking about today," I said, feeling the latch give a little.

"I don't have any idea."

"What about on a pirate galleon?" I said, as with a screech of metal the latch burst open and the padlock skittered across the deck.

I lifted the hatch.

"You mean this galleon?"

"Let's see for ourselves."

I climbed down the ladder into the hold, Cassie right behind me. Although the galleon was an accurate replica of an old seafaring vessel it did cheat by having electric lights. I flicked the switch. Against the far wall of the hold lengths of tarpaulin lay over some large rectangular objects.

We walked over and each took an edge of the tarpaulin. We lifted it.

"I hope you two aren't up to no good down there," I heard Stacey call from the deck. "I know what a rascal you are, Nick Madrid."

"Come down, I've something to show you," I said. "And get the others."

"I've seen it before, Nick, don't forget. And, without being rude, I have to say that I don't think the others would be much impressed either."

"It is what it is," I said, remembering that I was empowered now. "But I wasn't referring to that."

Stacey clambered down and came over to us.

"Joseph is getting the others."

There were half a dozen wooden crates before us. I would have preferred leather bound chests but that's the modern age for you. I tried the lid of one, expecting it to be nailed down. It wasn't. Cassie helped me lift it and we laid it against the wall.

We peered in.

I think we were hoping to see the crate brimming with doubloons and pieces of eight, pearls and necklaces, rubies and rings – all glittering, glinting and, for that matter, gleaming.

The crate was brimming right enough. But we were looking at lumps of silted-up metal – black, green, covered in all kinds of gunk and encrustations.

"So that's what treasure looks like," Stacey said. "I have to say, I'm not impressed."

"It needs a bit of brasso and elbow grease then you'll see – it will shine up a treat."

"You say," Cassie said.

We were lifting the lid of the next crate when the others trooped down into the hold. They clustered round us.

"They've been salvaging scrap metal – great," Bridget said. "The end of a perfect week."

Yves leaned in and picked up a cruciform shaped object from the second crate. He rubbed it on his shirt sleeve. Where he had rubbed the gunk away there was the dull glint of silver.

"Beautiful," he whispered. Or, okay – last time though – "*beoooteefull*".

"We've found the treasure," I said.

"Captain Kidd's treasure."

"It's not but never mind."

"So what do we do now?" Greg said, looking from one to the other of us.

Stacey too looked round the group. When she came to Mollie her eyes widened and a look of anger suffused her face. She pointed at Mollie.

"What the fuck is that bitch doing here?"

We were all as startled as Mollie, who looked at Stacey in bafflement. However, before Stacey could say more we were interrupted.

"Can I help?"

We turned as one. A tough-looking man in a wetsuit was standing at the bottom of the ladder, a harpoon gun in his hand. Two other men were hanging from the ladder above him.

"I don't think so," I said.

"Me neither," Bridget chipped in.

He gestured with the harpoon gun.

"I think you'd all better get off the ship."

"But this is our film set," Cassie said.

The man looked her up and down.

"Not any more. Haven't you heard? The film's been shut down due to the unexpected death of the director." He jabbed his harpoon at Cassie. "And you, darling, are fucking tasty."

He stood to one side.

"Okay, up on deck."

It was unspoken but all the men, when we shuffled over to the ladder, made sure we stood between this geek and the women as they filed by. There were another half dozen men in wetsuits on deck, some with harpoon guns, some with machine pistols.

The second unit vessel was moored beside the galleon. I

looked up at the sky. The clouds were dense and low. I looked out to sea. Two speedboats, some quarter of a mile out, were heading through an increasingly high swell towards the bay. And behind them, something bigger was approaching.

The man with the harpoon stood before us, grinning. He gestured with his thumb to a bearded man holding a machine pistol.

"Actually, my colleague has pointed out that we can't let you leave the boat until we've concluded a certain transaction." He reached out and brushed the end of the harpoon gun against Bridget's breast. "So I'm wondering what we can do to pass the time."

There was a prop iron bucket beside Bridget. She bobbed to her right to pick it up then swung it with all her might at the man's head. It clanged dully as it made contact. He stumbled then fell to his knees.

Not a prop bucket then. Actually, it was. That was the weird thing about this ship: some props were made of the real thing, others were balsa. It was difficult to know which was which.

"Hey!" the bearded man said, raising his machine pistol.

I stepped between him and Bridget and gestured past him.

"We're not the ones you want to be bothering about."

The speedboats were getting nearer, the whine of their engines just audible on the wind. And behind them the larger vessel was now clearly identifiable. It was a submarine. The man turned to look out to sea.

"Shit," he said. "The pirates are back."

He had a pair of binoculars round his neck. He trained them on the incoming boats.

The one who Bridget had walloped was back on his feet, holding his head. Dazed, he looked towards the submarine and the boats. By now the speedboats were at the mouth of the bay. We could clearly see their skull and crossbone flags blowing in the wind.

"They've got machetes," the man with the binocular reported. "I can't see any guns."

"No – that's because if they start shooting we'll get the local police and coast guards here," the man with the harpoon said, his voice hoarse. "And that's no good for anybody. If they only have machetes, we'll use harpoon guns and knives. Prepare to repel boarders, lads."

"*Only* machetes?" I heard Joseph mutter.

The leader pointed his harpoon at us again.

"Below."

"Are you going to clap us in irons?" Bridget said. "I haven't had my timbers shivered yet."

The man with the harpoon rubbed his head and leered.

"Oh I've got plans for you, darling, so don't go putting other ideas into my head." He glanced at Mollie, Stacey and Cassie. "We're going to have a little party afterwards and you girls are *all* invited."

Two of his men hustled us back to the hold. Once we were all below, the men closed the hatch. A few minutes later I heard something heavy shifted onto the hatch.

"Did anyone count how many men were in the boats?" I said.

"I counted about seven on one boat," Chuck said.

"Assume the same on the other then. And there are about seven of the salvage divers."

"That we've seen. And the Pirate King will have more men on the sub."

Although the heat was stifling below decks Mollie gave a little shiver.

"What are you thinking, Nick? Can't we just stay below and let them get on with killing each other?"

"They're not going to let us be," Chuck growled. "Whichever side wins it's going to be bad news for us."

"Chuck's right – neither one is going to want us around." I gestured towards the four women. "Then there's the little question of what the salvage divers have planned for after the battle, if they win."

"What do you suggest then?" It was Joseph, looking anxious.

Chuck was over by the crates of treasure but he was more interested in the wall behind it than pieces of eight.

"The other hold is behind this partition," he said. "We have weapons there."

"Prop weapons," Greg said.

"Some of them are pretty robust. They're real enough to cause some damage."

He kicked at a plank of the partition. It shuddered.

"Come on." He gestured to us.

We all set to work. Within minutes we'd made a hole big enough to get through. We climbed into the other hold, where all the props and costumes were held. We could hear yells and the sound of men running up on deck.

Chuck walked over to the props and costumes stacked in the corner of the hold. He picked up a cutlass.

"See. We've got weapons here."

"But they're not real," Cassie protested.

Chuck swung his cutlass in front of him.

"They'll do."

Joseph walked over to join him. He picked up the much slimmer rapier that was to have been his weapon in the climactic fight with Blackbeard.

"But who do we attack?" he said.

Chuck shrugged.

"Everyone."

Bridget frowned. Well, tried to.

Chuck was standing beside the rack of costumes. He reached for the long black frock-coat that was part of his own costume.

"If we're going to do this, we may as well do it right."

Bridget walked towards the rack.

"Not you," I said. I waved at Mollie, Cassie and Stacey. "None of the women are going."

"What," Bridget curled her lip and seemed surprised she could still do that. "You five against twenty of them?"

"You don't seem to have much faith in men," Yves said.

Bridget didn't even bother to look his way.

"Girls, your response, after three?" she said.

"We'll wait," Chuck said. "It won't be twenty when we get up there. We'll wait until they've decimated each other."

Decimated. Posh word for a cowboy but then I'd already concluded that Chuck wasn't simply the old cowpoke he seemed.

Bridget, obviously overcome that she had *any* movement in her face, curled her lip again as she looked at Joseph quivering over by the porthole, at Chuck looking decidedly paunchy without his corset – and at me. Well, I'm a fine figure of a man but maybe she could see my hands trembling.

"These people are ruthless," Greg said.

Bridget picked up Pierre le Peg's leg and swung it as if it were a baseball bat.

"That's why I don't want any of you men at risk. I think you need a little assistance from the gentler sex."

"Is that such a good idea?" Cassie said, sitting down in one of the director's chairs.

"Well, we're all at risk if the men can't handle the job," Bridget said. She looked at Cassie. "I thought that hole in your head was partly about empowerment."

Cassie laughed nervously.

"You must have a hole in your head to think empowerment means getting killed by pirates."

"Nobody is going to get killed if we do this right," Chuck said. "Nick – do you still have the flare gun?"

"Sure," I said. "It's back by the crates."

"We get on deck, we fire the flare gun, the police come down to investigate. Game over."

Bridget had gone over to the rack. She took a leather waistcoat off a hanger.

"If we do nothing, chances are we'll be raped and killed anyway. I think I'd rather have some control over that."

There was a table piled high with pistols, swords and peg legs. I assume they must have got a deal on the legs.

Bridget turned and threw a pistol towards Cassie. Cassie caught it without thinking.

"But these don't work do they?"

"They do if you wallop someone over the head with the butt end."

"Not all of them," I said, hefting each of the pistols on the table in turn. I picked one up and tapped Bridget on the head with it.

"Hey you." She jerked round to face me.

"Just demonstrating – about half of these are balsa wood."

"They're for my bandolier," Chuck said, reaching across and picking up two of the pistols. In fact he was wearing two bandoliers. They ran over his shoulders, crossed at his chest and were attached at the hips to a thick leather belt. He started tucking the pistols into the bandoliers.

"Pity we can't load these," he said.

"They're still not your six-shooters, Chuck," I said.

"They'll do," he said, thrusting two more into the big leather belt.

Chuck was a big man and with the hat and bulky jacket on he looked massive. Stacey glued on the beard.

Yves and Joseph got into their regular costumes. The rest of us found stuff that was easy to move in. We armed ourselves with the most solid things we could find.

Chuck stood below the hatch looking up.

"By now they must have done serious damage to each other,' he said.

He turned to Bridget.

"Ma'am, I'd be honoured if you'd light my twine."

"Haven't had an offer like that in a long time," Bridget said.

Stacey handed her a box of matches.

The twine was dangling down either side of Chuck's face. Bridget lit it. It started to fizz and billow smoke.

"That's a cue if ever I saw one," Chuck said and he pulled himself up the ladder and pushed open the hatch.

"Hi Ho Silver!" he yelled as he burst out on deck. "Awaaaaay!" His rallying cry sounded distinctly odd as he was brandishing a cutlass – but then what hadn't been odd these last few days?

"Okay, let's inflict war and petulance," Yves shouted.

"Petulance!" the rest of us roared as we spilled out after Chuck and fanned out across the deck. I pointed the flare gun into the air and pulled the trigger. Nothing happened. I wasn't altogether surprised – I'd been underwater with it more than once these past few hours. I threw it at a large black man with a scarred face who was bearing down on me. It bounced off his chest and clattered to the deck without slowing his advance.

I had a cutlass and knew how to use it. As you may know, before I discovered the delights of non-competitive yoga – the main delight being that lots of women do it – I used to be a competitive fencer. I slashed at the side of his neck as he raised his machete. It was a blunt blade so I wasn't trying to cut him. I was just aiming to stun him by hitting him on the jugular. I missed.

Cassie didn't though. I saw her barrel in from the left and hit him on top of his head with a wooden leg. She was taller than him so the blow came down with some force. He toppled.

We hadn't timed our attack quite right. I don't think we'd taken account of how long it would take the pirates to climb aboard whilst being attacked by the salvage divers. There still seemed to be quite a number of people on the deck.

Numbers didn't matter, however, once our women went into action. Cassie had just demonstrated that she had overcome her fear. In fact she, Bridget, Stacey and Mollie were like berserkers. I'd seen Mollie outraged and Bridget was – well, let's just say the walls of Jericho would tumble again faced with Bridget. But Stacey and Cassie too showed real grit.

Their weapons were peg legs and they wielded them with gusto. Pirates and salvage divers were going down like skittles as around us all I heard was the hollow thwack of wood hitting head.

Joseph and I found ourselves hard pressed by two machete-wielding pirates. Joseph's problem was that his blade was too thin to be able to inflict damage by wielding it as a cutlass or sabre. He could only stab and his point was deliberately blunted. He spent a couple of frantic minutes keeping this guy at bay.

"Lunge for the neck or head," I hissed at him.

I was in what in competitive fencing would be a sabre fight.

The pirate facing me, sweat rolling off him, kept slashing at me with his machete. It was a heavy weapon but my fake cutlass had enough weight to hold it off – though I couldn't help noticing the roughly honed machete was hacking lumps out of my blade.

Joseph's opponent was pressing him tightly.

"You have to attack," I hissed, "or he's going to get you."

Joseph was pale. His problem was that he was used to stage fencing. In that, you don't aim for the person, you aim for the other person's sword. In old-fashioned duels – which is what competitive fencing developed from – aiming at the person was the point of the exercise.

I'm a pretty good fencer but that's mostly because I'm terrified of being hit. Makes me fast on my feet. Especially when the guy I'm fighting has a machete.

I glanced to the side and saw Joseph's opponent start to make a swing.

"Go, Joseph," I cried.

And he did. He lunged at the guy's stomach. It was a good lunge, off the back leg. And he hit him firmly. I saw the sword go in. And in.

Joseph was surprised at how deeply he'd thrust. The pirate, I suspect, was even more surprised. He stood, one arm raised, machete in his hand. He looked – almost in slow motion – down at his belly. He started to bend double. Looked from the sword sticking out of him to Joseph's surprised face.

A puzzled look crossed his own face. He put his hand down to the blade sticking out of him.

I was ahead of him. Bloody movie special effects. Joseph was fighting with a retractable sword.

Just then the whole deck listed and the boat swung away from the dock. I assumed one of the lines had come free of the mooring but I was busy trying to figure out how to stop Joseph from being decapitated by the man with machete whilst I was fighting my own opponent. Then I heard that familiar thwock and I saw Pierre le Peg's leg fell Joseph's opponent.

Bridget, bless her. She clouted my opponent too.

"What's taking you two so fucking long?" she said.

I saw Chuck bend. With a grunt he picked up one of the cannon and raised it above his head. The two pirates who had been about to attack him looked on in astonishment as he raised it over his head. They cowered. He roared. They stopped cowering and instead turned and scrambled over the side.

I heard the splash as they hit the water together. Chuck tossed the cannon after them. It hit the surface, sending up a plume of water between the two men. They struggled backwards, then looked wide-eyed as it popped back up and bobbed on the waves between them.

Most of the cannon weighed half a ton. Some didn't. That balsa wood is an amazing substance.

A salvage diver struggled with me. He knocked the cutlass out of my hand. I fell back and reached for a bottle on top of a barrel. I smashed it against his head. He carried on struggling with me. Sugar glass.

He'd spotted the knife in my belt, pulled it out and stuck it hard into my stomach up to the hilt. I punched him as hard as I could in the throat before he realised it was a prop knife with a retractable blade. He clutched at his throat with both hands. I kneed him between the legs. Joseph, who had come up alongside me, whacked him in the face with a wooden leg he'd picked up. The man went down.

I looked round. Bridget was straddling some pirate, belabouring him around the head with her peg leg. Mollie was showing a diver the error of his ways by thrusting an oar in his belly, pushing him towards the side of the boat. She was in demonic, bring-em-on mood.

Chuck came up unnoticed on a pirate and a diver locked together in a struggle for a machete. He pushed them over the side.

By now I *was* Errol Flynn. A pirate had grabbed Stacey from behind at the far end of the deck. There was a mêlée between me and her.

I jumped up onto a bowsprit and grabbed one of the many ropes hanging from the masts. Resisting the urge to do my Tarzan impersonation – too much cross-referencing is confusing – I grabbed the rope and launched myself over the heads of the men struggling in the middle of the deck.

My plan was that my swing would end in a collision with the man who was threatening Stacey. And it would have worked, dammit, had the rope I'd grabbed actually been attached to anything substantial.

But it wasn't. So moments into my athletic leap the rope tumbled down, as did I, landing coiled in the rope just behind the scrapping crowd of men.

One of them looked down at me. Almost casually he swung his machete. I twisted away and he hit the rope.

The next thing I knew Joseph was beside me. I heard the crack as he hit the man across the side of his head. Half of Joseph's wooden leg fell on the coil of rope. The man fell heavily. Joseph was still looking at what remained of the leg when one of the others turned on him.

Joseph backed away and tripped over me as I was trying to disentangle myself. We sprawled together.

I was the first to my feet. The wind was fierce now and a boom swung my way. I grabbed it and sent it flying towards the man. It swung easily and hit him hard in the face. I was surprised when it bounced back from him and he was still standing. Some you win.

Yves came to our rescue. I knew he'd been in quite a few costume dramas in his time – they go down well in France – and he was in full romantic swashbuckler mode, setting about to right and left. He barged into the man then kicked him hard when he was down.

I looked at Stacey and saw Joseph making a dash right out of *Last of the Mohicans* through the fighting men to rescue her. The man holding her had his machete raised above his head. Joseph was still about ten yards away. Without aiming he hurled his wooden leg at the man's face. Unfortunately it hit Stacey in the stomach – but then what do you expect when you don't aim?

Next Joseph grabbed a barrel and hurled that. Given the ease with which he lifted the barrel I knew it was balsa wood but it still caught Stacey full in the face.

At this rate Joseph's rescue attempt would kill Stacey before the pirate did.

I saw Mollie on the fo'c'sle above the man. She had a bucket in one hand, a leg in the other. She leaned down and dropped the bucket over the man's head then walloped it with the leg. The man released Stacey and dropped his machete. He staggered. Stacey pushed him in the chest and he fell through the hatch into the rear hold. He fell so heavily I could heard the clang of the bucket from where I was standing.

I looked around the deck. There were a couple of pirates and one diver still standing. The diver was the leader of the salvage team and he was backing towards the main mast waving a knife at Bridget and Cassie. Stacey was coming up behind the mast, a machete in her hand.

The man pulled a gun.

"If you use that you'll attract the coastguard,"

"Six bullets?" he shouted, his voice snatched away by the wind. "In this? I'll take my chances."

Stacey was standing by a rope holding one of the booms taut. The man glanced across at her and up at the boom. He grinned.

"I shouldn't bother, darling. You know half of this boat is balsa."

She raised the machete and brought it down on the rope. The rope separated, the boom swung, the man ducked, keeping the gun pointed at Bridget and Cassie. He grinned again. Then the boom swung back again and hit him hard on the back of the neck. He fell down.

As I said, on this ship it was trial and error what was prop and what was real.

Yves was sitting on a barrel. He was knackered. Chuck was knackered too. He was leaning against the fo'c'sle, his head down, gasping for breath. His lengths of twine had gone out and he was half-heartedly trying to relight them with a box of matches. Half-hearted because by now the wind was blowing fiercely.

I looked up at the sky. It was a tumultuous black. The galleon had quite a roll on it now. Moored by only one line it was almost at right angles to the dock.

Bridget went over to Chuck and lit his twine with a lighter, shielding the flame with her hand. I made my way over to them.

"You okay?" I said.

He was wheezing.

"Having a great time," he gasped.

Mollie came down from the fo'c'sle.

"I think we're nearly done here," I said.

"That submarine is leaving the bay."

"Great. We need to get off this boat before we drift any further out."

"And the Russians are coming."

"Not so great."

In fact the Russians had already come. Four of them were clambering over the side of the galleon. Joseph, Cassie and Stacey hurried over and each pushed a man back into the bay. I saw another head appear further along. Pynchon.

The fourth man jumped down onto the deck. As he straightened he pointed a machine pistol at Greg, Yves and me. Then something snaked through the air from his left. The next moment the gun was yanked out of his hand and flew through the air towards Chuck.

Chuck had not only got his second wind, he'd also got his lasso. The Russian looked from his empty hand over to Chuck. Chuck's face was framed by sulphurous smoke and sparks of fire. He was big, broad-shouldered and looked bloody frightening. The Russian took one look, turned and jumped into the sea.

Pynchon had flopped over the side of the galleon and now lay on the deck like a beached whale. He was wearing tan shoes with a black pinstripe suit. Somebody had to tell him but now wasn't the time. There was a prolonged gust of wind and the galleon listed sharply.

"We've got to get off this boat before the storm breaks," I shouted to the others. The wind was really tugging at the rigging. The metal was screeching. The sky was fiercely dark.

Joseph looked at the sky.

"I think this is what they call the pathetic fallacy."

"You talking about Nick again?" Bridget said as she looked over the side at the various men thrashing in the water.

I realise I've talked quite matter-of-factly about people toppling over the side of the boat. If this were a comedy film that would be the gag and we wouldn't think anymore about them. But this isn't a movie, it's real life I'm describing. In real life actions have consequences. A man falling unconscious in the water may well die. This account should reflect that. It shouldn't treat such things lightly.

Okay, that's my sensitivity established – now where was I?

"How do we get off the boat?" Cassie said. "I don't want to go into the sea when it's this choppy."

Joseph was on the fo'c'sle.

"We can climb down the other mooring line. We're only a few yards from shore."

"Like hell we can," Bridget said.

"Look, Stacey and I will show you," Joseph said.

The two of them clambered rather cautiously over the side of the galleon – which was dipping and rolling heavily – and then, hanging below the line by their hands and feet, half-slid half-walked their way down it.

They waved back from the dock.

"What about the treasure?" I said, glancing over at Pynchon. He had got to his feet and was now staggering towards the hold containing the crates.

"Nothing we can do about it now," Chuck said. "C'mon ladies, let's move."

Cassie, Mollie and Bridget went next. They employed a different method, hanging by their hands and going hand over hand down the line. They seemed to sway alarmingly in the wind.

When Chuck was halfway down, using the same method,

we heard a crack and the line sagged suddenly, almost dislodging him. When he landed on the dock he called back: "Be careful. I think the cleat the line is tied to on the side of the boat is coming away."

Yves crossed himself before he went jerkily down the line. Greg looked over at Pynchon.

"What are we going to do about him? And these other people on the boat?" he said, looking at the bodies strewn across the deck.

Pynchon was struggling to open the hatch.

"You'd better get off this ship," I shouted, "before the storm breaks."

Pynchon gave me the finger and disappeared down into the hold. The hatch cover slammed back down.

"They'll just have to take their chances," I said.

Greg went next and then me. The cleat came away some more when Greg was almost at the dock. He fell the last three feet. I looked down into the seething water. Looked at the rope swaying between the ship and the dock.

I remembered a stunt from that *other* pirate film and picked up a wooden leg lying nearby. When I clambered down to the cleat I saw it was attached to the boat only by two of its six screws. I lay the leg on top of the rope, gripped both ends of it then launched myself. I slid down the line at some speed and barreled into Chuck and Yves, sending both men flying.

As we got to our feet, the rain began. It fell in solid sheets and we were all drenched within seconds. Then over the wind we heard a loud ping and the splintering of wood. The line sprang away from the galleon and dropped into the water.

The galleon seemed to leap forward now that it was unrestrained. At remarkable speed for a vessel so large and apparently ungainly it was carried away from shore and into the middle of the bay. Riding the waves it was caught by a current and pulled out towards the open sea.

Was it my imagination or did I see as it passed between the two headlands of the bay into the heaving ocean beyond a solitary figure standing on deck waving frantically back at us? The rain was blinding so it was impossible to see clearly and certainly the wind was by now so strong any cry for help would have been snatched from a man's lips almost before he could utter it.

As one we turned away from the boiling sea and went to find shelter from the storm.

Tropical storms start at sea. They develop once winds exceed 38 miles per hour. During one the sea is so rough ships are warned to steer clear of the area. Tropical storms have a column of warm air at their centre. Strong winds near the surface of the water draw heat and water vapour from the sea into that column. As that column of air gets warmer so the pressure at the surface of the water falls. That falling pressure sucks more air into the storm. And more air means stronger winds.

Tropical storms are given names. The names are in alphabetical order – the first storm of the year gets a name beginning with A and so on. The World Meteorological Organisation used to give only women's names but since 1979 has used men's names as well. You can look up the names on their website – the WMO has provided names through to 2009.

There'll be storms called Beryl, Kirk and Nadine in 2006, for instance. It must be a bit humiliating for an all powerful thing like a storm to be called such names – or Melissa (2007), Arthur (2008) and Bill (2009). Maybe that's the point – it's a way for humans to cope with such powerful natural phenomena. I would have been inclined to call our storm Bridget, for obvious reasons, but it was designated Cindy. I kid you not.

It raged all that day and all the following night. For a time it seemed we might have to endure it out in the open since our hotel, when we finally dragged our bedraggled selves to it, was pretty firmly boarded up and barricaded in.

Grudgingly, the proprietor let us in after we had rung the night bell for about ten minutes and offered bribes we had no intention of paying. With scarcely a word we all went to our separate rooms to get warm and dry. Mollie came with me. We showered (separately) then raided the mini bar and devoured the sandwiches room service had brought us. All the while the wind howled at the shutters outside the windows, trying to tear them off their hinges and force a way in.

We talked in monosyllables then stretched out on the bed and both fell heavily asleep for a couple of hours.

She shared my bed that night and – as a thank you for rescuing her so gallantly, she said – made love with me. She was ardent and passionate. I was my usual hopeless self. Although she must have been unsatisfied and frustrated, she kindly didn't comment. I didn't comment either, when I heard the sighs coming from the bathroom when she was alone in there for quite a long time.

Nor did I ask her the question that weighed most heavily on my heart.

When I woke in the morning she was sitting by the bed, already dressed, looking sorrowfully down at me. The storm had passed and she had opened the shutters and the windows.

"What is it?" I said.

"I need to go back and see if my hotel is still standing."

"Will I see you later?"

She bent and kissed me on the forehead then walked to the door.

"We need to talk," I called after her.

"Do we?" she said from the open door.

I sat up in bed.

"We do."

Without turning she raised her hand in a little wave and walked out of the room.

My phone wasn't working and there was no electricity in my room – I assume the phone and power lines had come down sometime in the night. My mobile had a signal so I spent the morning making calls for as long as my battery held out.

I didn't feel like seeing any of the others, even Bridget, quite yet so I slipped out of the hotel to survey the damage the storm had inflicted on the village.

The hotel had suffered remarkably little damage, although trees were uprooted in the grounds and branches and debris were everywhere. One tree was sprouting out of the middle of a car which had its roof stoved in. Other cars had been overturned.

I walked down to the waterfront set. There was scarcely anything left of it. The bay was full of lumps of wood. The half galleon had been smashed and splintered. The floats it had been built upon, bizarrely, were still bobbing at the dockside.

I walked across to the beach.

That too was covered in debris. The water was calm as it lapped at the sand. The sky was a watery blue. I sat cross-legged on the beach and tried to do some meditation but it didn't really take. I had too much going on in my head.

At lunch I found all the others looking much better than the last time I'd seen them.

"Nick," Bridget said as I sat at the end of the table. "It's around that time when traditionally you explain to me what's been going on."

I nodded.

"So what happened, Shylock?"

"I think you mean Sherlock."

"Whoever."

"I spoke to the coastguard. They found the second-unit boat in the harbour at Cancun. They recovered Dwight's body. It's with the pathologist. It will eventually be flown back to Los Angeles for a family funeral. His wife has been notified."

Bridget looked down at her plate.

"The galleon?" Yves said. "Captain Kidd's treasure."

"It's not – nothing, nothing. The galleon has not been sighted. The coastguard was very doubtful that it could possibly have survived the storm. If it did, he couldn't even imagine how far the storm might have driven it. The probability is that both the galleon and the treasure are scattered on the ocean floor."

"There were men on board. There's no way they could have sailed it?"

"In that storm? Doubt that."

"So, Zane–?"

"I think his chances of survival are virtually nil too."

"Serves him right," Bridget said.

"What a way to go though."

"The coastguard doubts that the wreck Pynchon's men were salvaging the treasure from will still be there. In such shallow water, he said, it would probably have been broken up by the storm."

"So this film is never going to be completed, is it?" Joseph said.

Chuck put a big hand on Joseph's shoulder.

"More to the point, my young friend, we're not going to get paid."

Cassie perked up then.

"But we've got contracts."

"Yes – with Pynchon. He's no longer a going concern."

"I still think Pynchon killed Larry too," Bridget said.

I shrugged.

After lunch we sat in the bar and congratulated each other on our heroism and endurance.

Stacey was wriggling in Joseph's lap as only Stacey could. Joseph was clearly enjoying it. He was looking much more confident since our return. No sign of his earlier timidity.

"How's the celibacy?" I said.

Joseph flushed.

"We've reached a compromise," Stacey said with a quick wink. Joseph's face reddened more.

"Stacey, can I talk to you for a minute?"

Unwillingly, Joseph let her leave his lap. I walked her over to the window.

"On the galleon, before the fighting started, you said something about Mollie."

"I asked what the fucking bitch was doing there," she said, fierce again. "I know she's a friend of yours Nick but watch yourself – she can't be trusted."

"Why do you say that?" I said, though I thought I knew the answer.

"She's the cow I saw Larry on the beach with. When he was swearing undying love to me he was shagging her."

Carlos's bar simply didn't exist any more. All that remained were piles of splintered wood and torn fragments of beach umbrellas. I surveyed the scene for a moment before I stepped down onto the sand and walked over to Mollie. She was sitting near the water's edge, her knees tucked up to her chin, her arms wrapped round her legs.

I sat down beside her. The sand was wet here. I felt it soak immediately into my trousers. She didn't turn. Instead she smiled wanly, which wasn't something I'd seen anyone do before.

"My hotel's still standing. Just."

"I know," I said, "I went there looking for you."

"Poor Carlos, though it looks as if he got the drinks and his precious sound system out first."

"They get good warning of storms these days."

"It was quite something wasn't it?" she said.

I nodded. She turned to me now.

"So that's the film over with?"

I nodded.

"My time here is done too," she said.

"What about the turtles?"

"My report is in. It's up to the local authorities now."

"And the coelacanth?"

"With the film unit gone it's out of danger of being discovered. For now, anyway."

I looked at her profile as she turned back to look out to sea. She was so beautiful. I've been looking all my life – well, all my adult life – for a woman to settle with. I want kids, I want all that togetherness stuff. I also have an unerring knack for choosing the wrong woman.

"Do you want to tell me what happened with Larry?" Mollie looked at me sharply.

"What are you talking about?"

"Don't," I said. "Please. I know."

"What do you know?"

"Remember when we were first in this bar together and you said you didn't go to the movies."

"I don't," she said, but there was caution in her voice.

"Yet you knew about dailies."

"That's just stuff you pick up," she said.

"From who?"

"Whom," she said.

I took her hand.

"Tell me."

She gave my hand a little squeeze.

"What do you want me to say?"

"I want you to say that you and Larry were lovers. That he was a brute who treated you badly. He beat you and abused you in so many ways. You happened to have a knife in your hand the last time he attacked you. In terror and fear of your life you pointed the knife at him and he walked on to it. It was an accident, you didn't mean to do it." I squeezed her hand now. "That's what I want you to say."

She took her hand away from me and brushed back her hair with it.

"Phew," she said. "This is a big thing to deal with."

"Yes it is, yes it is. So are you going to tell me that?"

"Okay, if you want. He was a brute…" Her voice trailed away.

"Or tell me that you knew he was a lad who tried to get every woman he met into bed but you fancied him anyway because women like rascals. So you started this thing with him – maybe after a few beers in Carlos's place on a balmy night when you were felling a bit frisky. Then, even though you knew what he was like you took it hard when you found out he was seeing other women. And you lost it – I've seen you do that so I know you can. A crime of passion they call it in France. You get a reduced sentence for it. So you stabbed him before you could stop yourself. And immediately regretted it."

"Is that how it was?" she said, almost to herself.

"Or tell me that you stumbled – I know how clumsy you are – and the knife went into him. Ten times."

"I wanted to be sure the bastard wasn't going to be getting up again."

I could see the veins starting to stand out in her neck.

"You have no idea what kind of shit that man put me through," she hissed.

"I'm sure," I said.

"He was a triple-timing bastard."

"I'm sure," I repeated mildly. I could sense her going. How to stop her? "So what happened?"

"So what happened? I got angry, that's what happened. I got *very* angry."

"How long had you known him?"

"A week."

"He got to you in a week?"

She said nothing.

"He was a big guy–" I said.

"When you're lying down, big is not necessarily an issue."

"Not in my experience," I agreed. "Were you on the beach?"

She nodded.

"He'd come to get his leg over on his way to a meeting. Didn't intend to stay long."

"Why did you put up with him?"

"Well, I didn't, did I? That's the point of this conversation isn't it?"

"You're sounding very cold," I said.

She tilted her head to look at me.

"Am I?" she spoke quietly but fiercely. "It's just that I have rules that I'm strict about. And the main one is this: nobody messes me about. Absolutely nobody."

"You left him on the beach?"

"The tide was coming in. I thought he'd be swept out to sea. I didn't expect him to be washed up so quickly."

I closed my eyes and tipped my head back.

"What are you going to do about this?" she said.

I shook my head and looked at her profile again.

"I wish I knew."

Epilogue

I like to think that when Pynchon's boat went down there was a peckish coelacanth with a fondness for fatty meat swimming by. If this were Hiaasen-Land maybe there would have been but I don't think real life works like that. Although the unlikeliest things do happen.

I remember reading a newspaper report – in *The Times* no less – about a young girl who was blown out to sea on a set of inflatable teeth. She was rescued by a man on an inflatable lobster. The kicker was the comment from the coastguard spokesman: "This sort of thing is all too common." As the Great Hiaasen once remarked: "sometimes fiction is a futile mission".

My other favourite you-wouldn't-believe-it-if-you-read-it-in-a-novel true story comes under the heading of unlikely scenarios. I read this in one of the UK's right wing tabloids. I read that particular paper in the mornings rather than having a cup of coffee as its outrageously hypocritical and bigoted articles give the same jolt to my system as caffeine would.

Guy on a country road rounds a bend a little too fast to find there's a railway crossing barrier just coming down. He puts his breaks on and screeches to a halt.

Waiting at the crossing is a woman on a horse and an old man with a small dog on a lead. Behind the car there's a guy on a motorbike riding too close. He goes into the back of the car and falls off his bike.

The collision startles the horse, which throws its rider into a hawthorn bush. The dog attacks the motorcyclist lying on the ground. The train approaches.

The old man pulls the dog away from the motorcyclist and goes to help the woman in the hawthorn bush. To do that he needs to tether the yapping dog. He ties the lead to the crossing barrier.

The train goes by. And the barrier starts to rise…

Good story but I know there's no real reason to tell it now. Except that it's a way of putting off talking about what's uppermost in my mind. The fate of the lovely Mollie.

She made a pass at me on the beach. One part of me – the gullible part – thought she meant it but the rest of me knew she was giving herself to me so that I wouldn't turn her in. She had the softest lips and I could have kissed her forever. But I was getting a bit fed up of people sleeping with me not because they desired me but because they wanted something from me.

"If you're going to worry about that you're never going to get any sex," Bridget said, quadruple vodka in hand.

We were on the plane back from Mexico. Bridget had, of course, blagged upgrades to Club Class. I only found out later it was by pointing at her frozen face and pretending she was a stroke victim and I was her nurse.

Bridget crunched an ice cube between her teeth.

"As you had the hots for her couldn't you have shagged her then turned her in?"

"Ever the pragmatist, Bridget. That wouldn't have been very moral."

She looked genuinely puzzled.

"Your point being?"

Actually, the thought had crossed my mind but I couldn't bring myself to do it. Instead I'd stayed on the beach and given her until the following morning before I reported my suspicions to the police. I figured I owed her that much.

And, indeed, suspicions are all they were – I wasn't aware of anything but circumstantial evidence.

Mollie had left Fuentes, destination unknown, by the time the police called at her hotel to ask her about Larry's disappearance.

"Morality didn't stop you shagging Cassie," Bridget said.

"Only once," I said.

"Twice actually." She reached across and squeezed my arm. "But I guess it was on the same night."

I leaned back and looked down at her.

"How do you know that?"

She slurped her drink.

"Cassie told me."

"When did you have time for that kind of conversation? Things have been a bit hectic the past few days, if you hadn't noticed."

Bridget flushed and concentrated on crunching another ice cube. Bridget flushing?

"Oh, that night you spent out on the beach," she said airily.

I had stayed on the beach all evening and most of the night after Mollie had left. I'd watched the sun go down a swollen orange ball behind one headland and rise the next morning over the opposite one almost obscured by clouds. Got bitten to buggery by sand insects but that's romantic idylls for you.

Bridget was focusing intently on her wine glass.

"Bridget, is there anything you want to share with me?"

She gave me a challenging look.

"Did you and she–?"

She held the look, gave a little shrug.

"Well, I thought I might as well try it once."

I reached for my glass of wine.

"How was it?"

"Typical bloody man getting turned on by the thought of two women together. None of your fucking business." Then she grinned. "I don't regret what we did…but I told her as gently as I could that I think I'm a woman who needs a willy." She squeezed my hand. "But hey you must have heard that loads of times from disappointed women you've slept with."

I ignored that – water off a duck's back, frankly. I was thinking about the way Bridget had been acting the past few weeks.

"Bridget, are you okay? You've been a bit erratic lately. Dumping Dwight, going off with Yves, then that creepy extra, Smythe. Now Cassie..."

She waved to catch the attention of the air steward, a gay guy with gelled hair and an officious manner.

"I've not been feeling myself," she said.

"Everyone else has," I murmured.

She gave me a scathing look.

"And you're Mr Observant but you haven't noticed why I might have been acting a little unpredictably?"

I shook my head. She tutted. There's a thing.

"Some journalist you are."

She had me stumped.

"I give up," I said.

She managed to look both smug and annoyed with me, even with the botox.

"You're such a dork, Nick." She was attempting to smirk, I could tell. "When was the last time you saw me with a cigarette in my hand?"

"Bridget–!"

My God, she was right. As a chain-smoker, Bridget had constituted a one woman health hazard for years. But I hadn't seen her smoking in all the time we'd been in the Caribbean.

She passed out soon after, blaming it when she awoke on

the travails of the past days and not on the six double vodkas she'd consumed since take-off. Given her extraordinary constitution that was probably true.

As she was yawning she said: "I feel I owe you, Nick. I invited you down to Mexico because I hoped it would get you out of yourself. Quite how out of yourself I didn't realise. I'm sorry."

I took her hand. The one that wasn't clutching her vodka glass.

"It's okay. I'm sorry about Dwight."

"He was a lummock but he was sweet."

"Greg said he had a family. I didn't know that."

Bridget drained her drink and turned harsh.

"What – you think I not only had a thing with a married man but a man with children? Well, yes, he has children but they're grown up." She softened. "Rather fancied his son actually."

"You never told me how Dwight knew you could sing."

"Because of you."

"Me?"

"Remember that old film you made me sit through at the NFT?"

"Which one?" There had been so many.

"A good one for a change – a Mel Brooks Frankenstein film from the early Seventies. This woman has sex with the monster who is a giant in every way and at the climactic moment–"

"Madeline Kahn breaks into song. Hang on – do you mean you break into song when you have an orgasm?"

"Just as a joke. Anyway he was impressed by my voice and given the intimate circumstances was inspired to offer me a part."

She waved to the air steward, who pretended not to notice.

"Problem was," she said ruefully, "he didn't realise I was joking and expected me to burst out singing every time – a real bloody pain that was. Especially thinking up different songs."

She dug a peanut out of the bag beside her glass. She threw it at the air steward.

"Another two vodkas, darling," she bellowed. "And whatever my friend wants."

Which last would have been generous had the drinks not been free.

The steward tossed his head and wiggled off. Camp gays have such a clichéd, limited repertoire, don't they? You'd think they'd come up with something different from time to time.

"War and petulance," Bridget said, watching him go. She took my hand again – after she'd poured two miniatures into her glass, of course. "I want to make it up to you."

"There's no need," I said, touched.

"Don't fucking argue."

Fair enough.

"What did you have in mind?"

"I'm going to get you to the Oscars."

"An invite to the Oscars?" I said, unable to keep the excitement out of my voice. "That's a pretty big gesture."

"Yeah, well." Bridget's voice trailed away.

Two months later I was wearing a tuxedo sitting between Michael Douglas and Catherine Zeta-Jones on my left and Cameron Diaz on my right. We were in a vast, gaudy auditorium, laughing at Steve Martin's shtick between awards of obscure technical Oscars. Jack Nicholson, Tom Cruise and Mel Gibson were directly in front of me.

I was, as Bridget had promised, in Los Angeles at the Oscars, although the experience wasn't quite what I'd expected.

I'd bumped into Hal Jones, the songwriter, in the foyer before things began to go askew. He looked like he'd just got out of his coffin – deathly pale and wearing shades, of course.

"Heard you had quite an adventure," he said. "I could have written a great song about a cannibal, though it would've been tough finding a rhyme. Maybe a half rhyme. Abominable? Viable?"

We'd phoned in about Ben Gunn – and the drug runners for that matter. The coastguard had taken Gunn off the island though I don't think they'd done much about the drug guys – I guess the fix was in somewhere.

First thing Gunn – real name Luther Foster – did was hire a lawyer to sue Neill Dodds for $100 million for putting him in a situation where he had to resort to cannibalism. Neill Dodds still hadn't been released by the pirates but given Gunn/Foster's claim he may well have decided to stay with them, catamite or not.

The Mexican authorities were all for charging Gunn/Foster with multiple homicide but he denied killing anyone and since he'd eaten the evidence it was hard to see how a case could be made to stick. Meanwhile six studios and at least four major stars were bidding millions for the film rights to his story.

There was still no word of Zane Pynchon or the galleon. Or Mollie Sanders.

I showed Jones my ticket.

"I'm not sure where I go with this – it just has a number on it."

Jones looked at it and smiled. It was a repellant sight.

"Hey, Nick, you're a sitter. This is a pass not a ticket."

"Some people have to stand?"

He smiled again and started to walk away.

"See you around, Nick."

I took my ticket to an information desk and the tight-faced older woman directed me to a chubby man in a too tight jacket with a film of sweat on his face. He looked at my ticket.

"You're my replacement sitter? About time. Well you missed the rehearsal but that can't be helped. Okay – you're clear about your duties?"

"Duties?"

He saw my perplexed look. Dabbed his face with a balled-up tissue.

"This your first time?"

I nodded.

"Okay, well you'll pick it up pretty quickly."

"You said something about duties?"

He gave me an 'Is-this-guy-going-to-make-trouble' look.

"That's right. I don't have time to dally here, fella – you're clear about your duties, are you?"

He thought I was an idiot, I could see that. Nothing unusual there then. And I was starting to get a feeling I often have in my relationship with Bridget – viz. that she hadn't told me the full story.

"I just want to know where my seat is," I said.

"Well, you'll have a range of seats. Depends which one is vacant."

"I don't get you," I said.

So he explained.

I knew that the Oscars went on for hours and, watching it on the TV I've always been impressed by the staying power of the stars – and others – in the audience. Whenever the cameras turn on the audience – which they do all the time – there's never an empty seat. Does nobody want to go to the loo or nip out for a fag and a drink?

Of course they do, though you never see their empty seats

on the TV. I looked at Catherine Zeta Jones and smiled. She smiled back. She had crooked teeth and a dark moustache. She only spoke Spanish. Cameron Diaz was about sixteen stone though she carried it well. Nicholson had thick black hair and a Zapata moustache. I won't even attempt to describe Cruise and Gibson.

Sitters everyone, occupying the seats vacated by the stars when the stars left the auditorium, often for a couple of hours at a time. I smiled as I thought of Bridget. We'd joked about me being the next Jude Law. I turned my attention back to Steve Martin. What the hell – here I *was* Jude Law.

Author's Note

I'm grateful to Nathaniel Philbrick's "In the Heart of the Sea" (HarperCollins, 2000) for providing me with information about the physical consequences of drink and food deprivation and arcane information about the practicalities of cannibalism. The survivalist's guide to eating people really exists and is a must read – er, sort of. The children's book Nick mentions, *The Boy's Book of Pirates*, also exists and though it was published in the 1950s was a surprisingly useful source – don't tell me I don't do deep research.